Edith Pargeter is better known as Ellis Peters, bestselling author of many crime novels including the *Chronicles of Brother Cadfael*, now into their sixteenth volume.

In *She Goes to War*, originally published in 1942, the author draws heavily on her own personal experience of the WRNS, and provides a wealth of fascinating detail about wartime Britain while also telling a moving and poignant love story.

She Goes to War

Edith Pargeter

HEADLINE

Copyright © Edith Pargeter 1942

First published in Great Britain in 1942
by William Heinemann Ltd

First published in paperback in 1989
by HEADLINE BOOK PUBLISHING PLC

ISBN 0-7472-3277-6

Typeset in 10/12 pt English Times
by Colset Private Limited, Singapore

Printed and bound in Great Britain by
Collins, Glasgow

HEADLINE BOOK PUBLISHING PLC
Headline House
79 Great Titchfield Street
London W1P 7FN

ARGUMENT

'I say again, we should never submit to an evil merely to prevent a war; in fact, we do not thereby avoid it, but only defer it to our great injury.'

Machiavelli: The Prince.

'When besieged by ambitious tyrants I find a means of offence and defence in order to preserve the chief gift of nature, which is liberty.'

Leonardo da Vinci: Notebooks.

'Orf'cers and their ladies,
    Sergeants and their wives,
Privates and their women,
    Fighting for their lives.

Daily deeds of valour,
    Heroes every one –
Crosses by the thousand,
    Medals by the ton!

Gallant British fighters,
    Mustn't hope to be
Treated on a footing
    Of equality.

Crosses for the orf'cer
    'Cos he is a toff;
Medals for the ranker
    Show where *he* gets off.

Democratic nation,
    Anxious to defend
Democratic notion
    To the bitter end.

Democracy's our watchword,
    Lifting up our hearts.
Democracy's the ticket –
    Wake me when it starts.'
                            – *Justin*.

I. JOINING UP

A Third Class Compartment (crowded),
The 11.40 to Plymouth, Just Beyond Hereford.
August 12th, 1940.

Dear Nick,

Now that it's done, it seems so odd a thing to do. My conscience wasn't involved; I had no more to do with making this war than any other of the millions of women doing semi-professional jobs like mine. I'm not utterly young, certainly not young enough to see anything but boredom and distaste in a uniform. I scarcely know what it's all about. My job was the women's page and the local gossip, and as for Strang's leaders, I haven't read one in years. Low is all I know about the Nazis, and even Low is more of a pattern-maker than a prophet to me. What in the world am I doing here, in a southwest-bound train, on my way to Plymouth, and a job about which I know literally nothing, and a uniform I shall certainly hate? And an *incredible* hat!

Do you know, Nick? You might. You know a great deal about the springs that make your old pal Saxon tick over, I think. If only I could have found time to rush over to Wastwood and have half an hour's talk with you before I left, I might have got things a little straighter in my own mind. As it is, you will have received an incoherent telegram, and probably still be wondering exactly what has happened to Saxon. Well, I have a seven-hour journey before me, and time enough to tell

1

you now. In full, and with trimmings. You always slanged my tabloid style.

I'm practically in the Navy. That's the long and short of it. The 'Evening Gazette' and my three-pound-ten per week are things of the past, and at Devonport (if this most erratic train survives so far) I shall become a common or garden Probationary Wren earning, I believe, one and eight a day. You will want to know the how and why of it, of course, the imbecile fact not being enough. And the how is easy, but the why is more than I can understand myself.

A long letter to you is the next best thing to seeing you; and this letter will be very long indeed. Seven hours is a long while to sit in a train, and I have exhausted 'Lilliput' already, and am far too securely jammed in my corner seat to be able to rise and claw down the case in which my library book is buried. But fountain pen and notepaper were on my knee, in an outsize handbag you may not remember giving me for Christmas two years ago. Hence this epistle. My mood fits the opportunity, too. So often I've written you long screeds about nothing, and now I've deliberately churned my world up into a fluid mass, and turned it blindfold into a mould, and am waiting to see what comes out; perhaps you'll be interested, too.

It was partly John's fault, and partly Mussolini's. Laugh and be damned! That's the way it happened.

We were out at Hillingham, dancing at a Red Cross ball. It wasn't a particularly inspiring sort of company, but the drinks were good, and the band was very good. After the third gin and lime I remember everything began to look pretty rosy to me. I was in form – the red dress and all my war paint, and John in his highest spirits which means a very attractive John, something for a plain woman of twenty-seven to brandish before the eyes of the world. You won't agree with that, I know. You never liked him. I wonder why I never held it against you that you couldn't see eye to eye with me about John? Not because your opinion didn't matter, believe me. It always has mattered, rather more than's natural.

They showed a short Ministry of Information film in the middle of the evening. It wasn't remarkable in itself, but it came as a jolt after that molasses of music and gin and slow foxtrots. All about the work of the defence services in London. You'll know the kind of thing perfectly.

Well, it's totally inexplicable, for I've seen them already by the hundred; but this one got home. It made me wonder what I was doing at Hillingham in a red velvet frock and silver shoes, with a gin and lime in my hand, and next week's gossip column in my head. Worse than that, it made me wonder what John was doing there with me.

For God's sake don't get any false ideas about me, Nick. This was no uprush of patriotism, only an inept kind of self-disgust because the whole scene, and he and I with it, just became monstrously unreal and precarious all in one breath. I love security. I'm twenty-seven, I have to have solid ground under my feet. Well, this sort of neutral ground isn't solid any more; so I'm getting off it, while the going's good. I expected him to see it the same way; heaven knows why he should, but one isn't reasonable about the workings of two hearts that ought to beat as one, and don't.

He wasn't impressed at all. I'd been taking him so

completely for granted that I didn't glance at him until the end, when he suddenly laughed, and said in my ear: 'What have I done for thee, England, my England?'

It jarred. You'll not need to be told how self-righteous and vehement I was feeling, being newly converted; and I turned on him and said a Catherine-ish thing for which I know you will slate me as I deserve. 'Not much,' I said, 'apart from pushing Fuller out of your father's office so that you could be sure of a reserved occupation.'

You would have sworn at me, but then if I'd said it to you it would have been a lie. Besides, John doesn't swear. I think he was genuinely puzzled; he has never yet awakened to the fact that I am the malicious creature you know me to be. He's so honest, in fact, that he doesn't know how to weigh up my more dubious utterances. However, he was hurt; of all the inept reactions! There was a chill in the air for the rest of the evening, but we didn't argue about it, we didn't discuss it; there was nothing to discuss, because we both knew it was true. I'd never found fault with the arrangement before; it had seemed to me the normal thing to do, the thing everyone was doing. But suddenly I seemed to have been caught up and transported to the other side of the fact, and the reverse view was a scalding experience.

That was how it began. I seem to see the famous Nick Crane smile beginning to glimmer. You know us both too well to take us very seriously. Or am I under-rating you? Did you ever see possibilities in me bigger and more individual than I cared to look for? I don't know. You always seemed to me to have within you a well of wisdom never altogether fathomed, from which you drew up at leisure pearls which surprised even yourself;

4

the result, I suppose, of so many years of inactive contemplation of humanity. At any rate, something has given you an insight I've never met in anyone else; and for all I know you may not be looking at a new Catherine Saxon even now, in this embryo-patriot probationary Wren, but at a slightly unusual angle-shot of the same old person. If so, there's no need to try and amplify this letter into a complicated self-analysis. Lucky, because I couldn't do it, anyhow. I leave all that to you.

Well, that was John's part. And now for Mussolini's. It's all very simple. He chose the next day as the safe and propitious time to stab France in the back. Probably you listened to the nine o'clock news that night, as I did. And afterwards – that bit about 'materially increasing the number of ruins for which Italy is famous'. That, and the grim satisfaction with which it was said, pleased me utterly. Ten days earlier I would have made austere noises, as smug people did in the newspapers afterwards, deploring an utterance so inhumane. Saxon, as you know, isn't normally an introspective kind of cuss, but she did notice this irrational-seeming change in herself, and took the trouble to examine it. I find myself a realist. If we must go to war, let's go to the trouble to find out how it's done, and do it with all our might. I always hated half-measures. If the systematic flattening out of Italy is going to be an ultimate economy in men, and time, and material, and bloodshed, then by all means let's flatten it and be done with it. And for God's sake, having been driven to the extremity of war against our will, let's not be ashamed of doing the thing thoroughly. The Nazis have certainly taught us a thing or two; well, I'm all for bettering the instruction.

So in the name of logic there was only one thing to do.

I don't know how many grains of national weight I represent, but it had to be thrown in, for what it was worth. And I threw it.

I said: 'I'm going to join up.'

Father was half asleep over the evening paper, making little deprecatory tut-tutting noises periodically in the direction of the wireless. Mother was rather more than half asleep after a baffled attempt to demolish the first chapter of 'Seven Pillars of Wisdom', which she has had in the house, unread, for about five years. They both looked up in a vague way, and stared at me as if it were dawning upon them that they had produced a dodo. I was glad then that I'd said it, that it was off my chest, that for cussedness' sake if for nothing better, I couldn't back out.

They tried to make me, of course. They talked about being old, and needing me; father is an able-bodied fifty-four, and mother is fifty and full of a troublesome kind of energy which makes her career about the country-side mishandling charity bazaars and knitting parties and whist-drives. I laughed; I couldn't help it. Then they began to be really concerned, and assured me that I was doing work of national importance in putting on record the new season's sensible trends in footwear, and the colour of Mrs Thingummytite's daughter's wedding dress. As if it mattered a curse whether we went barefoot or got married in dungarees! And when that was non-effective, they began to run through all the unmarried, unattached, able-bodied females we know, citing every legitimate and illegitimate reason why I should consider myself free of personal responsibility until they were all in uniform. Lastly, mother appealed to me almost tearfully to consider nursing or something of that kind.

'A nurse's uniform, dear, is the only one in which a woman looks *right*.' I said that I loathed the whole childish business of wearing uniform and playing at being a man, that I was temperamentally unfitted for it; but that I had no qualifications in the nursing line, and no time to get any, and no inclination either. Whereas after my unscientific fashion I could type, and my head was good for figures, and I could back myself to learn anything in the office line after my miscellaneous experiences with the Gazette general utility department. But loudest and oftenest I said that go I must and go I would; until they grew hardened to the idea, and finally accepted my going with the greatest complacency. They have even caught the infection, and begun to realise that this war has possibilities. When I left, mother was talking pensively about W.V.S. and evacuees, and father had a considering eye on the Sunday drills of the Home Guard. I think of him crawling over the Alden Hills on manoeuvres, and it gives me impish joy. He needed an interest in life.

But it's with myself I'm preoccupied, Nick, first and foremost. Thousands are doing it, but when one comes to the very doorstep of the deed it isn't easy. At my age the throwing overboard of a safe, congenial job within reach of home is a piece of heroism, especially to a confirmed grower of roots like myself. To snap off a whole set of contacts and set out to establish new ones in a place I don't know is harder to me than walking unmoved through air raids. But backing out is harder still; and here I go, uneasily but doggedly, well out into the deep end.

Why the W.R.N.S., you'll say. It just happened to be the first thing that offered. By sheer coincidence two

Wren officers came recruiting the following week, and spent what must have been a very trying afternoon interviewing applicants for a naval life. I was one. I hadn't thought of any particular service until then, but on reflection it seemed as good as any, and in I went.

Being interviewed is a weird experience, as maybe you found out in 1918, when you came back from France flat on your back, and crippled as much with publicity as injuries. But hitherto I've been at the dishing-out end, and oh, Nick, it's laughable, but I couldn't take it. Confronted by those two large, masterful women, Saxon felt like a dual personality – a very young girl applying for her first job, and a rather common insect pinned down on a board for dissection. Very salutary for the soul, perhaps, but bad for the self-esteem. However, being told I was willing and ready to go anywhere and do anything, they saw some virtue in me. Further informed that I could type moderately well, they saw me, as it were, taking shape before their eyes; and to them I began to look like a teleprinter. I beg your pardon, a teleprinter operator; teleprinter is the instrument itself. I agreed with a sort of slavish enthusiasm, like a spaniel expressing admiration of its owner's every word. And a teleprinter operator I shall be now for the duration.

I signed papers, very fairly worded as I remember them, and surrendered voluminous information about self and forebears and I was told that I should probably be called up very quickly. But not how quickly!

I lay back then on my accomplishment, and prepared to enjoy my last week or two. And they wired for me three days later! To report the following Monday! I hadn't even had time to complete the medical examination; that was done in a rush the day I received the telegram, which was Saturday. No time to make the round of my friends, and be fêted smugly at their expense on the strength of my grand gesture. No time even to come to Wastwood and receive your benediction. And how I wanted it, as soon as I knew it was impossible!

It's so long since I was at Wastwood. I think of it a good deal, whenever the small circumstances of life become too much for me. Time and anxiety stay outside the gate, and once I step over the doorstone – judging from the angle at which you lie, I doubt if you ever see how white that doorstone is – I'm safe from ever growing older. Write to me, Nick, just a line, not enough to tire you; and I shall hear the rustle and uneasiness of the wind threshing the rookeries, and see the evening growing blue around the eaves, bleu de pervenche, the only periwinkle-blue dusk in the world. When service life has driven me halfway to dementia I shall run away from Devonport, and you will see me streak to earth through your always-open door, and sit down by the fire and fold my hands, wrapping myself up in your supernatural security, and smiling at the worries and wars that dare not follow me in.

But I can't get to you, you can't approve me or slang me to my face; and goodness only knows when I shall have the satisfaction of seeing yours again. So write you must and write you shall, a line at least for the reams you are likely to get from me. All my grievances and all my amusements will know their way home to you.

So there you have it, all the tale up to the time of going to press. Shall I tell you where we are now? Under the Severn, somewhere in that astonishingly unimpressive tunnel. I've never written so long a letter in such a short time in my life; you see I still have more than four hours to spare. Shall I go on, or are you already tired of me and all my works? There's very little more to tell you. This is Monday, and I am on my way to report at Devonport according to programme.

What else? Don't – yet – ask me what a teleprinter is, or how it works. I've never seen one, though I believe the 'Gazette' has a couple tucked away somewhere. Such impressions as I receive on sight you shall get in your turn, faithfully.

Now be quiet while I read through this tangle of rubbish and see how little I've conveyed to you. There you come again, Nick Crane. When I write 'now be quiet' I can see you being quiet as the twilight, with your profile sharp and thin, pointed like fine pencil-work, against the glow of the fire; that queer, horizontal face. It was always fascinating to me to watch you; the human face recumbent – not just for purposes of rest, but for all its living and thinking and feeling, day in, day out – is an awesome thing; and as a coltish creature with plaits I was afraid of you. But when I got used to seeing you lie so still, and having you treat me, from your pinnacle of cripplehood, as man to man – even to that ready flow of language which shocked mother and satisfied me – then I began to take everything I had in my mind up to Wastwood for your examination, to be approved or damned as you saw fit. And I'm still doing it, Nick.

So, upon re-reading, I don't think I've said the half you will read here. No need. You must know what it's like to find yourself really at war, with this blinding suddenness. Perhaps it happened to you last time.

Expect news of me in a few days, and until it comes, consider that all's very well with your

Saxon.

II. LETTERS FROM PLYMOUTH

W.R.N.S. Quarters, Devonport.
August 15th, 1940.

Dear Nick,

This is a most extraordinary racket. I am sent for in palpable haste, two telegrams being lavished upon me; and when I arrive everyone looks at me blankly, and declines to be responsible for me in any way, unless my name is Smith. Alas, your Saxon, even to acquire supper and a bed, can pass herself off as no one but Saxon. I refused to be Smith, and finally they accepted me with a shrug, and consented to let me stay. At the time I thought it rather a pity, for I was tired and grubby from train and taxi, and my enthusiasm was at a very low ebb indeed, so low that the prospect of being thrown out, and set free to streak back to Wastwood with a clear conscience, was more inviting than you might guess. But I'm glad now that it didn't happen, because I hate to be beaten.

Let me try to describe the place first. It's a large, ramshackle building on a fairly busy street, not far from one gate of the naval dockyards. Four storeys high in stucco, with a black-out problem guaranteed to puzzle the best of domestic organisers. I'm told it used to be a hotel, and was condemned property until the Wrens took it over. There's a spacious entrance hall, relic of its days of glory, from which a spiral staircase winds up to the various floors, while the central well soars right up

11

to a blued-in glass dome. Necessarily very gloomy, and wasteful where electricity is concerned, for the lights burn in the hall all day; but what could you do with a glass dome except blue it in?

The surroundings are not beautiful – do you know Devonport at all? – but after all we need sleep and eat here only, and Devon is at our backs, and the sea not so far from our doorstep, and just across the Hamoaze is my Cornwall waiting to be challenged. You woo Devon, but you dare Cornwall. (I speak of the earth, not the people.) So I feel that there may still be more in life than wars and rumours of wars.

I don't yet know just how many women are quartered here. At the time of my arrival it looked as if the total population consisted of one leisurely Wren sitting at ease in the office (on the right as you go in) with a Boots' library book. It was she who implored me to be Smith. Smith they had been warned about, Smith they expected with some eagerness; but they knew nothing whatsoever about the imminent arrival of one Saxon. I felt myself to be suspect, but I stuck to my tale, and finally after consultation with an officer, summoned from somewhere upstairs, my mentor agreed to provide me with supper and a bed. She also showed me, praise be, a perfectly good bathroom, and the hot tap provided really hot water; and I began to feel a little better.

I located the common-room (ex-lounge) by the cheerful noise issuing from it; and the pugnacious part of me wanted to plunge in headlong and announce myself and get the shock over. But I couldn't do it. I was tired and despondent, and at my social and aesthetic worst. I decided to go to bed and refuse to face life until the morning, when I trusted the whole thing would look better.

'Breakfast's any time between seven and half-past eight,' said my guide, with one eye on her library book. 'If there's an alarm during the night you come downstairs and pile in with any of the others. They know where to go. Towels in your cabin. Goodnight!' And she swooped back into her eyrie, and I went to bed.

My cabin (sic!) – not exactly first-class A deck, but certainly not lower than tourist – is on the top floor; a long climb, but worth the effort, as I discovered next morning. It's large and bare, with three beds in it; two of them, when I entered, so rumpled and strewn with dressing-gowns, odd stockings, Penguin books and knitting that I had no difficulty in settling on the one I was meant to occupy. If all service people fare as well, ours is a fine country to live in. We even have two slips of rug, and the curtains are bright green; and the multiple and disorderly signs of occupation made me feel at once that I'd come into a place where people lived at ease. I examined – who wouldn't? – the photographs on the chest of drawers, and picked out by guesswork the family of Blue Mules from the family of Khaki-Knitting. Tons of gold braid on one side, and two very young army men, uncommissioned, on the other. I won't tell you what I guessed; it was all wrong anyhow.

I lay awake for some time, hoping one or the other would come in and give me an opportunity of breaking the ice. But they didn't, and I went to sleep a stranger still.

The next thing I knew was that the sirens were yodelling. The fourth time I had heard them since war broke out, only the fourth! I woke up trembling, as one does at a sudden noise, and remembered automatically that I had to get up and go downstairs. I sat up, and felt for my slippers. One of the other beds creaked, the most vicious and most mellifluous of voices said, 'Oh, damn and blast!' And up went the lights, and I saw my roommates.

The owner of the mellifluous voice was Blue Mules. She was sitting cross-legged on the bed, wriggling her way into a blue dressing-gown, and clawing up her gasmask from the floor with one hand. Not one of your fresh-from-school baby Wrens, but a tall, thin young woman of perhaps twenty-four, one of the incisive kind, one you couldn't miss. A lot of dark red hair, almost copper-beech-coloured, and a clear white face with high cheek-bones, and a long, droll mouth that had learned to swear from the two or three generations of gold braid in her family photographs. I like looking at faces like hers. I sat back and looked my fill. She was in no hurry.

She said: 'You're new, aren't you? Lousy welcome we seem to be giving you.'

I said: 'All in the night's work,' and began struggling into my slacks.

The other girl – Khaki-Knitting – was about nineteen, small and round and soft and perky-looking, rather sparrowish, with short, feathery hair. She was busily engaged – I remember thinking it a trifle odd at the time – in tearing her bed to pieces. With her gasmask slung over one shoulder, her arms clutching a blanket, a pillow and a travelling rug, and an almost paintless battle bowler cocked over one ear, she tottered towards the door and commenced to trip herself up at intervals along the landing, but all with an air of such bewildered boredom that I almost forgot to follow.

'Come on,' said Blue Mules, gathering up her pillow

under one arm. 'If we don't hurry, they'll pinch our table.' And as this seemed to be regarded as something of a calamity, I hurried.

All the lights were out under the blue dome, and streams of girls with pocket torches, like some curious midnight votive procession, converged from every corridor upon the spiral staircase and shuffled downward with a soft, slippery noise. Tall girls, short girls, fat girls, thin girls, black girls (black-haired, that is), tawny girls – you know your Pied Piper as well as I do. Girls in turbans, girls in curlers, girls in plaits, girls in kimonos, and siren suits, and slacks and sweaters and blankets and rugs. They surged round and round the staircase to the ground floor, and dived to earth in various eyries, of which I, faithfully following my leader, chose the common-room.

These picked spots, they tell me, are fortified as much as possible, since there's no cellar. At the time I was too sleepy even to wonder about my security, I simply doddered along after Blue Mules, and availed myself thankfully of the half-pillow she offered me in a sheltered corner of the floor. The table, as she had foretold, was already occupied by two blanketed bodies topping and tailing it snugly.

'Fine start!' said Blue Mules, rolling herself in her blanket and dropping adroitly into her corner.

'I'll get used to it,' said I, being considerably less adroit with mine.

Around us in the dark there were soft thumps of other girls throwing themselves down. The room composed itself slowly and reluctantly to a sort of quietness, troubled here and there by little explosions of ill-temper. Someone not far from us tried this position and that without comfort, and the upheaval as she turned over was like a tornado rounding on itself. Someone else exclaimed: 'My God!' at intervals, and betweenwhiles hissed at the company in general to shut up. Oh, very testing to the soul is discomfort, Nick Crane! You can't tackle discomfort on a pinnacle, as you can pain, and glory in it. I doubt if anyone but your Saxon really noticed that a heavy barrage had started as we came down the stairs, or that there were one or two dull impacts which shook the windows and dented the hearing and were quite certainly bombs. To me this snugly close presence of danger was new; to them, or most of them, it was familiar and contemptible and stale. They were more concerned with going to sleep.

This last, a problem to me, presented no difficulties to Blue Mules. She flattened herself, as it were, along the floor, and heaved a few long, easy sighs, and passed right out. Not so your Saxon. I tried every conceivable position, turning furtively to disturb as few of our human sardines as possible; but the floor got harder and harder and my blanket thinner and thinner, and the best I could manage in the way of sleep was a sort of stupor, in which I fervently wished myself away. But more by reason of aching bones than falling bombs. Which goes to show something perverse and vaguely reassuring about human nature, if I could but think exactly what it was.

Well, at the time it seemed as if this vague purgatory of bumps and shufflings and smothered swear-words went on for hours and hours. Actually you won't be surprised to hear that it went on for exactly thirty-five minutes. I suppose it wasn't much of a raid as raids go, though it ended in a very creditable burst of noise which wasn't all gunfire. The oddest thing was the way I could feel the reverberations of every impact coming up, as it were, through the floor, as if the earth underneath shivered. The effect was lulling, if anything. I believe I should finally have gone to sleep if the all-clear hadn't sounded.

One concerted sigh of relief went round the room like a very subdued echo, and next moment everyone was on her feet, hitching together blankets and pillows and rugs in a worse muddle than ever, and heading out for the stairs as if her life depended on it. Some, I swear, had been fast asleep a moment before; I know Blue Mules had; but she was out of the common-room long before I had disentangled myself from the blanket. I take it this faculty of getting smartly off the mark will develop in me only with time and practice; I understand one gets lots of practice here. This time I toddled along in the rear, stepping on the corner of the blanket at intervals of approximately three stairs, so that I got to the top landing in one piece by luck rather than judgment; and I drifted into my cabin in a daze, fell into bed, dragged the blanket over me and slept, all in one continuous and graceful movement. Really slept. Blue Mules and Khaki-Knitting had to shake me for thirty seconds to wake me the second time the siren blew.

Yes, it went again. The whole performance, just as before. Three flights down, and the long, irritated shuffling into position on that hard floor, and the barrage, and the voice hissing: 'My God!' and the numbness, and three flights up again, and at last a beautiful oblivion. And this somnambulist staggering round and round in interminable circles of stair and landing and stair, seeing nothing but the blonde pigtail of the girl in front, and hearing nothing but the puffing of the girl behind. I take it she was fat and scant of breath. I was incapable of looking round to see.

However, that was all for that night. The second time your Saxon fell flat into bed they let her sleep. I am getting case-hardened now, and can do the journey up and down (or rather, in this case, down and up) three times in a night without ever really waking up at all.

Khaki-Knitting shook me out of bed next morning, and I saw why the three flights of stairs really mattered so little. The room was flooded and overflowing with sunlight, and the sky was the colour of very clean primroses outside the window. Best of all, we have the top landing of a fire-escape just outside, like a private balcony, and ours being the highest building anywhere around, we have Devonport spread below us. Not beautiful is Devonport, but it looked good from above, in all that gilding sunlight.

Blue Mules was already up and away. I dawdled through my toilet, and Khaki-Knitting talked. Without stopping except now and again for breath. A funny little comfortable person, with a quaint, solemn face, and blue eyes with a twinkle one doesn't usually associate with short sight; but she wears pebbly-looking glasses, and reads her letters at a range of about ten inches at most.

She said her name was Dan Bartlett. She didn't enlarge on the Dan, but I rather think she was christened Danielle. Blue Mules, it seems, is Gwyn Mellor, more formally Gwynyfryd Mellor, and her father is a Commander, R.N., and hangs out at the Barracks. She said that I should have to report to Barracks, along with two other new arrivals (neither of whom, by the way,

18

turned out to be Smith), after breakfast, and that the
W.R.N.S. administrative office there would then send
us off to our various employments armed with intro-
ductory papers which would see us past the sentries; and
our respective departments would put us to work. Up to
then the future had been a closed book to me; I failed to
see exactly what form the approved gambit would take.
She cleared up this line of inquiry in about five minutes,
but her fund of information was inexhaustible. She told
me about her brothers in the Army, and her love affairs
(with all three Services and most departments of Home
Defence). I've known this process of receiving confidences to make me feel slightly sick at times; but hers
were such breezy confidings, and took so little account
of the confidante, that I was interested and amused. My
first Wren turned out to be witty, and totally devoid of a
sense of reverence, which is more than I had any right to
expect.

They are not all easy to talk to, of course, nor am I the
readiest of mortals to make friends with my own sex.
Do you remember calling me a taciturn little hedgehog
once because I erected my spines in Mrs Drummond's
well-meaning face when she came to tea unexpectedly at
Wastwood? I still do it, though the nature of the spines
has changed somewhat. I can remain sweetly com-
municative under pumping now, and still give nothing
away. A quality I think I shall need here, in a house full
of women. But Dan scatters her conversation like
largesse, and princely demands nothing in return.

Her forecast of my day's activity proved right except
in one particular. I was shepherded to Barracks, steered
up an iron stair in the first barrack block, and deposited
with the other neophytes upon a bench outside the

Superintendent's door to be left until called for. After three quarters of an hour I was received by an officer, and promptly sent off to an establishment at the other end of Devonport, where apparently the Command had its Signal Office. Which, I gathered, included me.

I found it in the end, Signal Office, Regulating Office and all. I acquired a pass which would give me right of entry beyond the barbed-wire barriers for some time ahead, and was informed of my allocation to B. Watch; but I was not put to work, for the simple reason that my watch had come off at eight o'clock that morning, and were not due on again until six o'clock the following evening. Very well managed, if by that time I hadn't been longing to take the plunge at once and get it over.

So here was your Saxon, with the better part of two days to kill; nothing loath, except that the fearsome mystery of teleprinting grew more enormous and complicated and awe-inspiring the longer I contemplated it from this depth of ignorance. Nothing to be done about it, however; they didn't want me until the proper time. So off I went to have an official photograph taken, and to explore Plymouth.

There are worse occupations for a fine August day, as you of all people must remember, who once, I believe, knew it so well. I sat on the Hoe, and Mount Edgcumbe was dark green and plumy across the water over the head of Drake's Island. I sat there and sunned myself through and through, and admired my beautiful golden-brown arms against my tussore suit, and altogether forgot my anxieties in a vague, pervasive satisfaction with everything. And betweenwhiles I did think of you in your very early flying-boats, before you broke yourself up; but I wasn't so presumptuous as to feel sorry for you, so hold me innocent of the sort of impertinence your lordship peculiarly abhors. Instead, I think I found a way of envying you. It isn't easy to endure patiently this apparently non-productive and non-progressive warfare of ours, when one remembers what Poland has gone through; and at times I am afraid that the only real satisfaction can be in putting oneself into the same appalling position with the Poles. Which is ridiculous. Nobody really wants to be tortured and killed. My God, I don't! You know Catherine Saxon too well for that. But there must be a guilt complex somewhere within me; or why was I so particularly happy after my first night in a genuinely dangerous target area? I suppose the most prosaic of us occasionally sees visions of himself behaving heroically in picturesque circumstances replete with shot and shell; and it might soothe this sense of being no use. But most of the time I'm sceptical, Nick.

Well, not that you want to hear about my unaccustomed wallowings in the introspective, I concluded that I was glad to be part of a bomb-target. Which argues madness in the family, but gives me a superiority complex which it will take more than Hitler to shake.

Back to facts! I used the rest of my free time in sliding into my environment, getting to know certain of my fellow-Wrens, skirmishing carefully with others I fear I shall never get to know, mastering the routine of quarters life. Of which more when I feel I have it more securely taped. But all with the ghost of the job I hadn't yet seen floating in my mind; so that I was glad when the time came for me to take the plunge in earnest.

It had its funny side. The first difficulty was finding the teleprinter room at all. I knew it was somewhere in the Signal Office, but the interior of the Signal Office turned out to be a veritable rabbit warren, and unhappily for me no one seemed to be heading for the same burrow I wanted. I asked the Marine sentry to direct me, and he did, but the results were not up to scratch. I turned left, according to his instructions, passed a row of red fire buckets, turned right, crept along tortuous corridors, shot into a blind alley to avoid a Rear-admiral, shot back again in the wrong direction, and found myself back with the fire-buckets. Starting again from scratch, I turned all the corners I'd missed the first time, and came out in an open office where a Petty Officer, two or three seamen and half a dozen Wrens were doing interesting things with sheaves of papers, bulldog grips, a stapling machine and other paraphernalia. I know it now as the Central Communications Office. At the time it was just a reserve of people from whom I hadn't yet asked my way. They turned me to the left, through a glass-panelled door with two traps in it for pushing signals in and out, and I was actually in the teleprinter room.

The overwhelming impression was of a demoniac, unremitting, inhuman noise. It came out and hit you as you opened the door, and wrapped itself lovingly round you the moment you shut yourself in with it. If you've ever been in a room with ten typewriters all going hell for leather, let me tell you here and now that you've heard nothing like our ten teles, all ticking over at once. This is a more insistent, more insidious, more pervasive noise; for besides the staccato effect of the keys there is the deep hum of the power which drives the machines; and if the one hammering on your senses from outside doesn't drive you crazy, the other will sneak in and complete the work from inside. The fact is, of course, that you get used to it in a few weeks, and it ceases to worry you at all; but the above is how it felt and sounded to me when I first entered the room.

Besides the din of the machines, there was a shriller din of voices. There were five girls in the room, and one seaman, and the whole half-dozen of them seemed to be yelling at once. Three of the girls were sitting at machines, the fourth was on the telephone, and the fifth was conducting a high-pitched and voluble quarrel with the seaman. The dispute seemed to be about a blonde and a dance and a broken date, but there was nothing private about it, for two of the other girls had joined in before it came to an end.

As for your Catherine, no one paid any attention to her after one quick, incurious glance. I took a comprehensive look around and explained to anyone who showed a momentary disposition to listen that I was the new member of the watch. They were quite blasé about it, unwarned but incapable of surprise. They told me that the fire-haired damsel engaged in skirmishing with the matelot was in charge of the watch, but held out little hope that she would notice me. They let me watch them at work, and gave me a machine in local (professional for 'not connected with any receiving station') to play with. With which measures my red-haired Leading Wren, having demolished and dismissed her matelot, had no fault to find. Indeed, she was completely disinterested, only if anything rather pleased to see that I was more or less off her hands.

And so to the point of the whole matter. What is a teleprinter? Well, it's a sort of overgrown cross between a telephone and a typewriter; and it looks rather like a typewriter with advanced thyroid trouble, in a black japanned cover fitted with a stand to hold the copy, and sticking out its keyboard from its undershot jaw like a bulldog showing his teeth. But in sex undoubtedly feminine, you would say, being capricious, incalculable and bad-tempered. It has a standard keyboard with slight differences; for instance, it has one key intriguingly marked, 'Who are you?' When connected with some distant station you depress (professional for 'tap') this key, and it answers its own question by producing the call sign of the station at the other end. It does this for me perpetually at the wrong moments, owing to a weakness I have for forgetting to put myself back on to letters after an interlude of figures. However, this insistence upon doing its trick has rammed home the principle of the thing, and I am one step upon the way to omniscience in the psychology of teleprinters.

But at first sight of naval traffic and teleprinter procedure I sat back in despair. It appeared to me that the job was beyond me. This is a failing I can't kill, Nick. You have tried cajoling me and cursing me both, without any effect at all; and heaven knows I have tried everything, even to concentrating upon that funny side which – do me justice – I never fail to see. But the gorgon's a gorgon yet. Let me touch something new, and I am always daunted. So I spent that first evening in a struggle with the conviction that I wasn't going to be any good. No use telling myself I'd never yet met the job I couldn't do; there has to be a first time for everything. So your Saxon was not very happy as she punched the usual silly sentences out of that teleprinter, and tried to make sense of the copy on her neighbour's stand.

The evening watch went like wildfire. They were too

busy to pay much attention to me, and I learned very little and that little chiefly by looking over people's shoulders as they worked. I left disappointed. I had expected to master at any rate the worst of the strange feeling, but I didn't feel that this frost had given at all.

But this morning was better. For one thing the signal traffic was not so copious, and so there was time to encourage me; and for another thing I did what I invariably do, with the usual results. I asked my Leading Wren – her name is Myra – if she thought I should be able to tackle the job. She looked really staggered, and said at once: 'Oh, yes, I think you'll be very good.' And I was satisfied. If she, after seeing my gingerly approach, had no qualms, why should I have any? Queer that a deep sense of misgiving like mine should be so easily allayed by this direct approach, and so impossible of treatment any other way. But the fact remains. I was quite satisfied. I sat down again and practised my unscientific fingering blithely until more traffic came in for transmission, when I actually sent two signals on direct lines, slowly but with deadly accuracy, and one – terrific achievement – through a switchboard, all the way to Chatham. I finished the morning in high spirits, and am now off duty until one o'clock to-morrow.

I am writing this from a seat in the colonnade on the Hoe, looking down upon the swimming pool. The water is a clear, pale, glistening green, and full of children; I think some local school has tipped its entire population into the pool, and I am seriously thinking of joining them. Dan – she's a telephonist, also in the C.C.O., but not in the same watch with me – is fast asleep in the opposite corner of the seat, with her hat tipped over her face. She was on duty all night – my fate to-morrow, so think of me struggling with my capricious allies, the machines, while you sleep.

Do you sleep? I wonder. I remember the Munich period. You weren't supposed to know that I knew how you lay awake night after night then, trying to work out a salvation for us in your own mind, or something impossible and Nick-Craneish like that. But I did know. As if because your physical self was irrevocably out of the combat your mind had to torment itself instead. No need now, believe me, Nick. You can afford to sleep.

I don't deceive myself that all's perfect in our particular national organisation; but I'm quite happy about the outcome of anything we set out to do. You had your turn earlier, Nick.

Write to me. I want letters. I have plenty to say in answer these days.

Salutations to Mrs Lane and the evacuee infant. When I get my first leave I hope to come over to Wastwood and see him. If I get any letters from America I'll send him the stamps.

Yours as ever,
Catherine.

W.R.N.S. Quarters, Devonport.
August 22nd, 1940.

Dear Nick,

Damn you, yes, you know everything. John did try to argue me out of joining the service, and we did quarrel, and so far neither of us has written to the other. But we shall. The devil of it is that I do see his point of view, as clearly as if I shared it. He's quite incapable of seeing anything outside his own narrow experience, and he's always been taught to regard his career as a sort of fetish to which circumstances must bow down. But is that his fault? The fact that I can't share his single-hearted devotion to John Randall doesn't mean that my feeling towards him has changed at all. I'm still wearing his ring, and shall be; that doesn't enter into it, as you jolly well know.

Your letter, you will have gathered, was irritating as well as sketchy. You were always a rotten correspondent. But being full of my own doings just now, I can't pay you back in your own coin. Mother expects only the merest personal scrawl from me, and I have to have a safety valve, and you fill the bill rather well, as a matter of fact. That was one job for which I never in my life nominated John, anyhow. So you'll go on hearing from me, indefinitely. No help for it, Nick.

John wanted me to stay home and marry him. You knew, of course, that he'd stepped into Fuller's job in the office; and that makes him reserved, especially since they've taken on so many experimental chemistry jobs for the government. All very attractive, or it would have been once. But while this business goes on, and especially as a pretty considerable portion of the population of this country is bound not to survive it, there seems precious little sense in personal attachments; except the biggest, which ours isn't, by any means. I don't suppose hell has any more use than heaven for marrying and giving in marriage.

So I said no. Me for the war, and whatever there was on the books besides could very well wait, and if we were both still alive and kicking after the war we'd talk about it then. He didn't like it, but we didn't go to extremes, and our engagement is still on. How you gathered so much from a long letter in which the poor lad's name wasn't even mentioned, only your uncle and namesake the devil knows.

Enough about that. Back to our sheep!

This grows interesting, Nick. Since my last letter, that is, in just a week, our office has migrated, lock, stock and barrel. It's the most amazing thing I ever saw in my life. We say good-night to eleven teleprinters in the heart of Devonport, and greet them next day elsewhere. How this is possible I don't know; unhappily we don't service the machines as well as operating them, so the mechanical side of this intricate defence network, how the connections are made and extended, and so on – all that part of it is still a sealed book. They're such intriguing things, too; they have character, and differ from one another in the most startling ways. They purr when they're pleased with life, they rattle and grow hot when they're angry, and I believe that once, exasperated beyond endurance, one of our most ill-used specimens burst into flames. I find them impatient with incompetence; they let me tap my slow and cautious way along a whole line, and then carriage return violently and spit a series of X's and figures across the paper, or cast up the answer-back of the station to which I'm transmitting – that luckless key-complex of mine again – to the accompaniment of a wildly ringing bell. However, I persevere, and am acquiring merit in my Leading Wren's unenthusiastic eyes, so there's every hope for me.

So much for the general set-up. And what a set-up! Working here, especially in the night watches, is a schoolboy's dream. The watches are brought out by bus now, an asthmatical grey contraption with an amazing turn of speed, commandeered from the Lord knows where. We stumble across an arena of grass in pitch darkness, a torch flashes on us, a rifle butt hits the ground with a bang, and we are halted in the most fearsome style, and bidden (if we give the right answer, as not all of us do) to advance and be recognised. Actually, of course, it's our passes they want to see, not our faces; and these being satisfactory, we're allowed to proceed. Into the bowels of the earth, no less! Think of it, Nick! If only we could be fifteen again, and going on duty by way of a subterranean passage a hundred yards and more in length, with obscure little box-like alcoves here and there in the walls, and a broken stairway diving away from it at one corner, away into goodness knows what complication of mystery. Who would mind working then? And that's what we do, almost every day. The most tantalising thing is that another sentry stands over that broken stair, so in all probability I shall never know where it goes to.

The rabbit-warren feeling is gone with the old office. Here we have twice as much elbow-room; and even something of the glamour of the approach colours the interior, for we have riveted steel stanchions painted naval grey instead of beams, and our walls are cream, and there is more than a distant suggestion of the battleship about us. Also we have a stunning canteen, deep under the ground, democratic enough to serve Wrens, but drawing the line at naval ratings. A pity, this last, because so far the naval ratings are by far the nicest and most satisfactory part of the navy.

Well, it will be no news to you that I was not cut out to

fit into a code of rigid behaviour such as a service necessarily entails. I have a tendency to say 'Why?' when told I can't do things. Why can't I take Bill into the canteen and buy him a drink? Why can't I walk through the main gate at the barracks, instead of sneaking in at one side? Why must I stand up if an officer enters? Why? It will get me into serious trouble yet before this war is over, but I'm afraid it was born in me, and I have to do it. It isn't good enough for me that a thing has been done so long that it's become a tradition; time was when the rack was a fine old English institution.

The affair of the barrack gate was funny. Gwyn took me there on Sunday morning to the church service. She has been in the navy just three weeks longer than I have, and has just gone into uniform – self-provided, I may add, for it seems the official kitting-up process is rather slow. In spite of a careless mental splendour which accepts and subdues every circumstance to her will, she's almost as ignorant of her new sphere as I am. And the navy – this is rule one, and a law of the Medes and Persians if ever there was one – tells you absolutely nothing of what you are supposed to know. You pick up your knowledge of their most sacred prohibitions by the simple process of putting your luckless foot through every one of 'em in turn.

Even so we. We came to the main gate of the barracks, a carriage-way in the middle, a narrow gateway on either side, a P.O. and a couple of ratings standing guard. Through the carriage gate we went blithely sailing. The P.O. let out a scandalised yell. We, being just short of the degree of greenness necessary to ignore such yells, turned towards him two smiles that were childlike and bland. 'Here!' said he indignantly. 'You can't go through there!'

It was a silly thing to say, but we capped it. Gwyn said: 'Too late. We have.'

I, in my usual line of thought, said simply: 'Why?' I think it was the 'why' that did it. He took fire like a Chinese cracker, and exploded in a shower of shibboleths and customs and naval thou-shalt-nots. He told us we were in the navy now, and we must pay proper respect to the traditions of the navy. He even dragged Nelson into it. I'm all for Nelson, but frankly I don't believe he would have cared a hoot if Gwyn and Catherine walked through all the main gates in R.N.B.

Well, we escaped from that lecture with a properly awed front which covered, I fear, nothing better than two acute fits of the giggles. And to cap everything, in our innocence we promptly walked clean across the quarter-deck without saluting. I was all right, of course, being still in plain clothes, but for Gwyn, in her brand-new tiddly suit, it was practically a hanging matter. Luckily the officer who spotted us and pulled us up was a fatherly old thing who thought fit to explain rather than rave. So we survived.

But the cream of the joke came after the service. We met Gwyn's father, and he walked out to the bus-stop with us. And it seems that when walking with an officer you borrow his glory and are allowed to share his privileges; so out we strolled three abreast through the centre gate, very conscious of the P.O.'s thwarted glare, and humanly rejoicing in it. So the score was beautifully evened up for us, and my introduction to the perils of visiting R.N.B. was not altogether discouraging. I grow inured to the fact that I shall inevitably step upon every naval corn in existence before my career closes; and I'm willing to take a sporting chance on tradition, and learn by experience without undue seriousness.

Our existence tends, I find, to separate itself into two water-tight compartments, work in one basket, quarters and leisure in t'other. All the more noticeably so in my case as all my fellow-teleprinters in the watch are immobile, living locally in their own homes and thus collecting to themselves the best of both worlds. On watch I hobnob only with Myra and her Plymouth stalwarts; between watches my company is Gwyn and Dan and their kind; and the two are no kin. Both sides, I think and hope, are to be friends of mine; but they look at each other with alien eyes, and their minds are full of criticism and distrust. Brother Nicholas, these things ought not so to be.

I know what you will say to that. Too early to judge yet. Wait and form your judgments, instead of leaping on them and squashing them flat. And I will. But an impression is an impression, not to be dismissed, however judgment may be reserved on it. Evidence, but not proof.

I have a feeling that there may be some doubt among civilians about the degree of usefulness of the women's services. Are they really earning their keep? Does the work they do justify the money that's being poured out on them? Perhaps it's rather early for me to have an opinion on that point, too, but on the whole I think we do. As you know, I'm extremely sceptical about the 'service' side of it, I hate uniforms and rigidity and regimentation of every kind; but aside from that part of it, which is a mere attitude of the organising or committee mentality and will never justify itself to me, I think we are giving the country good value for its money. My own job, by no means one of the most important or intricate a Wren can do, pleasantly surprises me every time I go on watch by its close and constant link with the actual fighting ships. So my conscience didn't tumble me out of the 'Gazette' office for nothing, and no one need refrain from joining up for fear of finding herself wasted. In certain unfortunate circumstances I suppose it could happen, but it would be exceptional.

So much for the primary satisfaction.

As for entertainment, in a community of females we don't fall far short of the standard set by a community of males. You won't have forgotten how high – and how peculiar – that is. I don't pretend that women are cut out for a communal life as men are. It's pretty obvious that they aren't. But a good deal of the original unselfconscious Eve comes out when there are no Adams around, and as one surprised rating remarked after a short visit to his girl in quarters: 'Why, a lot of girls together are no better than a lot of fellows.'

I used the word 'unselfconscious'. There is a selfconscious element, a small minority of girls who by nature or training or both are incapable of forgetting themselves for a moment. I think they are the losers. But even they add to the pattern. All human reactions are grist to my mill.

So we are not entirely dull even in quarters, while the job itself is one continuous entertainment. Can't tell you anything about it, of course, apart from what I've already said. The noise, I think, is less noticeable in our new home, unless I am already getting used to it. That's quite possible; I seem to have been here a great deal longer than ten days.

I must stop writing rot to you now, and go and get ready for evening duty. It's already half-past three, and tea is at four, and I have a hundred and one things to do after that before the transport leaves for never-mind-where fort.

Write me a line soon; and leave John out of it. You have been warned!

> Yours (as you are much too well aware) ever,
> Catherine.

> W.R.N.S. Quarters, Devonport.
> September 11th, 1940.

Dear Nick,

Do you know Cawsand? And the way to it, for that's important, too.

Plymouth is a lucky place for watch-keepers, with a thousand and one beauty-spots within easy reach whenever you have an afternoon off; but the two chief favourites are Cawsand and Yelverton – Cawsand over the water in Cornwall, and Yelverton on the Devonshire moors. Since last writing to you I have visited the first, and to-morrow week I am booked to visit the second.

Gwyn had done the Cawsand trip before, and when we happened to talk country-and-sea over our going to bed – it must happen to everyone in this hostel sooner or later – she naturally (I speak as one who has now seen it) said: 'Have you seen Cawsand?' And I said: 'No.' And she said 'You must,' and set to work at once to see that I did. We had a whole free day together the same week, on my side immediately after a night-watch, but I find I do my best walking after a night-watch. So off we went.

It wasn't an encouraging day, slightly misty and rough and damp, a day which looked torn and bedraggled in Devonport, but changed to a wild and wholly admirable half-gale storminess once we were well out on Cremyll Ferry. The feel of the open water comes in when you are half-way over, and you feel the little boat suddenly heave and strain under you, and the spray comes aboard at every dip, and the middle-aged and sane sneak away into the tiny saloon. But we sat up on the gunwale, where it is strictly forbidden to sit, and turned our backs on the wind and let the water pound at our oil-skinned backs and heave past us to flatten itself with a splattering splash on the deck. And we felt, heaven forgive us, that we had at least touched with one finger-tip the sensations of being at sea. Lovely Cremyll Ferry! I shall never forget it. The green, lush, feathery pinnacle of Mount Edgcumbe ahead of us, and the Royal William slipping away on our port quarter, and the long fingers of the true Atlantic reaching out without warning to touch and trouble and haunt us for a moment as we passed.

On the other side of the water is another world. The differences between Devon and Cornwall are so many that it would be much easier to number the resemblances. They practically begin and end with the cream and the visitors. Devon is charming, and I have still to see the best of the moors; but Cornwall, with its soul still in love with the lost centuries and unconcerned with this present one, is haunted and haunting. I know the interior is harsh, and speckled with clay deposits and mine-dumps and old tin-shafts; I know the coast is bleak and scornful and terrifying; but I know I love it utterly. It is less beautiful and much less twopence-coloured than Devon; but it is intensely personal, and vigorous, and turbulent, I think nearer and kinder kin to the Atlantic than to England. No wonder half the legends and more than half the fairies come from there. None of your comfortable little domestic fairies, either, but those dim, passionate, formidable beings, always above lifesize and seen against a background of storm, working out purposes dark and incalculable and ferocious as the sea that gnaws the blue-slate beaches of Arthur's Tintagel.

The corner of seaboard beyond Mount Edgcumbe is certainly softer and kinder than that coast, but still there's no mistaking the county you're in. First comes a long country walk up over the headland, with one amazing vantage-point, a curve of the road circled by a low wall, from which you can look out as if from a balcony over the whole of the intricate system of tidal water which laces Plymouth and Devonport. The Hamoaze, with all its attendant inlets, spread out below and to your right, and tucked immediately under the steep slope you are climbing the bowl of Dead Man's Lake. Go when the tide is well in, or it will be a large basin of smooth grey mud with a few meek little runnels of water threading it like veins; but we saw it at its best, with a fast tide flowing strongly towards its highest; and the grey, torn rags of weather were a princely wear for the sky over it, not beggarly as you might think.

Then you are under the trees of the Mount Edgcumbe grounds and climbing the last slope to the crest of Maker Heights, and Maker Church which sits most splendidly in a cedary loneliness above the steep drop to the outward sea. There is a churchyard wonderfully level and tranquil; you look down from it and see the white of breakers between the cedar branches, and hear the incessant thunder and long receding sighs of the waves coming in under the cliff. But you can't get back to the sea – yet. There is a short detour inland, and then a sharp plunging lane takes you down between trees, the sound all the time growing more insistent in your ears, and the smell more salt and wild in your nostrils; down to the gate which opens on a red earth path slung a third of the way up the cliff, with Cawsand away on your right at the other end of it, and on your left as you turn into it nothing for I forget how many thousand miles but the awesome Atlantic Ocean.

There's a path for you, Nick Crane! A steep slope up on the right, broken red and green of earth and waste grass and furze, with trees climbing it sideways; and on the left a smooth slope of meadow for twenty yards or so, and then the eroded edge of the short cliff, and a drop of maybe thirty feet or so into the ridges of black rock where the foam boils like a cauldron. That day the wind was lifting the spume from the last stress of the tide so that it came sharp on our faces like salt mist, and the tumult under the cliff, with its long recurring roar and longer frustrated moan, seemed to make the solid Cornish earth uneasy under our feet. We left the end of the boom and Breakwater Fort away behind us, and the headland of Mount Batten was a shadowy hump away in the slight haze over the water. And at a point where the path stands high I caught my first glimpse of Cawsand Bay, a semi-circle of cliff and beach round which the little town sat clustered, with a big grey fort set into the high slope behind it; and beyond, the long wooded jut of Rame Head shot out a mile or more into the sea to hold off the worst of the weather.

You come first into Kingsand, which is the newer part
of the town; and you are met by dogs, all of them hospi-
table and princely in their attitude, who make you free
of the place at once. Our welcoming committee consisted of two spaniels and a bull-terrier pup, who
accompanied us down a steep little cobbled street to the
first bit of open beach, and there parted from us with
mutual expressions of regard. A beautiful bull-pup he
was, snowy white, touched up with pink round the eyes
and inside the ears and under the pads of his feet. He
had one lop ear and a leery grin and a brand-new red
collar; and I wanted him, my hat! how I wanted him.
But even if his owner would have parted with him for all
the money I hadn't got, one couldn't ask a self-
respecting dog to live in quarters at Devonport.

We had lunch at the first hotel we could find, in a
room looking out on the boiling sea among the rocks;
and afterwards we walked slowly through the maze of
cobbled back-streets and brief bits of sea-front which is
Cawsand. The sea was running so high that when we
walked inland of the painted houses perched on their
painted rocks, we could feel as well as hear the
spray threshing their shuttered seaward walls, and
spasmodically it came full over them and spattered us
like heavy rain. How I should have loathed a day like
that at home, and how I loved it there! Blown to a wreck
and glistening wet and totally happy, I walked with
Gwyn up through the tiny square and away over the
narrow neck of the headland beyond the town.

Most of the salient bits of the coast are in possession
of the military now. I think they pick out a nice-looking
place in Spring and settle down there for the summer.
And who's to blame them? On the other side of the

headland is Whitesand Bay, all fifteen glorious, bleak, overwhelming miles of it, cruel coast, treeless, lofty, plunging into long black razor-edged rocks, up which the foam runs roaring like thunder.

We coasted downhill, easily at first through damp furze and bramble, and then by crumbling paths doubling back upon themselves in zigzags like bent wires. The end was a wet slide on our tails down red clay, but we reached the beach. Apart from ourselves, there was nothing human within sight, nothing living, even, except the sea-gulls. I wonder why some people dislike this tremendous feeling of being alone? But you're the last person who'd be likely to know an answer to that.

We climbed to a vantage point among the rocks, and took a general survey of our kingdom; blown gulls, and skirling winds, and great rollers that came in ten feet high and ten miles long and as green as jade, deep green, solidly green, only the crests of them glittering white; so terrific that while they kept their stature they were monstrous, and so beautiful that when they shattered they were tragic. We walked along the beach, just out of touch of the waves, for about a quarter of a mile, and came upon a rock; down we sat and looked at the sea, and were happy.

Gwyn Mellor talks very little, but she talked then. She sat there with her arms round her knees, and her hair streaming, and her green eyes watching the green sea. And she said suddenly: 'What's to become of us afterwards?'

I didn't ask what she meant. You won't need to ask.

What is to become of them? People like Gwyn, whose lives have been put, as it were, on a war footing; not only their work and their bodies, but their minds and their souls as well. My God, it isn't going to be so easy putting them back, all these strong uprooted trees.

She talked about herself. I never knew until then that she was engaged; she wears no ring. This is a love created by the war. He knows her only as a child of the navy, active in half a dozen home war jobs before she joined up. She knows him only as an air ace in the ascendant, a fighter pilot with fifteen enemy machines to his name, a survivor of two crashes, twice alive only by a miracle. A hero of the new romances, wearing a D.S.O. and D.F.C. They have no background but the lurid glow of the blitz, and the stormy darkness of the world's catastrophe. What's going to become of them when the fire goes out? None of us will be sorry, but a lot of us will be lost.

What is to become of her? She wonders about it with a sort of analytical detachment, but as one examining a bigger thing than herself, not a smaller. 'What are we to do,' she says, 'with this sort of love? It has nothing to do with domesticity. I never think of him as sitting by our hearth, or of myself as having his children. He used to work in a bank. It doesn't seem possible. The Johnny Fairmile I know just flies, and fights, and wins decorations, and shoots down Huns. If there ever was another, he means nothing to me. What are we going to do with a feeling like this? And how are we going to do without it?'

It's all a little obscure. No one can foresee what will happen to these relationships larger than lifesize when the stress is over that held them taut. No one can help the people like Gwyn, who have the wit to wonder about it. As for Johnny, I haven't seen him, but I doubt if he has any qualms. I doubt if he has realised that he's become a giant.

But to me it isn't easy to get that picture out of my mind, Gwyn sitting there on the rock all blown by the winds and glistening with spray like a mermaid, looking at the sea with her green, deliberate eyes, and talking in her mellifluous voice about the fundamental personal problems of war. Reality for the day had consisted up to then of Cornwall and weather; she brought the war back into the picture as all the barbed wire and gun-emplacements couldn't do. And why not? Very little in the world matters just now except the war; not even the ultimate fate of the Gwyns and the Johnnies, let alone the Catherines.

But I wouldn't be safe, I wouldn't be out of it for all the money in the world. I'm glad I was born at the right time to be a useful age now, an age to know what I'm doing, and why.

Well, we sat there until the rain began, and we had to make a wild dash back into Cawsand. We had tea in a little café right on the foreshore, where the wind drove in with such violence that the front door kept hurtling open with a shuddering crash, and had to be locked at last to save all the china from blowing away. Then back to Cremyll in a small springless bus, which took an unconscionable load quite lightheartedly up the most dizzy hills; and over the ferry and back to quarters just in time for supper.

There you have the story of one day in my service life. A marvellous day, too. Some day, Nick, if these continual operations come to anything, as in the end they must and will, you shall do that walk with me. But after the war. It must be afterwards. And there'll be no green-eyed mermaid sitting on the rock. God knows what will have happened to her by then.

As for pygmies like me, we take to war from a sense of duty, I suppose, and with both feet still firmly planted on the ground; a wrench to go, and a bigger wrench to come back, but at any rate no fear of not being able to come back.

Why should one have to go to a desolate bay, out of sight and sound and touch of the war, to examine its deeper implications? I give up.

I must stop, Nick. Ten minutes past lights out already, and P.O.'s on the prowl.

Goodnight!

Yours, Catherine.

W.R.N.S. Quarters, Devonport.
Sept. 20th, 1940.

Dear Nick,

Nights are getting dark and long here, and consistently noisy, but don't believe one tenth of the damage yarns you'll be hearing. Or perhaps I'm wrong there; you may not get them up at Wastwood, unless Mrs Lane has changed her nature. But mother, bless her, writes me long anxious letters full of bomb-stories, every one from Plymouth, but received by such roundabout routes I wonder even she listens to 'em. Still, to do her justice she doesn't use her maternal feelings to reproach me as she would have done once. She seems to have discovered the possibilities of this war with a vengeance, and a certain brisk impression of mother dashing round managing every war sideline in Yeatbridge and

Hillingham seeps into her letters and comes over to me strongly. Father has joined the Home Guard; and it seems there are soldiers in the neighbourhood, and they have two of the boys billeted on them. Mother, incalculable as ever, reacts with enthusiasm where I should have expected martyred indignation. It's certainly a wise child that knows its own parent. Maybe you're right, and my exit woke them up to their proprietary interest in the war. Anyhow, Hitler must be shaking in his shoes now if he's heard about mother's revolver practice.

Even nearer to the scene we get perpetual surprises on the subject of raid damage to Plymouth. Dan took me to tea one day with an aunt of hers who lives in Horrabridge, and the good lady seemed if anything rather startled to find us alive to keep our appointment. She commiserated with us on the mess the raiders had made of Plymouth. A large section of the town, it seemed, had been burned down, and some bad holes blown in the dockyards at Devonport by heavy H.E. All news to us. But she seemed disappointed rather than relieved when we undeceived her. I wonder why people do so love a blood-curdling bomb story? Personally there's nothing I enjoy more than listening to these yarns in buses and trains, and then solemnly squashing them flat. Not patriotism, or anything like that; just a streak of sadism in me. You always said I had one.

As it happened I was on duty during the worst night raid we had. It started about nine o'clock – they seem to favour an early start – and lasted until half-past ten, which made our relief nearly an hour late and annoyed us very much. From inside you don't hear such trivial things as sirens, and none of the varied noises of the raid comes down to you. The thing to do is to send out the whole watch singly, at suitable intervals, use their eyes, and collect information. Half-way through this particular raid the view over Plymouth was certainly alarming. It was a clear, starry night, and a steady, slow wind was picking up clouds of dun-coloured smoke over the city and driving it in a solid screen across the sky; and over and through the smoke there was a dark red glow that pulsed regularly. It looked as if half the town was going up, but the next dove from our ark, half an hour later, reported the fire out and the smoke clearing rapidly. Next day, being off-duty, I had a look round for the burnt-out sector, but couldn't find a trace of any fire. It must have been considerably less than it looked.

The all-clear went just before half-past ten, and our relief finally turned up twenty minutes later. A couple of matelots were strolling about over the knoll picking up the burnt-out ends of incendiaries, and the transport driver had a bouquet of them, and parted with a few to some of his particular favourites. I (said she modestly) have one. There was no sign then of raid or raiders, and on the ride home we caught only an occasional hint of damage in the bright moonlight. One flattened warehouse gave me a bad moment; it happened to be about fifty yards from a large gas-holder, and in an area crammed with little houses. Still, a miss was as good as a mile that night as always, and the cottages and cottagers are still on their feet. Apart from a deserted tram standing in a lopsided attitude in the middle of the crossroads at Milehouse, we saw nothing else of any interest. So much for the Plymouth blitz up to the present.

It will warm up, of course. Sooner or later we're bound to get it in earnest. Just now it seems to be London's turn. Some day it will be ours, and the Hun, who is damnably methodical over these things, will arrive punctually at the same hour night after night here as he's doing now in London, and things of which I hate to think will happen to this charming and gallant town. I am getting fond of Plymouth, Nick, deep down fond, and it angers me to see, as I can't help seeing, that the shelter accommodation is miserably shallow and inadequate, and that no effort whatever has been made to evacuate children from an area quite obviously booked as a precision target sooner or later. As usual in this idealistic but apathetic democracy of ours, nothing will be done until it's too late to do anything. The principal civic occupation seems to be hoping for the best. As if we hadn't done enough of that, during the past twenty years, to sicken us for life! I don't wish to be a prophet of evil; but there are several miles of naval dockyards at Devonport and a very large barracks, which make it a peach of a target; and the enemy, whose cardinal failing certainly isn't dumbness, must be as well aware of these facts as I am. In the meantime, the wise smile tolerantly, and say: 'It hasn't happened yet, has it?'

I quite forgot to mention, by the way, that I am now a fully-fledged Wren. I was enrolled last week. In theory the ceremony takes place two weeks after the probationer's entry, and if in that space of time she can't fit herself in – well, she's at liberty to get out of the service and scuttle back to Civvie Street. I've never heard of anyone who did, though; the most miserable misfit in the world isn't going to admit she's licked, no matter what her own opinion on the subject may be.

It was totally unimpressive. We filled in more forms with still more details of our private lives, and our undertakings were then read out and explained to us by a Wren officer. The proviso that no Wren may publish in any newspaper or periodical any article relating to service matters was skipped over with an indulgent smile. 'I don't think any of you would be likely to write for the press,' she said gently; and I endeavoured to sound as amused as the rest with my murmur of agreement, while my mind was on the woman's-interest mush I used to trot in to Strang daily. Tell me, Nick, do I look so impossibly unlike a newspaper woman? I used to think I had 'Press' written all over me when I did the round in that snappy little tweed three-piece and the Homburg with the you-be-damned brim. Definitely a swagger of a literary kind. Incidentally I'm still wearing 'em. I couldn't kit up earlier because I wasn't enrolled, and I can't kit up now because there's nothing in the clothing store except ultra-small sou'-westers. Some inconsiderate Jerry dropped H.E. upon the stored accumulations of Hector Powe's natty tailoring in Greenwich, and left us destitute. It becomes annoying to have to sit one's tweeds shiny on our swivel chairs; later on I suppose one's sole ambition will be to get back into tweeds again for a day or so; by then, of course, it won't be possible. Women are never satisfied.

Gwyn and I did our trip to the moors yesterday. Not alone. We had an air escort. The great Johnny Fairmile turned up quite unexpectedly with an inarticulate Sergeant-Pilot friend of his in tow, and the affair

turned into a foursome. Johnny's appearance in the
hall at quarters caused a considerable fluttering in
the dovecote, and at least half of those who happened to
be in quarters at the time have made occasion to pass
through the hall and look him over. Not that Gwyn
has spread his reputation ahead of him; but she has a
large and very captivating photograph of him on her
dressing-table now, and the curious have no inhibitions
about asking anything they feel they'd like to know. A
certain element here, which makes a hobby of lion-
hunting, grudges her the possession of anything so
desirable. For a naval man's daughter she's cavalier
about the trophies they value, and I feel the thought in
more than one mind here that one of their own circle
would wear Johnny with a better grace.

I can hardly credit that he used to work in a bank; and
I can't help wondering if he looked then as he looks
now, or if the achievement and realisation of his own
latent power has matured and changed even his face.
For he's pretty startling, Nick. He's burned a tawny
colour, with copper cheeks like a Red Indian, and his
hair is bleached flaxen, soft and straight and thick like a
child's. He has blue eyes, not pale blue but seeming very
light and brilliant in a face so tanned. He's big, maybe
just over six feet, and as quiet and agile in his movements as a cat. He talks a good deal, not at all badly;
and laughs almost all the time. If this sounds rather a
tiresome young man, mea culpa. He isn't.

I'm a little dazzled still. It isn't every day I sit on top
of a Devonshire tor with one of the heroes of Asgard.
We went up to Yelverton by bus, and from there set out
to walk to Sheepstor. Not by road but by a longer and
lovelier way; through Meavy, which is the Americans'

dream of an old Devon village, though thank God they haven't discovered it yet; across a small stony river by way of stepping-stones to Marchant's Cross, and from there by a steep climb to the crest of an outlying ridge of Dartmoor, and along it in the teeth of a high wind. As soon as you breast the ridge you can see Sheepstor, a hunched hogback in the distance, mottled red and grey with autumn bracken and outcrops of rock.

The road here is treeless, but trees are plentiful in the valleys on either side, indeed they run with rivers of trees, rivers in flood. On the very highest point of this part of the moor, exposed to every whim of the weather, stand Ringmoor Cottages, two little houses in an arena of trees obviously planted by man, but how long ago I can't guess, for they're very big, and I should say of considerable age. The effect is eerie. The wind in them is never still for a moment, and sounds like the running of a high tide on a broken beach. It reminded me of Wastwood for a second; the way the rookeries used to thresh and cry on winter evenings at the end of the garden, and how the sound came in mournfully after the curtains were drawn.

After Ringmoor, whose shape is so regular that it has an air of druidical ceremony, the road emerges again into full sunlight and the cheerfulness of the present day. It becomes a lane again, with hedges, and swoops down full tilt into Sheepstor village, with the tor soaring huge on the other side of the valley. We spared a few minutes to have a look at the church, where the Brookes of Sarawak are buried; only a few minutes, because that exhausted Johnny's interest in the subject, and the Sergeant-Pilot never had any. His name was Bill, and my finest efforts could prise only a few shy words out of him, but after his own fashion I think he enjoyed himself.

We let Gwyn and Johnny lead the way up the tor, which they did by the straightest and steepest way, scrambling over the first slope of broken boulders weathered from the rock-face, and tackling the higher reaches with toes and fingers and knees, like a couple of monkeys. Some surprised sheep looked over the top at them, and retired in indignation. Johnny forged ahead, hauling Gwyn behind him by the hand over the difficult bits; we followed more cautiously; and we all sat down together on the summit, blown and dishevelled, to empty our pockets of the apples and chocolate and biscuits we'd brought out with us, and eat them in companionable silence.

Johnny doesn't talk about his job. Gwyn just says: 'How are things?' and Johnny says: 'Oh, not so dusty;' and their service news is exhausted. But in his presence one is persistently and disturbingly conscious of his service identity. Some emanation of that reputation of his clings to him even while he plays like an irresponsible school-kid over the rocky top-knot of Sheepstor, and prevents him from being a mere pleasant young man. I see what Gwyn meant. No, I don't see him sitting by the marital hearth. A Titan must be an awfully awkward thing to have about the house. And yet having seen them together, I fail to see how they are ever to have any sort of separate happiness. They're exultingly, unreservedly in love; but 'in love' somehow suggests an impermanence which isn't to be found or looked for in their relationship. I am not a sentimental observer; you'll admit that. But I tell you positively I've met nothing so final and irrevocable as the passion those two have for each other.

My own capacity in that direction seems to be strictly limited; but I know the thing when I see it. And it bothers me. What's time going to do about it? Separate them in the reasonable fashion and let them go through life lame? Or marry them off and shrink them through a process of disillusionment down to normal stature? Either alternative seems pretty horrible, and yet there's nothing else for it. I wish I knew.

The spectacle of your well-trained cynic sitting on top of a hill and concerning herself to distress point with the fate of two responsible adults may seem to you odd, to say the least of it. But these are no ordinary times, and even a cynic may find it strangely easy to grow fond of people.

That's enough of that.

We walked back from our eyrie in time to catch a bus to town in the early evening. Gwyn wanted to take the boys back to quarters for their last hour or so; we have a fire in the evenings, and the place is fairly cosy. But there Johnny struck, digging in his toes and stating mutinously that he was *not* going into that den of lionesses again. Gwyn taunted him with being frightened of a bunch of girls. He admitted it, said they scared him to death. By no means a self-conscious or conceited child, but apparently not without perception of the predatory designs of nice girls at their worst. Anyhow we couldn't get him in; so we all went to a club in Plymouth, and filled the odd hour with a very good supper; and then we saw the two boys off from North Road, and took ourselves home in rather subdued spirits.

He has an odd effect on one's senses, has Johnny Fairmile. I find I tend to remember him as bigger, and blonder, and bluer of eye, and more sudden of movement even than he seemed when he was here. Probably we shall see him again at Christmas, but Christmas seems a long way off just now, and rumour, which knows everything and then some, says that changes are hanging over us here. Therefore we cross our fingers and hope to be able to see him again at Christmas.

I'm finishing this letter in bed, as indeed I usually do; and at great personal inconvenience I've hunted out your very scrappy note to see if anything in it needs answer. I see you've noticed that I have very little to say about my work. Conclude, therefore, my dear sage, that my work goes very well. Myra is pleased with me, and to tell the truth I am rather pleased with myself. These Devon people are not easy to know, but solid Jake when you do know them. The watch explained to me, when I was well into their confidence, that their casual attitude on my arrival was due to a natural fed-upness with training novices for service in other stations. Times without number, they said, they had laboriously instilled the elements of teleprinting into the most improbable people, only to have them snatched away just as they were getting useful. They added that I was the best beginner they'd had. So why should I report progress to you, when the job is running so satisfactorily?

Yes, John wrote me quite a nice letter ten days ago. Short, but he never writes the lengthy epistles I do, and in any case this was a feeler. I must answer it to-morrow.

Yours ever,
Catherine.

W.R.N.S. Quarters, Devonport.
October 17th, 1940.

Dear Nick,

I performed – or delivered, or maybe just gave; the right verb eludes me – my first salute on Sunday morning. In style. And who do you think was the recipient? The Commander-in-Chief, no less. And did the great man acknowledge it? He did. And if he was not pleased he gave a very good imitation of pleasure.

It happened thuswise. Dan and I got up early on Sunday morning and went to Communion at the Dockyard Church. There were only a handful of people there, and one of them was the C. in C. in person. I didn't know him, and his gold braid was out of my line of vision, but Dan nudged me, and whispered the momentous news.

We didn't particularly want to salute anyone, much less an admiral, the art being completely new to us. So we sat tight after the service for what seemed a reasonable time, and then, trusting that he would have got himself and his car safely out of the dockyard, we sallied forth. Just as he drove slowly past the steps on his way out! There was nothing else for it. Salute we must, and salute we did, drawn up in a sort of inadequate guard of honour as he went by; and he gave us a most charming smile and returned the courtesy.

For a first effort, most satisfactory. At any rate we started at the top, and what was good enough for the C. in C. had better be good enough for any other officers we may happen to meet. We toss off our salutes now with an insouciance and aplomb which staggers no one so much as ourselves. The ice is well and truly broken.

You will have gathered that we were in uniform, and newly in uniform, that day. Word went round, in that sourceless but accurate way it has, that the clothing store had received an unexpected windfall of kit of all kinds, and before they could so much as cut the string off the bundles, the place was besieged by a queue of determined Wrens, a queue that went twice round the hut and tied at the back. Every one of 'em armed with a chit to prove that she had been enrolled, and therefore had a right to her kit. The storekeepers, returning from lunch, found this greedy reptile waiting impatiently with its chin, so to speak, on the doorstep. They were not pleased, but there was nothing to be done about it except rip open the parcels as quickly as possible and push our kit over the counter to us with as little time wasted as possible over fitting. However, we had ideas on the subject, too, and tartly refused to move until we were satisfied we had the best bargain we could hope to get.

The sizes of these things appear to be totally erratic by any other known standards of measurement; and few candidates have the peculiar figures necessary to wear a Wren uniform unaltered. Mine – and I drove my unfortunate vis-à-vis half-crazy before I was satisfied with it – fitted well on the shoulders but bulged like mad in the waist, besides being inches too long in the arms. The accompanying skirt ended only six inches or so from the ankles, but the fit of it at waist and hips was not bad. Greatcoats seem to give less trouble; at any rate I walked straight into mine without having to alter a stitch. But the hat! No tales told against the Wren hat can possibly be an exaggeration; nothing can exaggerate that shapeless gaberdine orphanage horror. I put one on and looked at myself and went into shrieks of laughter. I couldn't help it. Never have you seen anything so forlornly grotesque as Catherine Saxon in a Wren hat. Added to the natural disadvantages my face is of a shape peculiarly designed to look its worst under that dilapidated schoolgirl brim turned up behind. Wait until my first leave – somewhere round about Christmas – and I promise you shall have an opportunity to judge for yourself.

Have you noticed, by the way, how advertisers who want to use service-women in their illustrations shirk that hat? They don't mind showing you an A.T.S. or W.A.A.F. ranker smoking their cigarettes or riding their bikes or using their shoe-polish; but if the Navy enters at all, it's bound to be in the person of an officer. The Hat deprives us once and for all of any show-value. Incidentally I actually know of a small Wren who was approached in the street by a kind – and inquisitive – old man, and asked if she was from the Seamen's Orphanage. Too bad one can't think of the appropriate answer until afterwards.

The rest of the get-up, however, isn't too bad after treatment by a decent tailor. Those who have the gift, alter and pad and persuade it into shape themselves; those like myself, who haven't, trot it along to Hepworth's and collect it the following week. Those who don't have to do either are so few that they don't count.

By way of parenthesis, how I hate collars and ties!

This personal excitement – the old girl all put away with my tweeds, and the new girl all put on – tends to eclipse the general excitement. But there's no denying times are getting livelier here just lately. They say there were some sharp raids here early in the war, before London found out the meaning of the word blitz; but since my coming we've had a moderately quiet time until the past week. Then it began. I hesitated to drag it into my letters, but the newspapers, I see, are quite free about it, so I gather the subject is not tabu.

I was on duty the first night. The alarm went while the transport was on its way out, and we travelled to the accompaniment of a steady barrage and under a vivid illumination of searchlights and gun-flashes. Later the barrage died down and the skirmish, I think, went out to sea, for only the gun-flashes continued at regular intervals; an odd effect, like rose-coloured sheet lightning, quite silent, the reflection of the firing of ships' guns well out of the Sound. Fascinating to watch because of its silence, and because it disappeared again almost before our eyes had time to see it.

Once safely arrived, nights on the job are always quiet. What goes on outside doesn't reach us except perhaps as rumour, often not even as that. Consequently it was something of a shock to find, as we drove back to quarters next morning, that all the windows of some familiar streets were sprayed in powder over the pavements, and the window-frames hanging out by splinters of wood and strips of black-out curtain. Besides one or two gaps in the rows of houses and shops, and some tired A.F.S. men trudging away from heaps of smoking masonry. However, this affair was showy rather than dangerous, and few, if any, lives were lost.

The next night there were five alarms, and five times we staggered up and down those abominable three flights of stairs, walking in our sleep and holding one another upright only by an eccentric but effective unity of movement. It reached the stage when we got tired of carrying our blankets and pillows and simply dropped them over the banisters and tottered down the stairs to collect them on arrival. After the third all-clear Dan refused to move. She slept happily through our fourth and fifth arrivals and departures, and was still asleep when we came down to breakfast next day. On the whole she had the best of it, but hope springs eternal, and every time we went up the stairs to bed we kidded ourselves we'd be allowed to stay there.

The third night the raid started earlier, halfway through our evening duty, and the first we knew of it was when lights and power went out on us together, and left us in sudden darkness. All our machines were going full blast at the time, and the way they checked, and coughed, and slowly ran down to silence was positively eerie. I've never heard the room so quiet. Myra grabbed her torch and dashed out to borrow a box of matches, while we switched off all the machines and groped our emergency lanterns – one candle power – out of their dusty corner. By the time the Duty Signal Officer came round to see how things were shaping we had the room looking rather like Christmas, and were all being frightfully British at the tops of our voices. Rather bucked, if anything, to find ourselves on duty the night a spark of excitement came into the evening round. He asked if all our machines were safely switched off, and had to implore us not to answer all at the same time.

In about a quarter of an hour the emergency plant was working, and lights and power were restored, and off we went again. By the time our relief was due the raid was over, and we got away on time, and picked up two special constables and a stranded – and very fuddled – sailor on our way back to town. Entering Devonport we found we were travelling over a carpet of broken glass, and at one point we had to make a detour because a street was closed; but it was too dark to see very much of what was going on.

The rest of that night was quiet, but during the hour the raid had lasted more damage had been done than in all five alarms of the previous night. A good many lives were lost, I'm afraid. Seventeen people from one shelter all sallied out together the minute the all-clear went, and made for a nearby fish-and-chip shop; and one of the raiders on its way seaward dropped its last bomb at random and caught them in the street, killing them all. I walked up that way yesterday. In the walls of the houses which are still standing there are holes you could put your head in, spattered thickly up the walls from ground level to perhaps seven feet high, and diminishing as they rise. I always understood the thing to do was to fling yourself flat on the ground; but as far as I can see the only way to escape there would have been by an inspired exhibition of levitation.

Needless to say some parts of the town have now no electricity and no gas. They're working hell for leather to get these services restored, but my mind misdoubts.

No letter from mother this week, but last time I heard from her she sounded at the top of her form, and her prime preoccupation seemed to be the feeding of her two searchlight boys. She sent me a photograph; two nice-looking lads, very young and fresh and high-spirited, playing ukuleles in father's old hammock in the orchard. All very sunny and peaceful. I suppose Yeatbridge is; I feel a good deal more than two hundred miles away from all that now.

You ask me if I'm satisfied, Nick. I wish I knew. On the job I suffer from an illusion that I am, but in my comfortable, well-fed off-duty hours I wonder. Is this enough? I doubt it. Are we, collectively, doing all we can? I doubt that, too. But not being in a position to see the thing whole and judge effort and performance accordingly, I have a feeling I may be letting a purely personal frustration colour my outlook on things impersonal. I always wanted to be a man. I doubt if any degree of risk or exertion or excitement tempered to a feminine measure can ever satisfy me. And yet who is this Saxon woman to think she can perform more than's being asked of her?

You see how it goes. Don't, for your own sake, think of me as a Freudian introspective for ever tormented by these improbable scruples and counter-scruples. Most of the time I forget to think at all, and then there's no longer the slightest doubt that I'm enjoying myself utterly, and wouldn't have missed this life for anything. Which is nearer the truth than I'm likely to get if I try and think it out.

I've just read this letter through, and was on the point of tearing it up, but decided to let it stand. After all, none of the foregoing egotistical rubbish will be at all new to you, coming as it does from

Your unsatisfactory Saxon.

III. HOW TO LIVE WITH WOMEN

W.R.N.S. Quarters, Devonport.
November 12th, 1940.

Dear Nick,

This trotting up and down stairs several times a night is beginning to get monotonous. If it goes on much longer I fear we shall all revert to type, and then heaven help the illusion of civilisation with which we contrive to cover our claws in this communal life of ours. They've stopped hunting us out of our beds for every siren, and we scramble downstairs now only if we get a second signal by 'phone; which happens only when the raiders are actually over our end of the town. A big improvement, but just lately they seem to have spent a good part of every night over our end of town. The merry-go-round continues to function; and so do the watch-keepers, but only just. One can lose a certain amount of sleep without harm but there's a limit. We begin to have circles under our eyes, and to fall out rather too frankly over our proprietorship of certain bits of floor. It matters more than you might think, because of the number and variety of draughts which rove round this ramshackle home from home.

Very testing to the soul, as I once remarked, is hardship. We kick against the pricks with a vigour worthy of a better cause. The contemplation of so much spleen arouses in me the moralising mood. Sit back and listen, Nick Crane. You're never likely to have a chance to put my observations to the test, so you can afford to listen patiently this once, and anyhow you can't prove me wrong.

The plain truth is that women are not cut out for living in a community. There have been quite a number of successful attempts, but they're notable chiefly because they're unexpected. It's against all the probabilities for a household of women to function smoothly. The female instinct among a hundred and fifty other females is to look round quite cold-bloodedly for a small number of congenial spirits, cement an alliance with them and declare war on all the rest. The occasional rare people who can and do mix unreservedly with all are always rather strikingly masculine in outlook. Which goes to show! We have a characteristic specimen in Dorothy Lord, who not only has a man's broad, tolerant, optimistic mind, but a man's face as well, and given an Eton crop could pass for a man whenever she chose.

In case this should seem to praise men at the expense of women, let me tell you at once that your sex has social vices just as dangerous but at the opposite end of the lane, and perhaps not quite so difficult to live with. Vices of lethargy and over-tolerance mostly. Vices of union, while ours are vices of separation. This won't do! Let me get back to ground where I'm safe from contradiction; you may have views on men's social characteristics yourself.

So women never are a community, but only a collection of cliques, with a sprinkling of unfortunate exiles who don't seem to fit in anywhere. The cliques form upon ground which, for various reasons, is common to all the members. The most formidable factor in the splitting-up process is class. I hate the word, but there's no getting away from it. Girls born in comfortable circumstances, and accustomed to luxuries and attentions, will gravitate to their own kind without hesitation. Working girls will associate with working girls, and avoid those who have not known similar ups and downs with them. There is a certain amount of friendly intercourse between the two sets, but only by way of oiling the wheels, since meet they must. Whose is the fault? Not theirs. There are fine people on both sides, people who would like and admire one another if they even spoke the same language. No, the fault is implicit in the system that produces and segregates half a dozen kinds of Englishwomen instead of one. Boys have more of the child left in them, I think, and that's why they find it so much easier than we do to climb over the barriers and fraternise; but there's room for improvement there, too.

What's the cure? Some drastic alteration in the educational system? The abolition of expensive private schools and establishment of a standardised education for all, with equal opportunities for those of all classes with a thirst for knowledge? The proud boast of 'equal opportunity' is heard a good deal now, but neither you nor I need to be told that that is so much poppycock. So it would be even with a standard scheme for free education, unless the family incomes behind the young people could be standardised too; otherwise there'd always be some who needed financial help from their children early, some who could afford to wait a few years more, some who could do without it for life, yes, and go on spending on the children for life if necessary. Which automatically knocks 'equal opportunity' for six.

How did I get into this deep water, anyhow? I was talking about women.

Class isn't the only dividing agent, of course. Locality has a good deal to say in the matter. Find three people from one county, or three with the same provincial accent, or three who share the knowledge of certain local words unknown to the rest, or three who played the same eccentric singing-games at infant school, and you have a highly promising nucleus for a clique. Shared interest in a certain civil profession helps to bring people together, too. But class remains the dominant factor.

Here we are, then, in a complicated system of small worlds inter-revolving and avoiding contact. All very well as long as things run smoothly, but when the system is shaken by some outside influence, such as the physical and mental strain of these continued raids, there begin to be collisions among our deflected worlds, and the sparks fly.

It's a highly specialised form of living, and the person who becomes involved in it soon develops a protective armament to deal with its peculiar dangers. The first essential is a complete indifference to other people's opinion of you. That's necessary because every time you leave the common-room you are bound to come under discussion, so you may as well grow a good thick hide and let 'em get on with it. The second essential is a proprietary form of expression to be used in verbal fencing matches with your enemies. Mine is a sort of placid sarcasm, but I know one cherubic child who uses a stare of preternatural innocence and bits of harmless repartee delivered as if they had a double meaning; a procedure which always leaves her opponent

wondering if she has missed the point. You get the idea.
Third in the list of essentials is a sense of humour. I
think I'm right in putting it only third, because there's
a sort of self-sufficiency in holding your own by tooth
and claw; it isn't absolutely necessary to enjoy the process. But a sense of humour is like a Li-lo to lie on;
which helps no end.

All this may sound very much like the primeval jungle,
but actually it's only very occasionally one takes it seriously. Only when the air treacherously oozes out of the
Li-lo and leaves you on the hard floor. So while I perceive
it so clearly, let me write it down; something *is* rotten in
the state of England. Not so rotten that one would wish
to swop it for any other country, but quite rotten enough
to urge one to look round at once for a remedy.

Betweenwhiles we have fun. I don't deny it. The service is in no way to blame for these conditions, indeed it
does what can be done to change them; but gulfs fixed
from birth are not so easily bridged. The comfort of
quarters must inevitably vary with the skill and understanding of those in charge. We do very well here. No
one seriously complains. Consequently except in these
rare stresses our civilisation functions in a way more
efficient than I've suggested. But I'm beginning to look
forward to my first leave, all the same.

Before Christmas I hope to be home, and if Mrs Lane
can make room for me, I'd like to come up to Wastwood for a couple of days. Probably on the 15th of
next month. I have some foreign stamps for Billy,
and will bring some candies in case your local supplies
are running low.

Until I see you,
Yours, Catherine.

W.R.N.S. Quarters, Devonport.
December 21st, 1940.

Dear Nick,

As you will see, I reached Plymouth safely in the end, though there was a time when I began to wonder if I ever should. I never knew a train spend so long standing still between miles. When it did move, it was at a spirited crawl, and every ten minutes of crawling led to such exhaustion that the poor thing had to lie down and pant for a while. I expect the railway companies are really performing major miracles in ever getting us to our destination at all, but it's hard to think so when one's marooned in an ice-cold third-class carriage in the Severn tunnel.

We were hours late in leaving Shrewsbury. The 12.40 came in at about 3.15, and was horribly crowded, though I was lucky enough to find a seat. I did a spot of lightning-calculating, and figured that with luck we might get in by ten o'clock if we made up a little lost time on the way. But it soon became pretty obvious that we weren't going to. Much worse, we went on losing it; consistently. After five o'clock, when we were still a good way short of Bristol, I just gave up worrying, and settled down to make the best of a bad job. It was bitterly cold, but after all one can't expect peacetime conditions, and at least we had a very decent set of people. I find travelling by train easier and pleasanter now I'm in uniform, though I can't flatter myself it's for my glamour's sake. Strange young men aren't afraid to speak to a girl in uniform; and servicemen assume she has a reasonable interest in adult affairs, or she wouldn't be in uniform. Results are satisfying. The pleasant young man in the opposite corner offered me a cigarette, and opened a general conversation. He was in civilian rig, but I wasn't deceived. He looked as if he had something to do with the sea. I don't know what it is that sets them apart, the men who mess about in boats, as Barney used to say; but it's there to be seen. This one turned out to be an engineer in the Merchant Service, coming home from one of many examinations taken between trips.

I still wish I'd had the sense to be born male. This boy couldn't have been as old as I am, or at least he didn't look it; yet he'd worked his way over most of the world's seas already, and was soon off eastward again. He was a good talker, too, modest as the morning but not the tongue-tied kind. He talked about the Chinese, to whom he gives credit for obstinate courage. From there we turned off to the national fortunes of the Chinese, and the entire carriage combined to wish General Chiang Kai Shek could sweep the little Japanese hellions into the sanguinary sea. The wish was formulated by a dour-looking man in battle-dress at the other end of the compartment, but even the prim little middle-aged woman nursing a Pekinese beside him murmured agreement. Maybe she wasn't so prim as she looked, or maybe the dignified friendship he'd struck up with the Peke – it was a jolly little dog – helped her to overlook his choice of adjectives.

Well, apart from two soldiers who were going only to Bristol we were all in the same boat. You couldn't hurry that train. We settled down resignedly, pooled all our papers and magazines, and from time to time fished out cigarettes or sandwiches and hawked them round. The wise travel heavily supplied these days, and we were all wise.

Not a bad journey, on the whole, but how it would have crawled but for the company! We read, and ate, and played cards – the engineer contributed the pack – and slept by fits and starts. It was past midnight when we reached Exeter, but I'd given up worrying by then. It wasn't as if I had any choice in the matter. I had to get back to quarters, no matter at what unearthly hour, because I was on duty at eight next morning. All I could do was grab a taxi when we did finally arrive. One is always curiously optimistic about taxis. Why I should expect North Road to be flowing with them at midnight and after I can't imagine, but for some reason I did.

After Exeter we ran into an air-raid alarm but nothing happened, except that the train lay down and had a snooze until the all-clear went. Then we crawled on again, and finally crawled into North Road, at something after two a.m.

As we ran into the outer approaches of the town there began to be an odd sort of glow round the edges of the blinds, like an unbelievable dawn or the after-glow of a super-sunset. The train lights had all been switched off during the alert, so we flapped up the blinds and had a look. Not that there was anything to see. Except the glow. It didn't seem to have any source, and on second thoughts it was more like an over-coloured aurora, for it pulsed at irregular intervals. We knew they'd had some lively nights down here, but the accounts hadn't been impressive, and you'll remember there were no details. The engineer said: 'Fire!'

It was an eerie business, coming into North Road at two in the morning by the light of that blaze. For one thing there was the most complete silence I think I've ever experienced. More than once I've noticed this quality about trains at night; the sound of the engine slips so far into the background that it doesn't count. And fire without noise seemed to deepen the spell, as a night of moonlight seems far more silent than one without moon or stars.

As we drew well into the town the glow had a direction, and later a positive shape. There was a column of it, wavering up into the sky like a red searchlight, and on either side of it in its upper reaches was an attendant garment of smoke. The roofs of the houses along the line stood up black and jagged against it, and the light of it made a sort of fantastic rose-coloured day out of that improbable night.

The little woman with the Pekinese was being met, but all the rest of us were hoping to snaffle taxis. So I imagine, were about a hundred other people on the same train. It was every man for himself once the train pulled up at North Road, and perhaps I wasn't very quick on the draw, for I'd been watching the column of fire so intently that we were in before I was aware. Anyhow, I never could bring myself to scrap for transport. I lost all my fellow-travellers, and all the taxis, too, for only two were standing at the kerb when I emerged from the station, and they were already loaded up. I stood by the exit, rather forlornly waiting for some opportunist to shed his load and come back, when someone came plucking my sleeve and muttering that he'd been looking for me everywhere. I expected to see the engineer, but it was the pro-Chinese private. He said he had a share in one of the two remaining taxis booked for me. The last person in the world you'd have expected to bother!

I said: 'What about you?' and he said: 'Oh, I don't need a taxi, I know where I can hop a lorry.' So we plunged across, and I made the sixth fare in the taxi. Lucky for me that the original charterers, two cadets from the Royal Naval Engineering College, were going my way. They and an elderly civilian were squeezed into the back seat, an infantry sergeant complete with kit sat beside the driver, a young boy sat on the knee of the elderly civilian, and I sat on the left-hand cadet. No one seemed to mind, though how we were all going to sort ourselves out at our fare-stages was rather a puzzle.

The private was gone before I could say thank you. I wonder how far he really had to go? An odd sort of chap. Looking back, I see I've called him 'dour'. Several times, incidentally, but I was never good with adjectives. Strang and Barney between 'em blunted my young perceptions long ago, when I was green enough to think their stuff the height of literary achievement, instead of goodish provincial journalese. Well, I take back 'dour', or rather I qualify it. It suggests a certain boorishness, whereas he wasn't even gauche. He just didn't seem to take an indiscriminately favourable view of his fellow-men, and my God, why should he? The engineer boy had an open countenance and a Derek Farr smile, but we can't all be born with that sort of nature. This other fellow was older, for one thing, and perhaps he'd been in action before Dunkirk, for he had a scar, not a long one, but ridged and puckered as if it had been a sizeable wound in its day, running out of his hair, and down one temple. I can't think of anything much more sobering than being caught in that civilian panic that littered the Flemish and French roads with dead. Or perhaps he just happens to be one of the dangerous people who think too much. He had a lean and hungry look, anyhow. Not bad-looking, in a saturnine way, but not cast for the lone female's champion. Well, time spent in wondering about travelling companions is usually wasted, for I notice I never seem to see mine again.

It must have been turned half past two when I struggled out of the taxi – third of the load to disembark – on the doorstep at quarters, and rang the bell. A discreet sort of ring; I didn't want to wake the whole house, and if no one heard me the first time I could always ring again. But one of the P.O.s, as it happened, was up waiting for another late arrival, so I was inside almost before I'd let go the bell. But when I got upstairs to my room, which faced the blaze, it was almost as light as day, a copper-coloured light. Lucky for the two sleepers it was, or I should certainly have taken a header over two cake-tins and a pile of books which Dan had left in the fairway between our beds. Dan has ways which have to be learned by hard experience. During her day-long comings and goings in the cabin she deposits all paraphernalia on her bed, and when she wishes to go to bed she collects every item neatly and stacks the whole lot in one tidy heap, squarely in the middle of our one rug. Her sense of design forbids her to push them on to the floor and leave them as they fall. She pats the pile into shape with fastidious care, switches off the light, and gets into bed. And as she is almost always first to retire, few nights pass without Gwyn or myself falling over this erection with a crash. Dan is always sorry, and invariably surprised.

This time the reflection of the fire saved my shins. Some good fairy had put a hot-water bottle in my bed, too, and wrapped my pyjamas round it. On the whole it was a good return. All that worried me was how I was going to wake up in the morning; and I don't know that I cared very much about that either.

I dawdled at the window for quite a time over my undressing, watching the pillar of fire and feeling rather like one of the Israelitish women in the wilderness. It was so light in the room that I stopped feeling tired, and even when I got into bed couldn't sleep for some time. How they managed to sleep at all for the first night or two I can't imagine; they had the window closed and the blind down, of course, but even so that throbbing glare would slide in round the edges and flicker up and down the walls of the room. Luckily my room-mates are two of the original seven sleepers.

Well, that's all about my return to duty. Things are much as usual here, and I see no sign of any other damage in town, though they tell me the worst of this bout happened on the other side of the Cattewater. In quarters there are two minor excitements, the preparations for Christmas, and a preliminary rumour of a general draft affecting most of us mobile people. So preliminary that I'll say no more about it now. You will be warned in good time if there's any real probability of me changing my address.

The prospect of Christmas in quarters has brought to a head the frayed feeling between our elaborate systems of society. A certain section, it seems, wanted to limit invitations to our party to officers; the idea being that those who did not know any officers, should I suppose, meekly submit to being partnerless rather than embarrass our young ladies and their commissioned squires by inflicting upon them the company of ratings, Petty Officers and S.B.A.s. Again don't entirely blame this attitude upon the service; the root of the trouble is in the minds of the expensively educated, who are uncomfortable in the presence of other types; and above all, as I think I remarked before, on the system which makes them types instead of individuals. But to our credit be it said, this motion of the minority was firmly squashed, and the party is to be a ship's company affair. Uniform, of course, unless you are lucky enough not to be kitted up yet. This navy blue is all very well for office hours and so on, but most of us would like to be allowed to shed it for parties. Dorothy Lord, who was not at the meeting which made the arrangements, had only one question to ask afterwards: 'Any drinks?' She's one of my own community of elders, who have been in charge of their own lives for years, and don't take kindly to being shepherded; but for her sins I doubt if she'll get anything stronger than cider-cup this year unless she goes out for it.

As for me, I don't know that I'm very keen on parties of any kind just now. I meant to have a hot time when I came home, but when I came to the doorway, so to speak, it didn't seem worth while going in. The house was decorated, the boys were fun, and mother had saved an unopened box of Terry's to greet me; and shops and shoppers looked much as usual, except for the Cinderella element of having to hie away home at black-out time. But it was all wrong. It ought not to have been the same. Nothing – to be thoroughly trite – will ever be the same again. I don't say Christmas will never get its meaning back again; I suppose the

children will take care of all that. But it will never be the
festival it used to be, of eating and drinking and gift-
making and absolute suspension of thought. The
energy and ingenuity we used to throw away on amusing ourselves we need now for the immediate end in
view, which is the annihilation of our enemies. Why
pretend otherwise? And after that – I think – I think
there will be other things to do. More than enough for
your lifetime and mine, Nick Crane.

It was nice to see you again, and to find you looking
so well. Do you think that you and Billy and Mrs Lane
could put up another visitor for two nights next week-
end? Gwyn and Johnny both have forty-eight hours
off, and time's too short for her to join her people in
Westmorland, while he hasn't any particular base at
all. Mother is having Gwyn, but owing to the presence
of the lads she has no room for Johnny. How about it?
He'd like to come to you, for I've told him who you are.
And you can talk flying with him in the short time he'll
be able to spare you in the intervals of dashing over to
mother's. With luck I should think you might see him
once a day, at breakfast. I expect he'll talk for you,
being one of the inner circle. I know better than to try
and make him, myself, though I did go up in an open
plane once; it cost me half a crown and a new set of hair
grips to replace those the wind blew out of my hair. I
was nearly seventeen at the time.

Let me know if you can have him, Nick. Or on
second thoughts, don't bother, because I've already
told him to come.

My love to everyone, but regard the choicest part of
it as earmarked for Nick Crane in person, from his
unprofitable

Catherine.

W.R.N.S. Quarters, Devonport.
Dec. 30th, 1940.

Dear Nick,

I've been thinking about what you said to me at Wastwood that night, about my ideas changing. But I don't think so, or at least not more than's inevitable in adapting myself to so completely new a set of circumstances. After all, I've never been an extreme case of the embedded conservative, have I? Every new experience adds another facet to the mind and the accumulation of experience gives it flexibility. If you can imagine a flexible thing with facets. Anyhow, I don't think I've suffered any fundamental changes. Leave that to the future.

Our routine was broken with a vengeance last night. I'm not fully recovered yet from the effects, but after sleeping all afternoon I feel rather more alive, at any rate, and desperately hungry. Supper will be half an hour yet, and I must keep my mind occupied somehow to avoid brooding. Hence this letter.

It was an ill-timed siren that caused the trouble, of course. Actually the siren went at about the usual time, around nine thirty in the evening; in fact we were rather congratulating ourselves that the alarm came too late to prevent the relief transport starting from town. True enough, but it came in good time to prevent the thing from arriving. We went on with our work placidly, and waited for the all-clear to go. It always had, within an hour or two, and we were getting used to cutting down on our sleep by so much. But this time the wretched thing simply didn't go, and that was all about it. For the first hour we were kept busy, and didn't pay much attention to the time. Then someone noticed the clock, and voiced a mild hope that we wouldn't be there all night. She must have had a premonition; we were. All, or most of it.

It could have happened to any of the four watches, of course, it simply happened to be us. But what aggravated the crime was that we'd done an extra watch already yesterday, being on duty from eight to one, and again on the evening watch. That's the way things happen, out of pure cussedness. Ridiculously, too, we had to come on again at eight after what looked like being a very short spell of sleep. For midnight slipped away, and still no sign of the all-clear. In fact the raid began to move our way. We don't often hear very much of the activity outside, but last night our one exposed wall shook periodically to the explosions of bombs and guns – largely guns, I think – and the window rattled at every crump like teeth chattering. Myra, working at the end machine, finally got sick of the irritating noise, and addressed it in a few pungent words which should have silenced it for ever. Teleprinters have that effect on one's language, I find. They refuse to be mastered even when they're well known and are liable to perform the most bewildering feats of unreason in the middle of long cyphers, which is fraying to the temper, to say the least of it. In fact, as one of our cypher officers once remarked: 'I used to be quite a nice girl before I started this job, but you wouldn't think so now.'

They're rather like cross-grained pets, of which, all the same, one gets inordinately fond. I should hate to be parted from my job now; the noise doesn't worry me at all, and the vagaries of the machines, though bad for the language, are only momentarily annoying. One gets into the habit of regarding them as sentient, malicious, fascinating beings, and talking to them accordingly.

More neatly, as Susan puts it: 'They're cautions!' But all this delving into the nature of teleprinters seems to have led me into a blind alley. Back to the night of nights!

In town they said afterwards it was pretty bad. Very few incendiaries this time, nearly all H.E., and some heavy stuff among it. But up there it was only the dull impacts from outside, and the window rattling, and the floor vibrating ever so slightly underfoot. Only it went on and on, steadily, by the hour, fluctuating very slightly, and giving us no rest. And how we longed to put our heads down on the machines and fall asleep. Night watches in routine are easy, but this involuntary night watch after a double day watch was not so easy. It was the time of day and the day of the week when our minds were accustomed to sleeping, and they struggled indignantly to carry out their contract. We found ourselves sagging and slowing in the middle of broadcasts, and pulled ourselves roughly out of the slough of sleep, and went on. In checking we found several very erratic things in our signals. I'd dragged a bulldog into one of mine; there was certainly nothing about him in the original, so I must have got him out of the edge of a dream; anyhow, there he was.

It sounds funny. It *was* funny. It was so awful that it was funny. In the intervals of nodding and shaking ourselves awake we went into gales of laughter at the improbability of our own predicament. There must be something crazy about the English character, Nick. There we were, some two dozen people in the C.C.O. who should have been growing hourly more weary, and desperate, and vengeful, and ill-tempered; and instead we reacted as the hands of the clock slipped round to one, and two, and three in the morning with faintly admiring exclamations like: 'Well, doesn't it knock you?' and 'Settle down, girls, we're here for the night!' and 'You can hardly credit it, can you?' And then we laughed. Swore, sometimes, too, but laughed every time. It may have been a spiteful joke, but it was a joke all right.

Our fat Chief felt it worst of all, I think. His round face gradually went a rather bad putty colour, and sagged into sad lines like heavy dough; but even he laughed. He sat there at his desk swearing quietly to himself over everything he did – swearing is one of his chief accomplishments, and he can go for hours without repeating himself – and at intervals uttering aloud, as if he had just made the discovery: 'Well, this is a bloody knockout!' Which it was.

When the work slacked off, as it did round about three o'clock, we kept ourselves awake by pulling his leg, an old amusement of ours. And the canteen, which habitually closes at ten, obligingly opened again and supplied us with tea and cocoa and cakes in the small hours, which helped considerably. So it was not such a grim business as one might have expected it to be.

Round about four the noise subsided, and at half past four the all-clear went at last. By that time we were hoping to be left in undisputed possession of the office until eight o'clock, when we should have been coming on duty again; but no such luck. Before five o'clock the long-delayed transport arrived, and our reliefs came trooping through, looking even more like the walking dead than we did. Such a bedraggled set of smudgy-faced wretches you never saw. We had at least had chairs to sit on, dry walls and roof to cover us, and the job to occupy our minds and make the time pass; but they, poor things, had spent the whole of the raid in an overcrowded, damp and grubby public shelter, with absolutely nothing to do.

There must have been a hurried conference somewhere as to what was best to be done; and it was decided that we should be taken home to snatch an hour's sleep, and come back on duty at eight as usual. It sounds hard, but either we or the other poor ghosts had to do that morning watch, and anyone could see with half an eye that we'd come out of it easily by comparison with them. So back to quarters we were driven, through a darkness as profound and silent as ever we had about us at Wastwood in those moonless midnights before there was any war.

Every soul on the transport fell asleep, naval and Wren ratings leaning cosily on one another's shoulders, and poor old Chief snoring in the back seat. But instinct woke them as they reached their own stopping places, and one by one they drifted away into the dark.

We arrived at quarters with just over an hour to go before early breakfast. It was still pitch dark, and seemed too early to have a bath, so I lay down on my bed and stretched my tired self for half an hour's relaxation. *Not* sleep. I was quite determined not to sleep, knowing the taste of it would only make me drunken when what I really wanted was twenty-four hours without interruption. So of course the next thing I knew was that I'd just awakened in a frightful panic, and it was twenty past seven by my watch. The transport left at half past.

Bath! Not even the flick of a sponge did I get. As for breakfast, it vanished into whatever limbo mirages use when they're off duty. Not a crumb, not even a cup of tea. It took me every second of that ten minutes to climb back into my collar and tie – in any case my usual time for this operation is five minutes – tidy my hair, dive back into my hat and coat and fall down the stairs.

I don't know how the others fared. Much the same, I expect. But there wasn't a single absentee. We came with swollen eyes half-closed and faces an unwholesome bluish colour like clay, and our gait as we shambled along that interminable tunnel of ours was eccentric, to say the least of it, with a tendency to tack from wall to wall like ships coming up into the wind. But anyhow we came.

The morning was so quiet that the only difficulty was staying awake; and when we were finally released at lunch-time even that didn't matter anymore. I can guess what the others did. I know what I did myself. I ate all the lunch I could get, had a warm bath, and crawled into bed; all in the wrong order, but what did I care? I slept all afternoon, and woke up hungry again. And here am I waiting for my supper, and whiling away the time by writing you a not very interesting letter about what seems to us a notable event.

I don't seem to have said a word about Christmas. I wonder why? It should have been the main part of this letter, surely, the date being what it is. But the truth is that Christmas away from home is not the same festival. There was more of it in that one evening by your hearth, the two of us alone in the firelight, than in all the noisy well-meaning party we had here, and the port (of sorts, but even so unexpected) and the carols. I was never so homesick as while I sat in a corner of the recreation room with an inarticulate R.A.F. corporal, and watched the very young dancing in (unauthorised) party frocks and paper hats. I lost the illusion that I was very young some years ago. After it was gone I was glad. To be very young is pleasant and heady, but to be merely young is more intelligent and has greater possibilities. Yet it needs so much more firm a basis for happiness, and our party wasn't enough. I wanted to come back and talk to you about books, and the letters of the great, and Tito Schipa's voice and the world of the future, and the strange bit of you and me that wants to talk about these things.

We did our best with holly, and paper chains, and a Christmas tree, and for most of us, the straight-from-school element, I think it covered the void fairly well. But not for me. There was the wanting to be home, the wanting to get away from the necessity for thinking of nothing but the war; and there was a sort of disappointment, too, with the spirit of the party itself. Some of our guests were of the élite, some were the no-account blokes you and I know best, some were the ordinary salt-of-the-earth ratings, quiet, jolly people with not very much imagination, perhaps, but a little of all the other virtues, and no vices to speak of. They had all of them (or shall I be cautious and say most of them?) the most affable intentions, but the effect was sad, and sad, and sad, my dear. Have you seen how animals of different species walk round each other stiff-legged and wary? So did they. They gravitated, as we do when we have no guests, into little conscious groups of their own kind, and were no happier then because the aliens were there. There's a good deal of the primeval animal about humankind. Do you remember that African wood thing of Grip's, the two monkeys clinging to each other, with that awful look of awareness about them? That's not gone out of us yet. We mean to mix, we try to mix, but the effort exhausts itself and we look round for company which requires no effort; and from that refuge look sidelong upon the defeating and defeated Others and puzzle to discover what ails them, that they should not be quite as we are. It isn't as obvious or as horrible as I've made it sound, my style being always a shade heavy-handed; but it's there as a disquiet under everything, and a conviction of waste and defacing and regret lives in it and evolves from it like mist from a swamp. Brethren, these things ought not so to be.

Perhaps if the men were by themselves it wouldn't be like this; almost certainly not to the same extent. I wish I'd been a man, Nick.

My letters have refrains, don't they? You must get a feeling of: 'This is where I came in.' But with you no one – no man, no woman – need erect protective armour. Being disabled from all the physical activities of humanity, and therefore enlarged from all its physical limitations, you have no social existence. You are a spirit with an intellect, someone quite outside the discomforts of age, or ugliness, or embarrassment, or any other of the small evils of the flesh. Something like Merlin. Remember?

The bell will ring any moment now, and I am so hungry that I intend to be first in the scrimmage. So I must end this letter here and now. The moralising mood will be gone by next time, so be easy, and think as mildly as you can of

Your unregenerate Saxon.

P.S. – I haven't said: 'I hope you are well,' but you know I do. I never ask: 'How are you?' but woe betide you if you don't tell me in your next letter.

W.R.N.S. Quarters, Devonport.
January 11th, 1941.

Dear Nick,

The rumour – no, Rumour, I feel it should have a capital – is gaining stature rapidly. I think it's true, though it may be previous. However, you can still write to me here for the time being, as the move isn't imminent.

It's given rise, this half-informed whispering, to a flare of sudden interest in promotion, because it seems there really is a strong chance of it. We mobile people must go where we are sent, but at least this obligation carries a correspondingly greater opportunity of advancement. Down here there are not so many of us, especially in some categories; and a little bird disguised as a Chief P.O. has whispered to me that if all goes well I may find myself a Petty Officer after the projected move. Personally I'm sceptical, but in the case of some others to whom the same bird has whispered, I fear the bait has been swallowed whole.

The Wren attitude to promotion is understandable but odd, from my point of view at least. But then, I am a rather special case. I have no business abilities to atrophy, and my career, if you can dignify my 'Gazette' activities with such a name, is only interrupted, not damaged, by this service interlude. I can pick it up again whenever I choose, without the slightest difficulty; and this not because I rely on Strang to kill the fatted calf for me, but because I know I am a competent hack writer of average energies and some small gifts, capable of making a living out of journalism as long as I continue to need one. My peculiar line of business thrives on muddled experiences like these present ones, whereas to most of the girls here the war means a total break with the professions from which they hoped to erect an ambitious future. By far the bulk of them are shorthand-typists, school-teachers, secretaries, general office workers, and the like; and every month of war means another coat of rust on their post-war earning capacity; since, apart from the ubiquitous typewriter, naval offices involve highly specialised procedure, none of which will be of much use to them afterwards. So I don't altogether fail to understand their urge to make a career of the war itself, and rise as high as they can in the job while it lasts. Rank may easily count in the quest for civilian jobs afterwards; and the increased money helps now.

But I have to keep reminding myself of all these circumstances in order to comprehend the workings of our mass mind. It never ceases to surprise me that they should care two hoots about an anchor on the sleeve. I beg its pardon, a killick; I never can remember to be conscientiously naval. The extra money none of us would refuse, if it came without a handle; but I'm quite at a loss to understand the slick way some people accept and pocket it without the remotest intention of doing anything to earn it, and without subscribing to the

service view of the importance of the position they're
filling. It seems to me about as moral as loaning your
name to bolster up a rotten company. My conscience,
as you know, has never been an overworked organ; but
I have got enough personal integrity to draw the line
at being a non-commissioned officer in name only.
Responsibility is a form of purgatory I loathe with all my
strength, but if I do assume it, by heck, I'll discharge it to
the best of my ability and according to my lights.

Servicely speaking, my lights might be considered a
trifle dim. I am not of naval stock, I have no automatic
respect for authority, I don't give a damn whether my
hypothetical subordinates sling their gasmasks, or hang
them from one shoulder, or trail them in one hand, provided they've got 'em. I don't think the country is in
jeopardy if Wren Jones walks along the Hoe with her
coat unbuttoned and her hat in her hand, and forgets to
salute a Commander or two; or that the beastly war will
be shortened by a second, or her speed on a teleprinter
increased by one word per minute, if she abjures all these
heathen practices. But I do care that she shall work as
hard as need be, that her interest shall be in her job, that
her signals shall be accurate, and a bit of her imagination shall follow them to Admiralty or Portsmouth or
Greenock, or wherever they may go.

I care a great deal about making the fullest possible
contribution to the winning of the war; but I cannot care
about the correct angle of a uniform hat, and the length
of the wearer's hair. Now don't think I'm objecting to
the harmless fact that an organisation like ours must
have rules. I know that, and I keep them. Believe it or
not, your Saxon abides by all the main laws of the Medes
and Persians. But there are rules and rules. The worst of

ours are puerile, and I value them for what they're worth; and these I neither can nor will help to enforce.

So you see that the higher my progression takes me, the more deeply involved I shall be with the tangles of red tape and tradition and conscience. It's all very difficult, and if this promotion does overtake me, I'm afraid it will take a few acts of Parliament to make your Catherine an honest woman. But she'll move heaven and earth to make and keep her watch the keenest, promptest and most efficient in the command, and devil take the length of their hair and the angle of their hats.

Nothing actually official has been said about the move up to now. Nothing will be said until the eve of the departure, I expect, but all will be known and discussed long before. This place seethes with a tide of suppressed excitement, everyone speculating upon her own chances and the chances of others. Only one or two of us who are jealous of our obscurity wander rather dubiously through all this greedy enthusiasm, and wonder if we shall be allowed to remain individuals when we don our killicks. And if, of course. I know enough about the service to take nothing for granted until I have it in my hands, and even then to retain one little doubt of its authenticity.

We have snow in the streets, Nick. That doesn't often happen here. Even on the Hoe there's a sprinkling of white, and every night a new frost holds it there until some second fall comes to fetch it away, according to tradition. Not a few of our steeper streets are treacherous walking now, and even the buses have trouble here and there; but so far the affair is pure comedy. As, for instance, the last time we went to squad drill.

Now there's one of the things I resent in theory, and find myself rather enjoying in practice. It's a nuisance at best, because it comes out of one's free time, and however scarce or however plentiful it may be, I do like my free time free; a legacy from the days before the 'Gazette', when I made my living in my leisure. Besides, we have to pay threepence in bus fares and use up a further half-hour getting all the way to R.N.B. and back in order to acquire something we didn't want in the first place. But the drill itself is almost always funny, which in this world counts for a good deal.

It takes place in the drill shed at Barracks, under the supervision of two or three P.O. physical training instructors. There are enough of us to make up three squads, and the shed usually holds, besides, a squad of defaulters who double up and down with rifles, and get as much fun out of us as we do out of them. The P.O.s play off their squads against each other in a most shameless way, and sometimes in sheer zeal get themselves and their pupils hopelessly mixed up. It warms us up on these cold days, and it does no one any harm; but my soul, what waste of a full hour of time when time is so precious and brief!

We came away from one of these drills in a sudden iron frost, not yet half an hour old, but hard and glittering as a diamond; and this on top of a moist day, so that every smooth road-surface was glazed and polished like the top of a glacier mint. We struggled up the steep slope from the drill shed, too precariously balanced on our feet to have any spare attention for officers; and at the top of the slope, towards the gates, our road joined the main barrack road at right angles. We had to cross this main road to reach the gates; and it happened to have a most decided cant in our direction, so that we went gingerly up a short but sharp rise of pure ice, like flies crawling up the side of a glass globe. Dan and I got over safely; Lord reached the crest of the rise, and her feet ran backwards suddenly and left her flat on her face in the middle of the road. It was such a gentle, such a gradual subsidence that we could and did laugh immoderately; so did the guards on the gate, only too delighted to have the monotony of their duty shaken by a few ripples of fun. Dan, out of the goodness of her heart, immediately re-embarked upon the glassy sea to the rescue of the fallen. But the moment she stooped to get hold of Lord the infectious, curved urge took her by the feet, they slid softly forward from under her, and she lay down by the first victim. But flat on her back, so that we had the droll speechless astonishment of her face to laugh at this time. We stood on the side lines, so to speak, afraid to advance a foot to help them for fear of adding ourselves to the slaughter; and we shrieked and wheezed with laughter in the frost until our chests felt like bursting and our sides ached. As for the guard, they emitted one grand concerted roar at the fall of Dan, and waited with breathless interest for the next item; being out of range where rescue was concerned, but in possession of a dress-circle seat for the performance.

At this farcical moment the Superintendent chose to come toiling round the corner on an auto-cycle, full into the mêlée. I hand it to her. She took in the situation in one glance, made a stately detour round the two prostrate bodies without seeming to see them, smiled benignly upon our helpless attempts to recover ourselves and salute, and sailed solemnly onward through the gates. An inspired piece of acting if ever I saw one.

But that wasn't all our traffic with that particular frost. When the victims had cautiously picked themselves up we sallied forth and boarded the first bus for home, quite forgetting the long hill it had to climb before it reached quarters. About halfway up the slope we awoke to the fact that our progress was no longer perceptible, and that the next bus behind us had just swivelled round on its haunches and broadsided. We could feel our own struggling to keep its footing, and just about managing it. People began to get off – hurriedly – until we were left alone on the top deck, debating whether to follow them. Gwyn was all for staying aboard, and we were not averse to risking it. So the crawl went on until we drew over the crest of the hill by painful inches, and soared triumphantly into a reasonable speed on the other side. Alighting at the corner nearest quarters, we found ourselves the sole survivors of a bus-load of passengers; and rather proud of ourselves, as if the credit for bringing the damned thing up without mishap belonged somehow to us.

These very small adventures help to pass the time, and keep our minds off our own unrest. But I hate being unsettled, Nick. I hate not knowing what is going to happen to me. I shall be glad when they make a definite statement, and set our minds at rest; no matter what the result may be, I like to take my steps forward tidily and deliberately, not in the dark.

I loved your letter. So glad you liked Johnny, but of course I fail to see how you could help it. Thank you for giving him a grand week-end. In these days of not knowing how many one has still to come every one is so precious. I like your remarks on him so much; I knew that childlike, candid thoughtlessness of his was genuine; I suppose you saw too little of him to discover all that lay dormant behind it. He interests me very much, chiefly because his interest in himself is practically nil.

Write again soon, Nick, in case the move happens before I can hear from you a second time. I'll let you know at once if we're told anything definite.

The afternoon post is just in. A letter from mother, and one from Strang. He's angry with me for leaving him, but he writes very nice letters, lighter than one would think possible from his stuffy leaders.

Yours restively, but resignedly,
Catherine.

IV. A.C.H.Q. IN MIGRATION

W.R.N.S. Quarters, Devonport.
January 27th, 1941.

Dear Nick,

It's about to happen. Yes, any moment. Don't write to me again until I send you my new address, as I will do the very day we arrive. We know where we're going, but I can't say any more until the move is safely over, and as for the actual address, I don't yet know it.

I'm not happy, Nick. I can't help it, everything is so fluid, I can't get hold of anything. I wasn't built for changes, my dear – or else I'm getting old, and just can't take it any more. Because although I was virtuous when they asked me my views on moving, and said I had joined up to do what good I could wherever I was needed; and although I do like being at H.Q., and want to stay with my job; and although Gwyn and Dan, thank heaven, are moving, too – yet now that it comes to the point I don't want to go, Nick, I don't want to go.

I've worked myself in here, and planted myself with little staunch roots that work their way out to Cawsand, and Mutton Cove and the Barbican, and even into the streets, the poor old streets with their sinister pits and their heaps of wood blocks ringed round with lanterns. I love Plymouth. These roots are going to cling like blazes when the moment comes; and it's on top of me now.

Do you know I can walk the length of Union Street alone in the dark, ricocheting off slightly drunken sailors as I go, and never have a second's uneasiness? Shall I be able to say as much where I'm going? I doubt it very much. Your Catherine is not yet quite so old nor so ugly that she can take her security for granted, but the back streets of Plymouth and Devonport, rowdy enough in all conscience, give her never a qualm. I like Union Street; I like it, pubs and all. I like the Octagon, and the Admiral's Locker, and the two South African soldiers who strolled ahead of me into town one night singing: 'Sari Marais.'

'Take me back to the old Transvaal,
That's where I long to be——'

But they sang it in Afrikaans, which sounds much better, and even more nostalgic.

When I write to you again, Nick Crane, you must hurry and send me a letter at once, because by then I'm going to need you rather badly. I don't think I'm very well, really, I tend to drop things, and I'm having disturbed sort of nights full of uneasy dreams. Sheer nerves, I suppose. I'm always like this when an assignment begins to look tough, and this one looks that way to me. So please, please write as soon as you hear from me, or better still have a letter ready and sealed, and lacking only the address, so that Billy can run and post it for you the moment my desperate note arrives. It will be desperate, I feel it coming on.

I have to pack now, because to-morrow may be der Tag.

> Goodbye for the present, and for
> heaven's sake bear with
> Your wretched Saxon.

PS. – I'm ashamed of using you as an outlet for my feelings, but we know each other too well, and anyhow time is too short for hiding what one wants to say. So I think you'll forgive me for worrying you with my worries, who have more than enough of your own already, if only you had time to remember them.

> W.R.N.S. Quarters, Liverpool.
> January 31st, 1941.

Dear Nick,

We're here! My, God, yes, we *have* arrived! This morning, the better part of three whole hours ago, and it feels like a hundred years of my life.

Oh, Nick, I know the first day of a new departure is always hell to me, and the first week only hell diminishing to purgatory by infinitely slow degrees; but I can't be wrong this time. It can't be just the newness; there must be more wrong than just that. I can't believe it will ever be any better. I wish I hadn't come. Not that I really had any chance to do anything else, of course.

I don't mind hardships, I don't mind privations; I'd expected both, in much more lavish measure than I've found them. But I can't stand this frightful wretchedness, this atmosphere of strain to screaming point. I think pain would be easier and lighter to bear. We are all of us unhappy. We none of us have anything we wanted, not even the company of our friends.

This is all wrong end round, I know. Let me tell you about the journey, because that was beautiful and fantastic, and I had Gwyn sitting beside me and Dan sitting opposite, and we had all persuaded ourselves that life was going to be at least fairly good. We all had chocolate and sandwiches for the trip, and most of us had some sort of music, too, so that we started off in high spirits, at six o'clock on a starry winter evening in the snow. Just out of Newton Abbot we ran into a raid alarm, and they put out all the lights. We flapped up the blinds, and sat looking out on a world of moonlight, wildly silent, through which we cruised very slowly. The moonlight and the snow and the trees, startlingly black and white; and Gwyn's guitar thrumming softly in the darkness by me. That was the fantastic part of it. It was peaceful, like a dream; as if we had set out from nowhere and were going nowhere. It was only when it became clear that we should eventually arrive that the uneasiness and depression came back. I suppose we slept a little; at one Midland station we stopped for tea, which made things look momentarily better. At dawn we arrived, and the moral temperature among us sank to zero.

Came the dawn! Did you ever see anything so desolate and discouraging as a winter dawn? It brings you up sharply against the hopelessness of effort, and makes you sit back and fold your hands and wait for the tide to roll over you; because by that light nothing looks worth a struggle, nothing in the world.

That was how I felt, and now it's high noon, or getting near it, and the feeling hasn't gone. Panic is the

wrong word for this unsuperstitious horror I have of
going on living, but I can't think of another. Perhaps it
is superstitious after all; perhaps it's all a manifestation
of the ancient evil bursting into malign activity and
swallowing up my faith and hope in action, and any
belief I had in the benefit of goodness. Mother would
say it's more probably a case of nerves. As for me, I
think it's really a bad attack of revulsion from the communal life, and the accumulation of wounds inflicted
by an organisation with its eyes tightly shut to all the
simplest rules of psychology.

We arrived here by coach from the station, tired,
depressed, desperate, all infected with the same disease.
The windows of the coaches were covered up with
fine gauze. We could see nothing but the vague colour
of unutterable dreariness, the colour of the last limbo
outside hell. We felt like animals in a cage. And then
this house. Breakfast wasn't ready for us; that didn't
matter, no one cared about that. If only we'd been met
at the door by someone who even looked happy it might
have helped; but they all looked harassed, and probably felt it, too. How can one make people realise that it
isn't hardship that makes service girls go out and drown
themselves, or hook themselves on to electric cables;
it's the aura of strain and tension that comes up from
their everlasting, inescapable, physical and mental
contact, like the noxious gas given off by the collision
of incompatible chemicals. I doubt if men know this
murdering poison to any considerable extent; but I
know how it paralyses women. I know only too well
how it's got hold of us.

Now with intelligence it could be mitigated. But see
how it was handled in this case. Arriving tired and

grubby and discouraged, we were shown to our cabins, which are on the ground floor for safety's sake, equipped with too many double-decker beds. Too many for our peace of mind, that is, not for our health; I've no doubt every possible precaution was taken against over-crowding. I found myself looking dismally round a room full of fifteen strangers. Gwyn was in with nine equally unknown at the other end of the house. Dan was stowed away in a wing with particles of two clans she detests, themselves lame with the lack of their own friends, she lamenting us. Dan is a child utterly dependent upon her company, and given to moods.

And after the cabins, the dressing-rooms. Upstairs, these, the ground floor being fully accounted for by the sleeping arrangements. Again we were all separate, and alone. It only remains for us to be in three different watches, and our despair will be complete. And I feel that this last blow will fall on us to-morrow, when we visit our new offices for the first time.

If only I could bring myself, just once, to accept things as they are! It would be better for me, and better for the others, too, for anyone as restless as I am now is bound to be a nucleus of unrest in other people. But resignation is utterly impossible to me. I suffer from an inexhaustible supply of hope; like Tantalus, who otherwise would have given up tormenting himself after a year or so, and grown indifferent to the beauty of visions he knew to be without substance. Even after it has become obvious even to me that I can't alter things, I go on questing for any small wire to pull, and after the worst has happened, I am discovered still at the same old unprofitable occupation. The only thing that keeps despair alive is that people are so reluctant to give up hope.

You see, I know myself rather well. Better than to waste time in trying to persuade myself that this horror of change will pass, that I shall become used to the new. I know it; it will happen this time as it has always happened, and I shall settle down and make myself another little rut. No need even to tell myself so any more; myself doesn't dispute it. But that doesn't in any way mitigate the misery of the moment. How could it? At that rate you could make pain itself an illusion by convincing yourself that death, at the latest, must end it.

So we are here, tired, separated, mutinous, unhappy every one. Discontent walks about the corridors and meets us at corners. I wish to God I was out of it. I wish I was home. I wish I'd gone on munitions, or been content to write up mother's W.V.S. activities, or followed Barbie into the Land Army, or something. I shall have a watch, yes, a watch of strangers.

There isn't much more I can tell you. I believe there's a garden, but I haven't the heart to go out and look. If there is, it will be frost-bound. I hate winter.

The only bright spot, so far, is that the bath water is scalding hot. Or was, until too many of us drew too much of it off.

Write to me quickly, Nick, though for the life of me, my long-suffering confessor, I can't think why you should. I am only the hag on your back.

Burn this letter afterwards. I don't want ever to see or hear or think of this mood again. Write as you like to me, you can do no wrong where I'm concerned; only write, and let it be long, and rough, and full of swear-words; I need a lot of you, and I need you neat.

S.O.S. Saxon.

W.R.N.S. Quarters, Liverpool.
February 7th, 1941.

Dear Nick,

You are much kinder to me than I have any right to expect. Your letter was better than a double brandy, and has me more or less on my feet again now, for which much thanks. I suppose in any case the edge of my ache would have been blunted by now in the normal course of events, but no one but you can really pull me out of my deepest ditches. I wonder why you never fail? You're not a bit consistent, really. When I expect you to be sympathetic, you snarl, and when I expect you to tell me to snap out of it, you decide to be gentle and reasonable and soothing. But whichever line you take is always the right one for whatever ails me.

Yes, it's passing. The worst phase is gone. I waited until I could tell you so without straining the truth, so you can be easy about the threatened sanity of your troublesome Saxon. I am getting used to it. What a description of lyrical blessedness it makes, doesn't it? I'm getting used to it! If I can say no more than that for it, it must be pretty well damned. But half the fault is in me or in my inevitable nature – more than half. I never pretended otherwise.

There are signs of regeneration, at any rate. I've reached the stage at which I allow my strange bedfellows one or two virtues, and can pass a whole night in one unbroken sleep. But I was right about the watches; scarcely any two friends are together.

Well, I'm approaching the point at which the humorous side of the business emerges upon one in its full sublimity. Up to now only facets of it have been perceptible, gorgeously funny moments at which, for love

of the ease there was in laughing, we laughed immoderately. As, for instance, the affair of the first night-
watch—— But let me tell my story forward for once,
instead of backward.

We had the day of our arrival free; free to recover or
free to brood, whichever made the stronger appeal. I
hadn't meant to brood, honest to goodness I hadn't,
but it was so hard to do anything else. Have you seen
Liverpool in the rush hour of a foggy February evening? I went to town by myself because I was not fit for
human companionship, and because I wanted to snap
out of it, and in quarters that was hopeless. I wandered
to the main road, boarded a tram, and set off to look
for Liverpool, and I found it and it found me. In the pit
of the stomach, with a horrible sinking feeling. I don't
care what anyone says in its defence, Liverpool, the
third (?) city in England, is the abomination of desolation. Bombed or unbombed – in fact I think the
bombed bits are better. It would be a good idea to
remove all the people to safety and bomb at least
seventy per cent of the town flat. Then they could start
afresh, and let's hope they'd make a better job of it.

You gather that it wasn't comforting. It wasn't comfortable, either; it was cold and damp and clammy; and
the only thing I could find of any beauty or grandeur
was the new cathedral. I must look more closely at that
some other time, and I feel reasonably sure it will pay
for discovery. But the rest of the town, apart from a
few of the better shops, is so squalid and depressing and
soiled that every step I took in the streets made me
homesick for Plymouth. So no more shall be said just
now about a subject I find wholly revolting; my judgment is probably jaundiced, and I should hate to have

to take it all back later. Anyhow I was utterly miserable, and in my innocence I did the final foolish thing – I dawdled until the rush hour, and then tried to board a tram for home. It took me three-quarters of an hour, fighting tooth and nail, and though I'm not good at fighting for transport, I did myself credit on this occasion; but I got back to quarters too late for supper, which didn't help in the least. So our first day was by no means a success, and the first evening had that end-of-the-world feeling about it, the feeling you have before something new, and presumably bad, is due to happen.

The following morning buses collected us and took us to look at our new offices, though we were not to begin work until next day. They unloaded us in a narrow street, at a hole in a wall, with the mere skeleton of a very large building looming over us. When I say a hole in a wall I mean it literally. Obviously it was going to be a door some day, but as yet it wasn't even a doorway; but our old friend the sentry was standing over it with fixed bayonet, which made it look rather more like our own place to us. The building was in keeping with the entrance, being only half a building, in possession of armies of workmen who marched about wreathed in wire, and caressing, besides innumerable and strange tools, such small arms as wood beams, festoons of lead piping, joints of steel shafting, and so on. As yet we saw only a small part of their kingdom, and couldn't guess how completely they had us in their power, but they looked at us with indulgent curiosity as knowing themselves proprietors and us mere visitors in their odd paradise. And how right they were! We only work here. They work here, play here, sleep here, cook here. We are hirelings; they are a free army of occupation.

We went down a staircase which revolved around a hypothetical lift-shaft. It's going to be quite a handsome staircase of faced stone some day, but just now all the edges of the steps are chipped with lugging beams and girders up and down, and the marbling is hidden completely under layers of mortar rubble and dust, which rises in an effective smoke-screen as your feet stir it. Every room below, every chair, every desk, was buried in the same very pale, very fine, very irritating dust; but our room, when we found it, proved to be the most completely shut off, and consequently the least soiled and trampled, of all. We thought and still think this a very considerable virtue; but it has its drawbacks, for our beautifully isolated room is going to turn out, unless we're much mistaken, unmercifully hot and airless. However, that remains to be proved, and if necessary rectified.

Well, we had a look at our room. We have a bigger switchboard here, and more machines, and the whole thing is on a more imposing scale, so I gather that expansion is in the air. Just then, however, we were not officially in service at all; not a cord up nor a light showing on the switchboard, not a machine talking. Even now, though we have been working for four days, traffic is very light, and gathering momentum only gradually.

We were divided into our watches on the spot – mine were strange to me every one, but in the end I'm not sure that that won't be an advantage, for it means we start without prejudices. We were to set the ball rolling with the first watch next day, and for two days we worked only the daylight watches; after that, the old routine; old to me, that is, but new to some of these innocents who had never done a night-watch.

For the first day that was about all we did, except roam around the building in a daze and lose ourselves by twos and threes in the wilderness of constructive material and just plain junk. The whole crazy place was only half-finished. Pieces of wall were missing in the oddest corners; there were temporary stairs of wood leading upward and downward at improbable angles; and the most remarkable thing of all was the way you walked along what appeared to be a finished bit of corridor, and found yourself suddenly under the murky sky, walking on mud and falling over miscellaneous bits of wood and masonry. The workmen had braziers burning here and there – or else it was the same brazier and I passed it several times on my peculiar way through the maze. Anyhow there was at least one brazier, and a nucleus of workmen round it doing anything but work. From this point it was not so easy to find one's way back into cover. I tried several directions without success, and finally collared a passing sailor, the first for some time, and asked him to direct me back to the teleprinter room. Matelots, as I soon found out in this racket, know everything; and this one didn't let me down. I not only found the T-P room, but the hole in the wall, and my dusty way through it. Then, having retrieved Gwyn and Dan, and found a thin cold rain falling, I took self and party to the nearest cinema, and forgot my woes in the (cine) adventures of Kit Carson. Not bad in some ways, but one had to close one's eyes to all previous knowledge of Cristobal the guest of governors and friend of Archbishops in order to enjoy this particularly rough diamond. However, this was a film, not a biography.

Others, I understand, became even more involved with the complexities of our new offices. Life can be difficult indeed, if you come to think of it, when marooned for a watch of five hours or more in a place more closely resembling an obstacle race than an office, in which you have no idea how or where to find even the simplest necessities of life. We spent two whole days trying to locate the one thing one must locate. Very awkward, my dear Nick. We, being all equally new, found no hope in asking each other, and had to rely on our own personal scouting. Maybe we're not very good at scouting; anyhow, I gave it up in the middle of our second duty, and did the obvious thing. I asked a matelot. Yes, he knew. Matelots are miracles of blithe, unselfconscious commonsense. He said it was a bit hard to describe how to get there; so he took me. More, my dear, he waited for me, and carefully steered me back to the T-P room. And *that* problem was solved once for all. Unless, of course, the thing moves around; I don't trust anything in this place to stay put for more than two days at a time. The shape of the whole building is changing all the time; it's very confusing.

On our first night-watch, which was the first ever worked in our new home, the possibilities of comedy became rather obvious, and we all began to feel much better. Laughter is so infectious, even more so than despair. The first performance of my anecdote about the sanitary arrangements went almost extravagantly well. Jean Perris, who is just eighteen and horribly homesick, laughed so violently after a long temptation to tears that I began to love my watch with a surprised, parental, jealous love. Odd that in all my life I've never felt personal responsibility for any human creature except myself, until now. I have a humble feeling, Nick. I think it's good for a self-sufficient woman of twenty-seven to be given a watch of young, spirited, vulnerable girls to look after. I know it dragged me out of the ditch – much shallower after your letter, but still a ditch. I began to look round for other easy laughs; and believe me, there was plenty of material.

The arrangements for night work are rather odd. The night-watch proper takes over at one o'clock in the morning. There's sleeping accommodation for the whole of one watch, the idea being that the off-duty watch comes aboard at a reasonable hour in the evening, sleeps until one, when the turnover takes place; and the dormitory is surrendered to the retiring watch. We took over at one on that first night of all.

Lord, but it was funny. We'd been told that three operators would be enough for night work for the time being, and I took on with me only young Jean, and a Welsh girl named Owen. The fun began as we were climbing the main stairs on the first lap of our hazardous trip to the dormitory, which involved the passage of the brazier and five minutes of wandering through the open-air section of our home from home. The first incident was a pursuit from the guard-room by the door, by a small, harassed, middle-aged sailor who plucked my rear-guard – Owen – by the sleeve, and uttered appealingly: 'Miss——!'

We stopped as one man. He seemed in some difficulty about putting his errand into words. He said very quickly: 'Will you take charge of this, please, miss? Some of you young ladies asked for it to be sent up.' And he presented her with a roll of Bronco, and fled before the spell could break.

I am almost sure he didn't hear us laugh. Owen behaved magnificently, thanked him with an aplomb of which I still think with admiration, and stood there holding the thing solemnly, her face quite bland. Not until we were a full turn of the lift-shaft away from the scene did the collapse set in. Jean began to bubble like a kettle boiling, and exploded in a fountain of sympathy and delight: 'The poor, dear little man!' And with the wild willingness to laugh which comes after acute depression, we let it rip, and wandered our erratic way through the resident army of Lancashire tradesmen in a daze of mirth, clinging together, helpless with laughter. In the dark that journey was even more of an adventure than usual, and it seemed to me, before we reached our goal, that someone had spent a considerable time thinking out the correct placing of the hazards. There was a coil of wire, for instance, so placed in a dark corner that no one but a confirmed and cautious pessimist with a torch should see it, and whoever did not see it should immediately stumble heavily into a heap of sand. I, being in the lead, got the full benefit of that, and went on with my shoes full; but I was still laughing too much to have any breath left for swearing. We made it in the end, of course, arriving minus a few bits of skin and plus a ladder in Jean's stocking, but well out of our despairs once for all.

The dormitory, so far from being the haven of peace for which we had hoped, was in the thick of things. A couple of picks and a length of steel tubing were leaning against the door. We lifted them out of the way and let ourselves in. Inside it looked deceptively calm and quiet, a long, low-ceilinged room full of beds; but I had a feeling that all things were not as they seemed, and the prompt rattle of the picks and the tubing coming back to harbour against the door had an ominously confirmatory sound. So matter of fact, so hullo-have-those-kids-been-meddling-again. Just picked 'em up and propped 'em back against the door. I told you we only work here.

We went to bed, optimists to the last. It's astonishing how sound carries in that room. The trampling and talking of the resident army sounded more like herds of elephants in clogs crossing a wooden bridge; and when we got so nearly used to this odd acoustic effect that there was a distant hope of sleep, quite suddenly from somewhere terrifyingly near, an electric drill went into action. The walls shook, and the beds took all four feet off the floor at once and jitterbugged in mid-air. That sort of thing should have had us hopping mad, by all the rules of logic. Instead, it made us laugh like hell. Another sign of lunacy in the English (female) character. I don't know of any other country where one's own physical discomfort is comic, though I gather that there are plenty of places where you are allowed to find your fun in other people's.

We'd locked the door, not out of any alarm we felt at the close proximity of the workmen, but because the whole show seemed so improbable that we had a feeling they might not recognise the function of our sleeping quarters, and there was an even chance they might come breezing in for a rest and a smoke any moment. If you saw how they take possession of everything you'd understand our coyness. But it was unfortunate, because the only person who tried to get in was an immobile telephonist who had come into town by the last tram, arriving about eleven o'clock. I had to get out

of bed to open the door for her, and I couldn't find my
torch or my way, so the operation took some time.
Again we settled down, screaming goodnights at each
other above the rattle of the drill, and trying to stay in
bed when the floor rocked.

At midnight, we had learned with pleasure, the
workmen had an hour's stand-easy. That should have
given us an hour's rest, at any rate. And sure enough, at
midnight a whistle blew, the drill stopped, and the gang
audibly downed tools. But alas for our hopes, they all
came and ate their supper round our door, of all places.
They brought the brazier with them, for we heard it
being stoked up, and the glow of it came under the
door; and presently they started up a poker game.

Noisy for a poker game, but unmistakable. It didn't
make the beds dance, but it was almost noisier than the
drill, and much less predictable.

We gave it up. In any case it was hardly worth the
struggle, for a possible half-hour's sleep. We made
the best of our beds, anyhow, until Dan, on behalf of the
watch we were relieving, came to tell us it was a quarter
to one. She must have tramped through the poker game
without even seeing it, and when we unlocked the door
she fell into the room helpless with a fit of the giggles. It
seems she found a dormitory, all right, at her first
attempt, and several sleepers in it; and with her usual
optimism she slapped on the lights, hammered a tattoo
on the nearest bed-rail and yelled: 'Come on, girls, one
o'clock – time to get up.' Then she seized the nearest
sleeper by the shoulder, and shook her, and was heading for a second when it occurred to her that our coats
do not have lighter blue rings round the sleeves. Always
quick on the uptake, she was out of the room before

any of the cypher watch can have revived sufficiently to recognise her. Officers have to be awakened, of course, but it isn't usually done Dan's way.

We left her prostrate on one of the beds, still giggling, and wound our way back to the T-P room, to a session almost totally devoid of traffic. I expected it to be quiet, but there were almost literally no signals at all. So we commandeered all the leather chair-cushions we could find, and made up three beds in the darkest corner. Off duty we couldn't sleep; on duty we slept very well, and had tea sent down to us by the guard into the bargain. Our chief, who – lucky us! – is everyone's favourite and – for good measure – knows his job backwards, forwards and sideways, came in with that tray of tea very softly, the tip of his tongue out like a kid's to balance it. Good tea it was, too.

Don't imagine that this state of affairs will last long. It won't. Already we're turning over a highly respectable night traffic, and I foresee heavy going on the way. Pretty soon we'll really be working. So much the better for us all.

You see the crisis is over. I don't know how those periods come or how they go, I only know experience is no armour against them, nor logic, nor reason, nor anything of the normality of life. Only from outside normality can I get these things in a true perspective; from a place in your mind, using your vision, Nick Crane.

It's been an odd sort of partnership, ours, when you come to think of it; and coming out of a shadow like this I do think of it. I couldn't, in my maddest moments, write to anyone of my own sex as I write to you. With you I have no reticences. What an appalling thought if you were anyone but you!

Let me tell you something I think you want to know.

Something rather odd, at least to me. I haven't written to John Randall for a month. I wrote at Christmas, and not a line since then; but I know now that I must write again soon – in the next few days – and send back his ring. You were right about that. It was only a very little discomfort, not so much transient – for I like him as much as ever I liked him – as an illusion, for I want and expect so much more now. Perhaps through looking at Gwyn and Johnny. Who knows? All I am sure about is that it never mattered very much, and doesn't matter at all now. A poor sort of epitaph for an engagement, I'm afraid, but better than some I have known.

I really must stop. This letter is getting out of hand. I promise you shall hear of me again soon, with perhaps a little less of me and a little more of other people than I've sent you this time.

Yours always, my Nick,
Catherine.

V. LETTERS FROM MERSEYSIDE

W.R.N.S. Quarters, Liverpool.
February 12th, 1941.

Dear Nick,

The weather is settling down, and so am I, and so are we all. It's odd how one does. A few nice bright days of clear frost and sun, and a week or so to get used to the communal living, and learn one another's sore spots, and we are shaking down into our jobs as to the manner born, and beginning to plan ahead instead of living for the next stand-easy: which is a very healthy state of affairs indeed.

This is a model hostel once you can adapt yourself to its initial peculiarities. The house is bright and sunny, and there's a garden, frosty now and full of rimy shrubs, but with considerable promise for the summer. I walked round it this morning, and thought it all out. There are two lawns, and quite a few summer-houses and seats dotted about in quiet corners; and I thought, thought I: 'Just wait until the Spring lets us expand into all this and stretch our own prickles without the risk of cramping someone else's! Then life *will* be worth living.' That's some months ahead yet, but it's grand even to see it in the distance. All we need now is room to escape each other. There will always be cliques; I mean always as far as this generation is concerned, and probably the next one, too. Certain people will go on peeping into common-rooms and withdrawing again because certain other people are already ensconced there. A condition in us which cannot be cured will at least be relieved when we have more lebensraum.

From which pearls of wisdom you will gather that your Saxon is herself again.

I'm beginning to scratch myself a new sort of rut, and I think I like it. I am now an Acting Leading Wren, with six girls in my charge, for the deeds of all of whom I am more or less responsible. A thing I've never had to say of myself before in all my twenty-seven years. And I'm a success, that's the amazing thing. They like being in my watch, and I like having them, and we're getting really into our stride. We're going to be – *I* think we already are – the best watch on this station. It's a pretty good sort of feeling, better than being good at a thing on your own. Some of my own operators can make rings round me, but *I* am the person who holds them together and keeps them happy – yes, it's possible to be happy here now – and co-ordinates their mixed efforts into one efficient whole. There are occasional gaps in our efficiency at the moment, but they're merely the breaks of inexperience, and we're closing them fast.

The office keeps growing, but there's no sign of the army of occupation leaving yet, or even stopping nightwork. As it happens, we've done very well out of them, for our canteen isn't functioning yet, and there's a certain young joiner named Charlie who habitually brings an extra can of coffee on night duty with him for the inhabitants of the T-P room. Very good coffee Charlie's mother makes, too. He works in the C.C.O., just outside our door; by the time he moves on we hope the canteen will be working.

We lack, of course, the one thing we had most lavishly

in Plymouth. You can take a short walk here, say round the park, and enjoy it, for it's about the finest park I've seen yet; but when the urge comes, as it still does, to pack up some food and go off for the entire day – well, you're sunk. There's nowhere to go. I believe there are spots in Cheshire worth visiting, but to reach them means a long journey by train or bus before you even take off. Down in Plymouth we had only to pop over into Cornwall by way of Cremyll or Torpoint, or take a bus out to Yelverton or Crownhill, and we were all set for a glorious day. There's nothing in this part of the world comparable to Cawsand, or Looe, or Anthony, or Newton Ferrers. No, in Liverpool you have to take pleasure in other things or die of stagnation. But there are certain lines in which Liverpool has the advantage, particularly in winter. There are very good shows here, both stage and screen, and excellent concerts. The initiated among us frequent the Philharmonic almost every Sunday, Sunday concerts being free to the Forces, and almost every Saturday, too. We've also been visited by some extremely good plays on tour, and rumour says the Anglo-Polish Ballet is coming soon. In Plymouth we had only cinemas to brighten the dark evenings; but oh, Plymouth was fun in daylight.

There are squirrels in our garden; that's one more thing we hadn't got in Plymouth, anyhow. They come up sometimes and sit on the galley window-sill and peep round shyly at the stewards inside, and wait for scraps. Little red squirrels, not the grey kind that's reputed to be killing them off. Beautiful little things with bright brown eyes and small questing hands. Paws doesn't describe the shape of them, nor the way they're used, so hands it will have to be. They told us, the first time we saw one of these little fellows twinkling at us from among the Virginia creeper, that in the park they're so tame that they'll climb up to your shoulder and eat out of your hand. So Gwyn and I bought some pea-nuts and went off one morning to look for them.

It was a fine morning, with only the mildest touch of frost, and there was a deceptive look of Spring about the trees in the park. We walked beside water for a little way, crossed by some stepping-stones, and turned down a narrow path among shrubberies; and in ten minutes we came to a small neat clearing where a man sat with a squirrel on either shoulder. His back was towards us, and we stood watching him for quite five minutes before he was aware of us. He was in khaki, his head uncovered. The backs of people's heads are interesting, I can't think why. This rear elevation was nice-looking, a fine firm neck, not too long nor too short, and heaven knows a neck has to be just so to look good in battle-dress; and a well-shaped head, with a lot of thick black hair cropped close enough to show its decisive lines, and left just long enough on top to curl. The hair was just beginning to grey a bit above the ears, but all the same it looked a strangely young and statuesque head. Anything else about it? Oh, yes, the lobe of one ear was missing; it looked as if it had been chewed off. A pity, because they were neat, close, alert-looking ears; a trifle sharper at the top, and he'd have looked like a faun. All the more so as he was engaged in shelling pea-nuts and handing them gravely by turns to the squirrels on his shoulders. The little things waited eagerly, and reached out and took them from his fingers with gestures so human and childish that it wouldn't have seemed particularly odd if they'd burst into speech at any moment.

They heard us before he did. One of them whisked down his arm and sat at the extreme end of the park seat, ready to bolt if we moved any nearer. The man sensed our presence then, and turned his head leisurely and took a good long look at us.

Good-looking back views like his usually have plain faces, and he was no exception. Thin and gaunt-lined he was, with a dark complexion and harsh gipsyish features. His eyes were black and sunken, but looked very clear and long-sighted. They looked at us without apparent curiosity, but oddly without annoyance at being disturbed in a moment so private. He didn't smile. I don't think he smiles often. I had a feeling at once that I'd seen him before somewhere, but I couldn't think where. It wasn't a very strong feeling, not one of the we-two-have-met-before-but-who-knows-where-or-when kind; just an idea that some-where or other I'd seen a fellow with the same dark sort of face. It didn't matter very much, but I can never quit nagging my mind until I've run these resemblances to earth, and this one was elusive.

Having butted into his private conversation with the squirrels we felt bound to account for ourselves, like people who have walked into the wrong house. Gwyn said something about being forestalled, and herself began to shell nuts and hold them out invitingly in the palm of her hand. I, as I usually do when out with Gwyn, kept silence and left her to be our ambassador. You've seen her, you'll know how wise I am.

The soldier said: 'Come and sit down!' An ambiguous sort of remark, but it was obvious that he was being helpful to our friendly overtures towards the squirrels, so we just naturally made to comply. At the first step the squirrels were off like two flashes of russet lightning, into the bushes and out of sight. 'Oh, they've gone!' said Gwyn, checking in dismay.

'They'll come back,' he said quite simply. 'Just sit down and keep quiet.'

And we did, and they did. They came back and climbed over us in the end, and took nuts from us as we'd seen them do from him. It was fascinating, the touch of the little quick creatures and the cool of their fur glancing over your skin. We almost forgot about the soldier, he was so silent; and quite suddenly when we remembered him, he was gone, without a word to us. He left, intentionally or unintentionally, an impression that he withdrew so stealthily only because we were engrossed with our pets, and happy; so the faunish feeling persisted, if you can imagine a faun in khaki.

Long after we went back to quarters with the remains of our pea-nuts I was still trying to trace that resemblance. And in the middle of the night-watch I got it. If he'd turned the other temple towards me, the one with the scar, I should have put my finger on it at once. Do you remember me telling you about him? The infantry private who talked about Chiang Kai Shek? And got me a share of an overcrowded taxi, that night I went back from leave and found the town alight? It seems a long time ago, and it was never so very good a light in the carriage; but I got him in the end.

I wonder if he knew me. I can't help thinking he did. Odd that he should, but my instinct tells me he recognised this very ordinary face at once. I wonder how he came to turn up here? He has as much right in Liverpool as I have, of course, but it's stretching coincidence rather far. Still, one does meet people at the strangest moments in the strangest places. Once! I don't suppose it will happen again; they always disappear after the first time.

I have nothing to say really, only an urge to write. No news from home; I don't mean no letter, but only that small sort of good news which is no news. At home all is peace, except that the dark boy has picked up an undesirable girl, or one mother considers undesirable, and the fair boy has taken father's watch to pieces, with the best intentions, and can't put it together again. You see what I mean?

In fact, this is a letter in which, I've discovered, the war has never once been mentioned until now. It's extraordinary that it should be possible to write about anything else; but the fact remains that since our coming here we seem to have been doing a routine job, rather oddly trimmed, but nothing to do with a war. Who would have thought, last year, that I should have been at leisure to spend a whole day chasing a fugitive memory? Or even to spare an hour of a wartime morning in the sylvan contemplation of squirrels, park shrubberies and infantry fauns?

I'll write you a better account of things next time. At the moment I am being harassed by a battle between Jean and Second Officer's friend's bull-pup, who has no respect for letters, even to you; and as it shows no sign of abating I think I'd better give up the unequal struggle, and lose no time in signing myself

> Your tired but not altogether discontented
> Saxon.

W.R.N.S. Quarters, Liverpool.
February 18th, 1941.

Dear Nick,

Something very strange has happened. I've seen him again.

It doesn't sound very much to make a fuss about, come to think of it. But in the growing calm of this month, with London half in ashes, and the face of the country mutilated beyond repair, and only our stony quiet isolated in the vortex of the whirlwind, this unexpected collision with someone whose interest for me had nothing to do with reason stood out at the time as an event quite unique. I thought it a coincidence that I should meet him again once; the second time its significance became less measurable because it stepped so far aside from all the rest of my life. Only abnormality is normal now; the very ordinariness of this meeting set it apart.

Even now I hark back to the moment with a kind of detached wonder. The war, you see, stopped the day we came north. Only the headlines have kept it before us, and headlines alone are not enough to make a war. But when I sat down beside him in the tram on my way home from town that night, and talked to him in the desultory way one does to a person scarcely known, and yet in a few minutes found that we were talking in a very different fashion—— Yes, there was a war. It was his whole background, though he had little to say about it. I know only that in that blue, subdued light, in which we looked to each other something like corpses of the drowned, the war came in and arched over us both like a vast anger of cloud and storm. And that was as it should be; as I wanted it to be.

It's too easy to forget all that's happened. There are even people who think it desirable to forget, as if it were a virtue to forgive easily the unspeakable wrongs of other people in other countries. But I think it one of the most deadly sins of this nation, the father of lethargy, and financial opportunism and selfishness, and tolerance-gone-mad; the mother and grandmother of half-heartedness, which will damn us in the end unless we learn to hate more generously.

What a lot of misapprehension there is about the nature of hate, the most feared of vices and the most maligned of virtues. Hate, positive and open and unrelenting, seems to me at least worthy of respect, and if it's directed against injustice and cruelty and retrogression, as it should be, wholly admirable. I used to know a pacifist who preached to me indiscriminate forgiveness; when I said that forgiveness without repentance had no significance whatsoever he didn't know what I was talking about. But you try standing in the path of a tank and forgiving it for destroying you; and what use is that to the rest of the world? No, I prefer to make some sort of counter-effort at destruction. So many people suffer from muddled one-way thinking about hate; it's an uncontrolled, blood-thirsty fury to them; to me, when I fall into this thoughtful mood it's a dynamic force under strict control; and what a weapon! But this country doesn't know how to use it. It accomplishes miracles, if it destroys the instruments; do you remember in 'Seven Pillars' how Talal drew his veil over his face and cried out, and rode into the retreating Turkish column, after he had seen the massacre of his village?

But it requires a great and selfless heart to house a

hate like that, an emotion which consumes and exhausts and enlarges our small human energies so that we forget to retain any limitations, and perform prodigies of heroism before we die. As in any case we inevitably should in the end. There's a Russian proverb which says: 'No man can find two graves, nor fail to find one.'

All this out of fifteen minutes of the company of a rather singular man. But some casual contacts have this way of stimulating the imagination.

I boarded the tram alone at the bottom of Mount Pleasant. Gwyn had done a cinema with me and gone back to duty; it was the first time I'd come back to quarters alone after blackout time. Almost every seat was occupied, but this one soldier was sitting alone towards the back of the car, reading a book. I sat down by him, and he looked up at me quite suddenly, a long intent glance, and I looked back at him, and it seemed quite right and meet that he should have a puckered silvering scar down his temple, and the lobe of an ear missing. It was momentous, but not surprising; you'll understand perfectly.

He said: 'Hullo!' and closed his book. He was reading 'Urn Burial', it had a good gilt title, readable even in that dim blue light, though he must have particularly good vision to have deciphered the type inside.

I said: 'What are you doing in these parts?' Harking back rather to North Road than to a bench in Sefton Park.

He smiled; rather a dark sort of smile, with odd effects; it made the scar whiten and a nerve twitch at the hollow of his cheek. 'Digging a sewer,' he said.

One hears things like that; and after all they have to

be done, and with a great part of the country's active man-power under arms—— But for a man like that – no new campaigner eighteen years old—— No, it couldn't be accepted complacently. I said: 'How does that happen to your sort of soldier?' and he smiled again and said: 'What is my sort of soldier?' And he slid 'Urn Burial' away into his pocket, and settled a little sidewise in his seat so as to be able to watch me. Can you see, I wonder, exactly how much and how little I mean if I say that it was intense pleasure to be sure of his interest in me? I think so. To have him put away Browne in order to talk to Saxon; and knowing him, as I very surely knew him, not the man to do so much for kindness or courtesy.

I said: 'Not a green sort of soldier. You've lost a scrap of your ear, and I think, though I won't be sure, that a rifle-bullet took it. And you have a scar on your forehead which is very irregular and very puckered, and may have been done by shrapnel, or perhaps by debris thrown out by an exploding hand-grenade. There shouldn't be any grey in your hair, but there is; and besides, if you were new to this you wouldn't be so weather-beaten.'

He looked at me for a moment clean in the eyes, and then he said: 'How if I'd always worked in the weather?' And I said: 'If you're from behind a plough, why do you talk with such a London voice?' And it was true, you know; not the Cockney note, but the cosmopolitan London which was yours once and never has been mine.

He was quiet for a moment, and then he touched his scar, looking intently at his fingers afterwards as if he thought it might still be bleeding. 'It was a booby-trap,' he said. 'Home-made mine. The man who sprung it was killed.'

I said: 'Flanders?'

He said: 'Spain. Outside Barcelona.'

Then I knew, or believed I knew, rather more about him. But who can be sure of a man like that? We sat there side by side, not looking at each other, the bone-shaker tram rattling along its lines in the dark, and we seeing visions. I don't know what his vision was. I wish I did. Mine was a stream of black-haired women with old, sad faces, filing through the Spanish frontier barriers into Gibraltar, and a starved horse grazing sickly along the dry brown grass of the neutral ground by the inexpressibly dreary road to La Linea de la Concepción. The only bit of Spain I ever saw, except the coastline as we cruised south. And that was after the war was ended, and all that prolonged, tragic splendour brought down to bitterness and loss.

I said: 'There must be times when all this seems a trifle stale and trivial to you.' But he said: 'No. That was only a rehearsal. This is the night.'

There was something final about the double meaning in that. This is the night, sure enough; the earth all one great dark place full of the abomination of cruelty. I was very keenly aware of it then. I thought of all the things one spends a good part of one's life trying to forget, and I thought of them peacefully, if it is peace to be without dissension in oneself. My mind all one iron stillness of remembrance and condemnation and resolve. I thought of the boatloads of pale dead children picked up after the 'City of Benares' sank; and a press photograph of an old woman's cart wrecked on a Spanish road, and she sitting in the mud fondling a little dead dog; and two Chinese babies lying in their blood in a street in Chungking; and the students of Prague martyred by outrage and murder publicly before their friends; and merchant seamen dying in seas of flaming oil; and little homes blasted and little people killed without haste or hot blood or consciousness of sin; and Guernica; and Coventry; and Poland. Only now and again do I realise how right it is that we should remember these things, and exact a price for them. Justice is not a vengeful thing; neither does it bend the other way. Only those who have not felt nor understood the stature of the crime can ever think or speak of forgiving it. Do we talk of forgiving the virus of a contagious disease?

I said: 'You've had experience of war as it's fought now. Of this war, because it's all one. Can't they find a better use for you than digging sewers?' And the dark smile came again, and he said: 'Is it all one? I'm not so sure. When I went to Spain of my own free will, the newspapers of this country called me a Communist. Nowadays I think they begin to change their minds about the use of that word. It was the dirty Reds then; it's the dirty Nazis now. Yes,' he said, softly, 'perhaps you're right. It's all one war. England's changed sides, that's all.'

I tried to sort out what I wanted to say; and I couldn't and he said it for me. 'A people gently-minded,' he said, 'and peculiarly prone to follow where they believe they lead.' And I said: 'But not much longer.' And he said: 'I do believe – not very much longer.'

It was all very brief and strange. There was a sailor at the merry stage singing: 'Bless 'Em All' right behind us, and a blonde girl perilously near the sick stage sitting

121

opposite. They might as well not have been there. All the ordinary small things of life existed, but none to any lively degree. Only his ideas, singularly naked and unselfconscious and erect, stood up in the middle of my world, and earth's foundations, if you understand me, were stayed.

I said: 'Are you a Communist?'

'It depends,' he said, 'on what you mean by it. If you mean a member of the party, no, not that party nor any other. If you mean one who's convinced the good part of life and opportunity and happiness is meant to be shared by all humanity instead of a comparatively small part, yes.' And all this he said not with detachment, not reflectively, as one being careful to sound judicial; nor passionately, as one proselytising; but in the cheerfully rational manner of direct conversation, as one satisfying a simple question with an answer as simple.

And I said: 'Is that why they find you fit only for digging sewers?'

Then he laughed, and he said: 'There are still a great many people who believe they can afford to look sideways on a man who got the mark put on him in Spain – on my side of the fighting. They've been sure the wall was blank for too long ever to see the writing on it now.'

I said: 'What happens to them when the landslide gets under way?' And he said: 'I wonder! In any other country it would be so easy to answer, but here no one can even begin to guess. Maybe that's what the peerage is for. It's not much more than a workhouse for outworn ideas now.' And I said: 'What would you do with outworn ideas? Destroy them?' And he said: 'No.

122

Destruction is easy to start and hard to stop. If I wanted this very inadequate system destroyed, should I be in uniform fighting to keep it?' And I said: 'Digging sewers for it, you mean.' And he said: 'Some day we may run out of sewers.'

And then, when we were nearing my stop, he suddenly said: 'When shall I see you again?' I said: 'Does it matter?' And he said: 'Yes.' No reason, no explanation, no compliments, simply yes, it did matter. So I told him when and where before I left him.

But now, as I write you this lengthy account of what must seem a very small incident, I wonder if I shall keep the appointment. To sit beside a stranger in a tram and exchange abrupt volcanic confidences, and feel the stimulation of someone else's positive ideas, is one thing; to meet him deliberately by pre-arrangement, like two people who have picked each other up at a canteen dance, is quite another. God knows neither his feet nor mine were ever off the ground, but to come down to that is like coming down to another earth.

These are odd things to be telling anyone in a letter; impossible things to be telling to anyone but you. But you will have known, certainly have known, contacts like this, so brief and so profound and so kindly-starred that nothing marred them; and you will know how bitter and shameful it is to tempt providence a second time and find even the first unique experience soiled.

There was a man once, I won't tell you who he was; I met him quite by accident, and we had the better part of one afternoon together, and I told him about everything I wanted to do, and he was interested and interesting, and we were terribly happy. Nothing very striking happened, nothing very exciting was said; there was no question of love as we know it; he was fifty and I was seventeen, and we could never have loved each other. And yet the thing was perfect. It still is perfect, because he died a month later, and we never saw each other a second time. I could never be sorry he died. It was hard not to be glad. That's one thing nobody can touch.

So I'm afraid, Nick, I'm afraid. There's so much to lose, and yet, who knows, there may be so much to gain. How if I should meet him, and it should turn out to be just a way of passing the evening, like any other date between two uniformed nonentities who don't even know each other's names? And yet I can't bring myself to believe in that; for he isn't a nonentity.

I really think I shall go. If I lose even what I've got, well, so much the worse; but if I lose nothing, and this time the relationship need not stop short even of love?

I've never been in love, Nick Crane. I know that now. John Randall never mattered in the slightest, nice though he is, fond though I was of him in a facile way; he was just one of my pleasanter habits, an agreeable companion, an accomplished dancing-partner. Every woman wants more than that; she's a liar who says otherwise. I for my part have been occupied and happy, enjoying a fairly full life and my share of fun. I haven't wasted time grizzling over the thing I hadn't got, being very much intrigued with all the things I had. But if I once see it, I tell you frankly, nothing shall stop me from getting it, nothing in the world. Smaller models in the same line are no use to me; I'm not hard up for interests, I don't have to put up with any second-bests. As far as love goes I want the real thing or none.

It is suddenly quite easy to say all these things one

usually scarcely thinks. Because time is so short, and we can't afford to waste it. Because any night a stray bomb may light on this corner of Sefton Park, and put an end to Saxon's powers of self-expression once for all; and there may be raw edges left which a few words in time might have smoothed. Life uncertain of its survival becomes singularly simple, instead of terrifyingly complex.

All of this you know very well, and a great deal more which still eludes me. But at least it may be some satisfaction to you to know that I've gained a little wisdom out of this titanic cosmic foolishness.

It's very quiet here in my cabin. Mine for the moment because for once I happen to be early to bed, and no one else has yet come in. After growing used to things one may even begin to like them; and I sit here in my top bunk, and write you letters, and am by no means unhappy. After the war we shall need very little, surely, to keep us content. We shall be the new ascetics who have forgotten how to covet. And some of us, perhaps, a new lost generation, developed before our time and spent before our prime; who have forgotten how to be tranquil, and exhausted our capacity for being troubled. Was that what happened to Lawrence?

I have some more Indian stamps for Billy, about four square inches of them from the envelope which held Geoffrey's Christmas card. Late but large, as always. But I'll save them for his birthday now, and hope to comb up some more to go with them. Tell me more about him when next you write, and send me some of his scribbles. It sounds as if he may be sprouting an imagination rather early for a boy (or rather late for a little boy, it depends how you look at it).

But this letter, of course, is only for you; and if it's sombre, and not as you would have it, neither have I ever been what anyone wanted me to be; and yet you at least have never quite washed your hands of your queer

Catherine Saxon.

W.R.N.S. Quarters, Liverpool.
February 25th, '41.

Dear Nick,

I am having an evening by the fire, before going on night duty. A lonely evening, for Gwyn has gone aboard a corvette with one of her innumerable naval cousins, and Dan is on duty, and half the personnel of the hostel have gone out to an R.A.F. dance round the corner. Our social life here is developing rapidly; our parties acquire a reputation. And the oddest difference obtains between quarters here and in Devonport; there they could persuade men over the threshold of a friendly-disposed Wrennery only with the greatest difficulty; here the crews of ships, and the R.A.F. from local balloon barrage centres, and any units of the army who happen to be around, compete merrily for our invitations. I don't know quite what the cause of this change of heart may be; maybe it's just the difference in temperament between north and south.

Well, I am glad to settle down and get on with all the jobs I've neglected for the past week. I have washed three or four pairs of stockings and a few other odds and ends, ironed three shirts, and written two letters. This is the third, and when it's finished, I shall be, from the correspondence point of view, out of debt.

On consideration, I think a few words deserve to be said in praise of this hostel. Starting from the very considerable handicap of ground-floor cabins holding anything up to twenty people, and communal dressing-rooms which allow no privacy and little space for one's own personal possessions, we have yet achieved here an atmosphere more nearly approaching harmony than I ever expected to find in a community of women. I think no one here can honestly profess to be unhappy; and our erection of content, a house within a house, grows steadily bigger and stronger. It is a process parallel to the expected one of 'settling down', but quite separate. Few of us, I suppose, think about it at all, but all of us feel the effect of it as an easing of tension. There are still cliques, of course; there will always be cliques; but here they circulate freely in an atmosphere of tolerance (or as near tolerance as you will get with women) which acts as oil between the wheels of our highly specialised machinery, and prevents the friction and heat we knew in our novitiate. It is all very satisfactory to the contemplative people, among whom I belong at the moment.

So much for our home life. It doesn't seem too much of a parody to call it that now.

All things but the worst, I find, improve on acquaintance. Even Liverpool looks less unmitigatedly villainous now than it did at first sight. In appearance it's still mean, hideous and sordid, but there are ways of enjoying it. You get to know the right shops (especially book-and music-) and the right cafés; you have a long list of cinemas to choose from, and a very good theatre; you can go and look at a copy of the painted limestone bust of Nefertiti in the Museum, or wander up and down to your heart's content in the Shipping Gallery; or you can visit the wartime art shows in Bluecoat Chambers, where there are some blonde domestic paintings of lions and cows (in separate canvases, of course) oddly attractive, by a man named Huggins. Don't ask me who he is or was; I never heard of him, either, but you should see his lions. Or you can get a good deal of pleasure on the Pierhead, watching the shipping on the Mersey; and there are always the horses of the mounted police – almost the most beautiful things in Liverpool – to brighten up the streets; and almost always flowers in Sefton Park.

Just now it's snowdrops, and here and there in sheltered places the first early crocuses. They're coming up in great clouds of gold and purple and white in the grottoes under the park trees; hastened, no doubt, by the period of warm rain which followed the thaw. When it does rain here it really rains; and if it brings on early flowers it does a lot of other things besides. Especially in a case like that of our offices – growing rapidly, but still no more than half-finished. There was one particular night – I still laugh when I think of it.

We were on the late watch, finishing at one a.m. Our dormitory has now migrated to its permanent quarters, and happens to be immediately over certain important offices. And that night it rained in upon one of the end beds and made a wet pulp of the mattress. When we have a proper roof over us I suppose all these little inconveniences will be overcome. But when we got to bed that night, stumbling about the cold room in the dark, and finally settling down in our blankets to make the best of a short night's sleep, there was the maddening drip, drip, drip of water on that invisible pillow, as regular as a

pendulum, and as loud as a grandfather clock. A noise
more like flop by that time than drip, the pillow being
sodden.

We stood it for as long as we could, and then Jean,
who was in the nearest bed, sat up suddenly, said 'Oh,
hell!' and leaned over and gave the thing a shove which
sent it on to the floor with a horrible wet plump. It was
out of range of the drip, anyhow; the rain came down
comparatively silently on to the iron mesh of the bed-
stead and the wood floor; and the dormitory settled
down with a concerted sigh to get some sleep.

No such luck. It seemed the drip was becoming a
public menace; having maddened us, it sneaked
onward through the floor to puzzle the Royal Navy in
the offices below. About half an hour later we were
awakened by the sound of agitated voices in the room;
masculine voices conferring violently about something,
one in a frantic whisper, the other cheerfully aloud. A
torch beam came wobbling along between the beds,
and the gist of the conversation emerged and made
sense. The whisperer was an R.N. two-and-a-halfer in
the last stages of embarrassment, the second party was
a workman, a single-minded creature oblivious alike of
the beds and their occupants and his companion's
reluctance; and the dialogue went something like this:

'It's right along here, sir, up this end. You come and
have a look at it for yourself, sir.'

'But damn it, man, we can't do anything about it
now. These girls are trying to sleep.'

'You won't get rid of the trouble, sir, until that
joint's shifted. It wouldn't be a big job. I could do it in
half an hour——'

'But you *can't* do it *now*, man——'

'Right up here in this corner. Here you are. Shine your torch this way a bit.'

'I tell you it's impossible. We can't do anything at this hour.'

'There you are. That's what's causing the trouble. Here, you can't see it properly by that light. Half a mo!'

And the workman crashed back cheerfully to the doorway, and slammed on the lights, and came back to display his rare specimen of Lancashire plumbing in the full glare of ten one-hundred-watt bulbs. By that time every soul in the room was not only wide-awake, but acutely interested and highly amused. Why not? It was damned funny. But the officer didn't see it. He was crimson; I don't think I ever saw anyone so literally crimson. The workman didn't see it, either. He had a one-track mind. He delivered a brief and loving lecture on the spot-lit pipe, and concluded happily:

'Of course, I can't do anything about it till morning. Haven't got the proper tools here.'

So they retired at last. That processional between the beds in the full glory of all our lights was the funniest thing of all; I doubt if that unfortunate two-and-a-halfer will ever do anything quite so brave again. We were all, I trust, sufficiently diplomatic to pretend to be asleep, but it was more than obvious that only the blind, the deaf and the dead drunk could have slept through that upheaval. Moreover, human nature couldn't altogether sustain even the pretence. The poor man walked a gauntlet of suppressed laughter, and I hand it to him that he didn't even hurry.

When the lights were off, the door closed, and the blithe footsteps of the impervious charge hand growing faint in the distance – naval officers make no sound in walking, by the way – the weaker spirits let it rip. I doubt if the victim was out of earshot, actually, but at least he was meant to be. And how we laughed!

The time will come (I hope) when it may rain and rain on our roof and we shall know nothing about it; but up to now that's the sort of thing that happens to us in bad weather. Still, that phase is over, and it hasn't frozen again so far, thanks be, so with luck we should keep our flowers, and they should be plentiful.

They say there are two seasons one must see in Sefton Park, daffodil-time and rhododendron-time. I've tried hard to find some colour film for my camera, but it seems to have disappeared from the market, in common with a great many other agreeable things; so I've given up the idea of taking photographs, for black and white couldn't do the place justice even now, and this is only the beginning.

I'm getting drowsy, Nick. The effect of the fire, I think. I wish you were here. I'm in the mood to talk to you now, the right hour, the right sort of fire, all one red glow, the right get-up – slacks and a sweater, our usual undress uniform – and the right fund of talk; not too garrulous, not too dumb, not too intimate, not too restrained. What should I say to you, I wonder, if you were here with me now?

I should say: 'Well, Nick, I went. I kept my appointment. And he came (I should say) and we spent our evening together, and there's no wreckage. Nothing is ruined. He didn't make love to me, he didn't take me for granted, he didn't treat me like a housemaid keeping company or a débutante slumming. He talked neither too much nor too little of himself, he was not shy nor bumptious. He was not anything that did not become him very well, nor anything I could have wished him not to be. I am quite happy, I should say, and I am going to see him again. And you would perhaps nod gravely and drag at your pipe, and say nothing at all.

I suppose I have never been satisfied with anything in this life except with those brief outbursts of singular happiness rounded and ended in one day, like that one contact of which I told you. Things too sudden and swiftly gone to be marred. Everything else has always suffered to some degree from the normal finger-marking of daily use. But it seems to me that this affair is steering its own course, and is afraid of nothing on earth. Something that never was idealised, and therefore cannot be defaced; something that never was seen from the beautifying distances, and therefore has no reason to fear close-ups. Something not enchanted, which can never behave itself gingerly for fear of disenchantment. Or am I on the wrong track? Perhaps the only circumstance which separates it from other intimate meetings is the fact that it has come to flower under the shadow of death, where mutual understanding is too urgent a necessity to permit of the usual qualms and pretences and conventions, the wearing of veils, and dramatising of ourselves and each other. At any rate, the strange conviction of intense reality is there, and it's rock under our feet. And I know he feels it, too.

I should tell you, I suppose, where we met, where we went, what we did; and you would listen gravely but not uncritically, and continue to look almost as wise as I know you are. There's not much to tell, of course. No tors here to climb together; no trawler hulls to sit on in the oily beaches here, only a sewer or two breaking out among the stones. We met by the number fifteen tram-stop, we went into town and saw quite a decent cast in a not very good play, and had a drink or so in the intervals and some supper at a nondescript sort of club afterwards. And then we walked back together from the same old tram-stop through the park, not by the quickest route because it was a fine night, and still early. It was a friends' night rather than a lovers', with a sky-full of stars jumping out of their sockets with cold, and all the roads turned to steel and glass, and the evergreens tinkling like old-fashioned chandeliers in a draught; and that depth and height and darkness of sky between the stars, as there is at Wastwood on such nights, too high and too deep for imagination. I used to spend hours staring out of my window at just such a night sky, not thinking at all, just watching it, much as children enjoy stroking velvet.

We walked home, and I told him my name, and he told me his. It seemed a good thing to do, useful but not vital, if you see what I mean. He's called Tom Lyddon. I don't know much more than that about him; just a few odds and ends I've picked up from casual remarks and mannerisms. He's a Londoner, I should think in his late thirties, but with a man like that how can one be sure? He was in Spain for eighteen months, entirely of his own will, by which I mean that no considerations of boredom and excitement and mere caprice entered into his going there, and only the consummation of the tragedy drove him out again. How he lives between wars I don't know, but I'm quite sure he has no money, and almost sure he doesn't write, or paint, or do anything in the artistic line. He joined up as soon as war broke out here, and has never been noticed or advanced in any way since, which doesn't seem to surprise him in the least. I asked him why he didn't try to make himself heard with the theories and lessons of the Spanish war, and he said because better men than he, and with better authority, were already crying in the wilderness, and would continue to cry until someone did pay attention. Tom Wintringham, he said, would take care of that angle without any help from Tom Lyddon. And the next best thing, and perhaps the best of all, was a personal hand in the fight. Even if it was run by men half-asleep, I asked; and he said all his life he'd been forced to live in a world not run as he wanted it run, and he'd got over the stage of wishing to wash his hands of its affairs on that account. Which is something I have been waiting for someone to say, though I didn't realise it until that moment.

That's it. That's what makes us tick. We can't just chuck the whole thing overboard because it isn't all it should be. Nothing is, as yet. The old argument between amelioration and destruction doesn't enter into it. The fellow who wants to patch the structure differs only in the quality of his strategy from the other fellow who wants to shatter it and rebuild it nearer to the heart's desire. Who am I to say one of 'em's right and the other one wrong? It's enough for me to pick my own way ahead by the light of my own ideas; and if the lighting effect makes me think 'Patch' to-day and 'Scrap' to-morrow, am I going to stop and try to reconcile the two? I think, I hope, that I continue to grow in wisdom, and my ideas may shed more light as I go on. The great thing is that one should not, out of pique or plain despair, sit down among the wreckage and jerry-building of the twentieth century, and put out the light and sleep.

All this, you see, out of a few words of his, and he the least sententious of men. The touch of him makes clear to me, within my mind, things I cannot make clear to you, or only in spite of the tricks I use, not because of them. Does he confess to any caring for the world? No. Nor deny it either. Does he preach to me any sort of formulated code of national or international behaviour, any faction, any faith? No. He is concerned only with his own path, and it is not a matter for discussion, only for action. I suppose the most complete individualist I ever met.

What else did we talk about as we walked back through the park, besides the conduct of the war and the shortcomings of the high command? Nothing very remarkable. About the play, a little and about the thousand and one differences between Plymouth and Liverpool. To tell the truth, we didn't talk nearly so much as you might expect. There was no need; there was no gulf between us to be bridged.

This has been a rambling, convolvulus sort of letter, if you like. From plumbing to progress, from dormitory to doctrine. But if you had really been here it would have been different. I write half a letter to bring you here, and then we can sit back and talk, and you get something of the truth of what goes on in my mind.

I must stop writing. It's high time I got ready for duty. Scarcely time left to ask for news of you, and you tell me so little. Why should we both talk so much about me? Isn't one of us enough to harp in this fashion on the affairs and experiences of

Your Catherine?

VI. EMBARKATION LEAVE

W.R.N.S. Quarters, Liverpool,
March 8th, 1941.

Dear Nick,

I am engaged to be married. If that's a shock, I'm sorry, but somehow I don't think it will be a shock. Very little, I fancy, goes on in my mind, even at this distance, without your knowledge. Sometimes you know my heart before I know it myself. And in talking to you about Tom Lyddon I have not tried to hide anything or to preserve any formality.

Yes, I'm going to marry him. Am I sure it's right this time? Yes, very sure. I'd known John Randall for nine years before I became engaged to him; I've known Tom Lyddon just over a month, but still I'm quite sure. The John affair was all wrong. The Tom affair is in a different world, Nick; there's no mistake this time.

Yet it might not have happened so soon but for the war. The war disposes all things, even our loves and marriages and antipathies. You see, Nick, he's leaving soon – I can't tell you when, but terribly soon – on foreign service. If there were time I'd marry him now, but there's no time. To-morrow he begins a short leave, and after that I shan't see him again until the war's over.

Everything is grown so ridiculously simple now. If you are in love with a woman you just walk into her house as he did into this hostel this morning, sit down beside her, and say: 'I have so many days' embarkation leave. There's no time left for all the usual approaches. I love you, and I want you to know it. How do you feel about it?' And she, if she is bewitched as I am, will say: 'I love you, too. What are we to do about it?'

I was sitting at the piano when he came in, playing, if I remember rightly, an epic called: 'You Don't Have to Tell Me, I Know.' There were three other people in the room; Jean was asleep in a chair by the fire, and two other girls were playing a pretty hot game of ping-pong all the while we talked; but the room is very big, and solitude can sit in one corner of it while the world walks in and out at the door opposite. I was not a romantic figure. I had on my usual brown corduroy slacks and a shirt as grubby as night-duty could make it, with the collar off and the sleeves rolled up; and all I was doing at the moment was killing time until the bath-water should be hot. When he came in I just looked up long enough to say: 'Hullo, Tom!' and went on strumming.

He sat down on the arm of a chair just behind me, and flipped his cap over my shoulder into the litter of music on the piano; and he said what I have told you, directly, as he does everything. And I, with the last chords of that silly song trailing away diminuendo under my fingers, answered him in the same tone: 'I love you, too. What are we to do about it?'

I would have married him to-day if he had wanted me to. I would have followed him out of the house then and there in my slacks if he had beckoned me; but he only took the onyx seal ring off his little finger, and put it on my marriage finger, and said: 'This, Mrs Lyddon!'

Those were the circumstances of my marriage, Nick

Crane. No church, no registry office, even, no orange blossoms, no white satin, no bridesmaids, no kiss for the bride. No music but the thump of my left elbow in the low notes, and Mona Levin shrieking triumph over a dirty return. No witnesses, no blessing. But I'm as securely married to Tom Lyddon as if we'd done the deed in the cathedral before our thousands. Afterwards, when all this is over and done with, we intend to get married 'properly'. The word is selected for the benefit of the outside world; I think we are very properly one person already. But that other marriage, strangely enough, must be in a church. No civil contract for us.

There was nowhere we could be in complete privacy. Outside it was raining, so the garden was hopeless. We went and sat on the rug in front of the fire, and talked about what we should do, and Jean, but from tiredness, not tact, went on sleeping.

Time is so short. We have only a few days together, and so much to say to each other, and so much to do. I don't want him to go, of course, or more truthfully I would prefer to go with him. And yet I'm glad that he's going, too, because he is glad. No more digging sewers. No more rusting in disuse, which seems to me the most ghastly thing that can happen to a man who goes white-hot to war. This time it will be action. I don't know, he doesn't know himself, where he's going, though I believe he has a shrewd idea of his own about that; but it will be a step nearer to battle, surely, and that is the greatest gain.

I told him I would try and get a few days' leave, and this afternoon I've been busy about it. It seems we aren't allowed to have less than seven days at a time, on

139

account of victualling difficulties; but I am practically
due for my next leave, and Owen is quite capable of
taking over from me, so I am taking a week, and after
Tom is gone I shall come home to Wastwood and spend
the last three days with you. What we are going to do
with the first four I don't know yet. Tom is going to call
me up at eight, and then we shall make our plans. It's a
quarter to eight now. I sit here listening for the telephone to ring, and everyone wonders, I think, why I am
so distrait and write only in snatches, for usually I find
no difficulty in concentrating even with pandemonium
– our constant condition – going on round me. No one
has yet noticed that since this morning I've acquired a
seal ring.

Oh, Nick, what can I tell you about the whole trans-
formation of my life? What is there to say that can
possibly make plain the thing that has happened to me?
Not in the exchange of a few words this morning, for
that was merely the lifting of a curtain from a thing
already in being. What is it like, this sudden instinctive
loving past the age of instinct? For I'm too old and
experienced to let myself fall into anyone's arms for
intuition's sake. I don't believe in love at first sight, I
hold no highflown theories about lovers star-destined
for each other. All I know is that the thing has happened, and is quite beyond appeal. A grand finality
about it, and there's satisfaction in finality. No difficulties of adjustment afterwards can hamper our rela-
tions with each other; ours is no winged haggard of love
such as the one Gwyn and Johnny share. Johnny soars
among the stars, spot-lit, singular, temporary, titanic,
a vulnerable victim for every arrow of circumstance;
Tom is one of a gang digging sewers. No one has heard

of him except me; moreover, his life has a continuity too tough to be dislocated by the mere ending of one phase of the fighting. Spain being finished, this other warfare remains; and this being over, there will be other battlefields crying out for him, as long as the world remains imperfect; which will more than outlast our time. A pretty precarious sort of married life, you may think; but I'm not so sure that I want security. If he takes me into a sort of twentieth-century sturdy-beggary, the new vagabondage, well, I always had leanings that way. I'm past the stage of caring what people think of me or anything of mine. The contentment of my heart with its own preoccupations is all I care about, and whatever he does and causes me to do will be satisfying. You see I have no doubts, no doubts at all. The atmosphere between us is too crystal-clear for doubts to live in it, and too realistic for illusions. Our feet have never left the ground, and never will.

And if this sounds to many an unexciting love, it won't sound so to you. Glamour is only a synthetic covering over something too mean to be seen naked. We don't need or value it. I've always preferred to look at my happiness undecorated, and I look at this so, and it doesn't disappoint me. But always it amazes me. I am learning by being in love, and that's a thing not all lovers can say. His range is so much greater than mine that it will take me a life-time to explore him properly; so curiosity alone will keep me a happy wife for as long as I shall need the guarantee. And over and above and beyond all that, I know my own mind, and it's fixed on him as it never was before on anything in this world.

If he has no rival suggestions, I want to take him away for these four days to a place where no one we know will bother us, where we could live in sin if we wanted to – though at the moment I think that would be a distraction from loving rather than an enhancement of it – and be mad or sane and merry or sad just as and when we like without conforming to anyone else's moods. A certain pub I know of, on a certain by-way I know of in North Wales; even to you I won't give it away, except to tell you that its name is The Little House, and it's a short walk from the lonely sea, and the woods, and all the things one wants with one's love. At this time of year there'll be no one there but us. I'm not afraid of boring him or being bored.

So far I haven't written the news to mother, or anyone else. I haven't had time, but in any case I'm not sure that I want people to know yet. Let's have a pause for the children's hour, and then, when he's safely out of reach, we'll let the rest of the interested in. So not a word, Nick, until I say go.

The telephone! So happy. Goodbye.

Catherine.

The Little House, North Wales.
March 11th, 1941.

Dear Nick,

It's raining here, the first rain we've had since we came, a green twilight rain softer than down and dimmer than cigarette smoke. It's cold, too, for we stand fairly high, and though the frosts are all over and done the air has a bite about it at night; but with a war on one can hardly expect fires in bedrooms, so I have to be content with a very small electric fire, the plug-in kind you can carry about with you. It makes a little compact glow in one corner, not enough to make me draw the curtains, though it's past black-out time. I am supposed to be changing my frock; instead I sit here in the dark by the open window, beginning a letter to you, a queer letter because it's already too dark for me to read what I've written, and so I cannot change any of it even if I wished.

It is still, here in the room, and the hush has no tension about it, as some silences have, but is quite tranquil and complete. Outside the window the air is greenish and faintly misty with the rain, and seems to tremble between me and the trees with the almost imperceptible motion of quiet water. There is no wind at all. Time seems to be standing still. I am very happy, Nick, I am so happy.

You cannot write to me. I made sure that no one from home could write to me. And yet I feel very near to you now. You and I have shared by sympathy so much of our lives that nothing can quite be kept apart now. Why, having cut myself off so deliberately from all my family and friends for these few days, do I write to tell you all about it? Unless because we have become so inextricably mixed that my pleasure is incomplete until it becomes your pleasure. And in that case, what happens to my marriage? Are you going to be an invisible third party in it? I've never contemplated polyandry, even of a spiritual kind. But perhaps I can afford to leave these worries for Tom, to whom they properly belong, and who will certainly never lose any sleep over them.

I sit here, and watch my reflection watching me darkly in the mirror of my dressing-table; and the face I

143

see is strange to me; and I think if you could sit here and watch it with me you would find it a little strange, too. I have watched myself change in these few days with him. That woman is mysterious and handsome in the twilight. She has dark hair and darker eyes, Byzantine eyes fixed and wide and assured; and her smile is a triumphant smile, sumptuous and serene at once, as if she has her hands upon everything in life she wants or needs. I think she has. She wants peace, perhaps more peace than she has, but I think she has the heart of it. She doesn't want or need safety. What is safety, any-how? One might go to earth through this war, survive it by infinite care and anxiety, and die slowly of cancer at the age of seventy-odd. No man can find two graves, nor fail to find one. There comes that Russian proverb again.

Tom is downstairs, playing darts with the landlord in the parlour; and I am taking my usual hour and a quarter to change into my pet house-coat for the evening. In the evening we don't go out; there's nowhere to go, and in any case no need to go. Here we are private and comfortable and lazy together over a fire, and want nothing more in the way of entertainment. During the day we walk, and row, and take out the landlord's spaniel pups, and come inside only for meals. In the evening we play the gramophone, and according as our mood is gregarious or solitary, we play darts in the bar, dominoes in the saloon bar, or shut ourselves into our own small sitting-room and talk the fire out. The war could not reach us here if we wished to keep it out; but we don't; it is an integral part of this thing which has happened to us. We brought it here with us; it was almost all the luggage we had.

To-morrow we go back to town, but not until to-morrow night, I am determined, for the journey shouldn't take more than a couple of hours, even allowing for possible hold-ups on the line. It took exactly an hour to get here, but that was by bus, and there's no bus back later than midday. And since we left there have been one or two rather lively nights over Merseyside. Not heavy, but ominous. Who knows what may not happen to-night?

But I know, as surely as one can really know anything in this world, what will happen here. It's our last night together. When we meet again – it may be before he leaves this country, or it may be after many months, even years – we shall manage to erect, I hope, a pretty good sort of happiness, but it won't be quite as these few days have been. This is something we shall never have again. Sometimes I think very few people have it at all, even for one perceptive moment, and we've had it for four days. A pause in the business of living, a bubble of a world caught in a fissure of time, peopled by only the two of us, though others look in at us from time to time without entering. Not an involuntary world, and therefore not an illusion; self-created and deliberate, a thing we made between us, a pause to draw breath for whatever follows. Those who love in these days are in need of all the endurance they can muster, even if they have walked into both love and war with their eyes wide open, as we have.

Afterwards other people will come into our joint life, mother, Gwyn and Johnny, all the people at home, his people if he has any; and you; but not in that order, for you'll be there first as usual. And you'll all be welcome, as you very well know. But we are here in our island, timeless and apart, building a very secret place into which you will never come, and we never again.

It's a strange place, Nick, as strange as secret, made up of little, insubstantial, dream-like things; and yet I think it will last out my lifetime. Afterwards, while he is overseas and I am back in the teleprinter room at A.C.H.Q., we shall both be able to draw on our memories of these few days. We shall remember how we came here in a flurry of sun and wind, greeted by an elastic golden riot of Cocker spaniels and a smell of baking apples; and how we wandered along the shore under the cliffs, in a half-gale, with the spray scalding our faces and the lip of the tide lunging at our feet; and how we took out a sailing boat, on our second day, to a rocky island of birds, and lived among the gulls all day long, and came home perilously at night through the boiling phosphorescent sea; and how we lay on the rug in front of our fire to dry our hair, and fell asleep there together, and two of the puppies crawled into the warm hollow between us and slept too; and how the smell of the pines came home in our clothes from the woods, and haunted us all night long. And I think we shall remember most often of all our last night together, and these things I am taking into my mind now; the dim rain green in the dusk, the trees grown shadowy and remote behind the veil of it, all the world withdrawn for awe of us, standing at distance and looking inward where we are. We shall remember the sweetness of the wet, soft air touching our faces through the open window and the slow deepening of the twilight over our woods, and the rare quiet. And I shall remember his face as it looks to me in this half-light, dark-featured and illusionless and weather-beaten, gaunt with shadows; and I trust that he will remember mine. On these memories we shall have to stand until the earth grows firm again, and we come together at last.

You see we have a long way to go and a long while to live in separation. Good reason why we should build ourselves a sanctuary while there's still time, and furnish it with all the graces and beauties left to the world.

The lights are on now, and the curtains drawn, and I am dressed. That woman of Tom's is not a bad-looking woman, at any rate not to-night. Her housecoat – it looks like a very sumptuous dinner-dress, and sometimes it does duty as one – is cherry-coloured velvet, and her slippers are red and black satin with very high wedge heels, one of her last extravagances, and to tell the truth brand-new for this interlude. Her hair is combed out into a dark brown cloud, and falls just to her shoulders, and her face is cunningly made up with iris-shadowed eyes and cerise mouth, but the glow is not in the painting, and she didn't have to put belladonna or anything else into her eyes to get that brilliance and lustre. Her arms are thin and fair, and she has a high-shouldered walk like a self-conscious child's. I wonder if he'll notice how handsome she is? Probably not, but she'll feel handsome, and that's the main thing.

I didn't know it would be like this, Nick. I knew it would be splendid, but there's no way of guessing how splendid until you have it in your hands; and this is beyond what I thought, more lovely, more terrible. There's no escape from it, and no appeal against it. From this haven I look back at my service life, and find it unspeakably horrible, though to-morrow I know I shall go back to Liverpool without a qualm. Oh, let the war end soon. Let me get back to myself, let me be a person again instead of an official number. A good Wren must wear her skirt not more than fifteen inches from the ground, and her hair well off her collar. Tom's woman has a cherry-red skirt that sweeps the floor, and her hair falls down over her shoulders, and she salutes no one and calls no one 'Ma'am'. There are times when one grows deathly sick of it all, when the nostalgia for peace and home comes over one in a great drowning wave; and this is a thing not to be confused with the mere human homesickness of the first few weeks, which by comparison is only a very small discomfort. All the same, if I could get out of it now I wouldn't; not until the job's finished. There'd be precious little happiness for either of us if we turned our backs on the world just to look at our own love. So we make a virtue, if you like, of necessity; and he is for overseas; and I am for the noise and heat of the teleprinter room at A.C.H.Q. until peace or death do us part. The more reason why we should hold this island inviolate, for a place of withdrawal when we feel the need of solitude, and a hiding-place when our anger fails us and the backward-looking sickness takes hold of our hearts.

I must go down. I've outstayed my time. Lovely just to sit here and listen to the whispering of the rain; but lovelier still to go down to our little sitting-room and put out the light and open the window nearest the sea, and sit there and listen to that more ominous whispering which will be in all our dreams after to-night. And to-morrow doesn't come, does it? Or if it does, we shall be ready for it. The more ready because we've had to-day.

In a few days I shall see you. He will be out of town by then; I cannot go with him, and I shall not even know the day when he sails; but other women have been through the same thing, and many of them have had not even one perfect day before the parting, while I have had four quite perfect ones, unspotted from the world.

Goodnight, dear Nick, and until I see you be easy in mind about the happiness of

Your Catherine.

W.R.N.S. Quarters, Liverpool.
March 17th, 1941.

Dear Nick,

So after all I couldn't come. You can't, believe me, have been building on that visit as I was, yet your letter has a tone of disappointment, for which earnest of your patient goodwill towards me I'm duly grateful. If you really wanted so much to see me, then I'm even sorrier than I was already on my own account. Needless to say, it wasn't my fault. Appendicitis waits on no man's pleasure. Poor Owen is in hospital, a part of her internal economy is in a glass jar, and I am back in charge of my watch. No alternative. There's no one else I could expect to take over, especially with the watch already two short. So back I went, the day I should have come to you, back to the heat and noise of the teleprinter room, to swear at the machines instead of confiding in you. Ah, well! Bigger plans than mine have gone agley in this world, and will again.

No use letting my mind wander back to Wastwood

now; as it will if I give it half a chance. I wanted – next to the wanting I had to go with him – to come and sit by your fire in the evenings, with the wind shoving at the windows and threshing the trees; and perhaps to tell you, as I've always told you, everything I had in my mind. Well, that's over.

He's gone, Nick. Out of Merseyside, I know. Out of England, I feel, but take it from me love isn't psychic, and I had no moment of knowledge, and no inner voice whispered to me when his ship sailed, if sailed it has. But there was a sort of haste about it all. Yes, I think he must have gone.

So that's that. It didn't seem so difficult to part on those terms as I'd been led to believe it would be. Perhaps the stress of outward events divides the integrity of love, and holds back the half of our emotions and thoughts fast tied to the war, and immune from any lesser pains and preoccupations. But in the end I don't think that can sufficiently explain the calm I feel. I think we go our separate ways tranquilly because we know where we're going, and why. I mean spiritually. Where he or I will be in the flesh a year from now is more than I can guess.

All is anti-climax here, after that stormy leave-taking. But I haven't yet told you about that.

We started back from our Welsh interlude at eight in the evening; by no means a wise hour, but that was my fault. I was reluctant to hurry the moment, as who wouldn't be? I think the raid began while we were still some little way out of town, though neither of us heard the siren. The first we knew of it was when they stopped the train and put out the lights, and for maybe twenty minutes we had front seats at as fine a firework show as you could wish to see. Or – let's be truthful – as you could wish to avoid seeing. Barrage, chiefly, and at that distance we could hardly judge where the actual firing-centre was; the south side of the river, we thought, probably towards Wallasey. The 'planes – we could hear that faint, persistent humming which meant there were several – held their peace for the most part, only that cruising noise always recurring as they circled. The searchlights interlaced like a sort of formalised aurora pulsing upward instead of down; but they couldn't find their target, or if found momentarily couldn't hold it. After a while the 'planes seemed to sheer off, and the noise died down, and the train went on again. By then I knew I should be late getting in, but I wasn't worried. Raids can and do bend every quarters regulation in existence.

It was after ten when we drew into Central, and dashed across the street to board a late tram. It was horribly crowded – at that hour they all are – but we got on board safely, and we began to think we were going to make pretty good time, after all. But halfway out of town the ominous hum, more concentrated this time, began again, came practically overhead, and hell broke loose.

I don't know how many 'planes there were, but it must have been a considerable number. The darkness, which was intense, began to blossom with violent rose-coloured explosions of light, and the usual bewildering miscellany of noises blazed out all round us, but particularly ahead. The terrible thing has visual beauty, there's no denying it; but its voice is plain hell. Like children and dogs I have an almost superstitious hate of shattering noises, and this was the loudest, if not the most dangerous, raid I've encountered up to now. I was glad when the tram thought fit to give up the struggle and decant us into a surface shelter in a side-street. But that was worse when it came to the point; all the noise and none of the beauty came over to us inside, combined with the native smell of surface shelters, damp and cold and musty, and a ghastly feeling of being nailed down in a coffin alive. Most of us, I think, have at least a touch of claustrophobia. I used to dream of crawling along a diminishing passage, on hands and knees at first, then flat on my front. That was in the problem days of my adolescence. This felt like the consummation of the dream.

I suppose we were there about a quarter of an hour, cramped into a corner by the doorway, trying to keep track of the raid by the noises. It's odd how one begins to pick out gun from gun; there's one somewhere near, not a great noise, only a sort of squeaking grunt, like a pig disturbed in its sleep. It was going constantly that night, like a punctuation mark separating the big stuff into suitable periods. I found myself listening for it each time; it was something to do; at least it gave me a sort of illusion of being occupied.

Strangely enough, for I'm not by any means the raw material of which heroines are made, I've never been frightened of raids. I take it to be a sort of temporary blind spot in the brain, a preoccupation with the excitement to the exclusion of more practical considerations. Anyhow it's quite general, whatever the origins of it. The chief reaction is a sort of mental stimulation rising crescendo with the noise; noise being the chief clue to the degree of danger, at least as far as the civilian population is concerned. That night I deeply disliked the surface shelter, but I still wasn't scared to any sensible degree; and when there came a lull in the row outside I jumped at the chance to get back into the fresh air. Tom had a look out from the door, and reported all quiet, and the Jerry 'planes no longer audible, So we risked it.

We took the quickest route we could find, and reached the near edge of the park without more than an occasional gun-burst at some distance. Then we heard the drone of engines coming nearer again, and the searchlights began their third hunt for the raiders, weaving slowly overhead like careful sweeping strokes of so many paint-brushes on a colossal canvas. It was a lovely night, fairly still, clear, black as pitch; and the pattern of the searchlights was startling and attractive against it, so that we walked with our chins in the air, watching the play and counterplay and scarcely noticing that ominous patient drone which was the enemy's invisible, but pervading, presence. When they finally forced themselves upon our notice, it was by way of a sudden shower of incendiaries. The guns burst into full song again, close to us, a shattering noise. The darkness flowered again in an astonishing profusion of starry fire-bombs, with dazzling petals that expanded before our eyes in a magical, monstrous growth. It was most beautiful, and most horrible. The night became lit from every side, with fire on the ground and fire in the sky, and a sourceless, palpitating glow which was everywhere and nowhere. One or two incendiaries came down at no great distance, and burned ferociously in the short park turf with nothing to feed their fire.

It was folly to saunter onward through that firework

display. We made for the first shelter, and dived into the doorway, and watched the blaze from there.

There was nothing living around those parts except the two of us in our bolthole. The park is like that late at night. We stood there shoulder to shoulder, fitted tightly into the narrow doorway, watching the sky shake and flicker and sprout fire. There began to be a smell of smoke in the air, and soon some of the outlines showed blurred and hazy with heat and smoke against the scarlet skyline. Most of the time it was too big and too noisy for us to make ourselves heard; but there were lulls in which I think we talked quite a lot, in the monosyllabic way we've developed between us. Once we saw a barrage balloon hit and brought down. An incendiary must have struck it full, for it burst suddenly into one wild red blaze from end to end, and came slowly down still burning bravely, and we lost sight of it beyond the trees at the other side of the park.

After a full half-hour of this fiery entertainment, the affair changed somewhat. We heard what we took to be high-explosive bombs between the gunbursts; not very heavy stuff, but a fair amount of it. Considering how long the show went on, I saw very little damage next day; but of course we could hardly come through a night like that untouched, and there are casualty lists outside the Town Hall now, and breaks in the continuity of the buildings here and there along several streets not so far from here. I keep thinking of my First Aid days: 'A wound is a break in the continuity of the tissues of the body.' Well, Liverpool has its wounds to show for that night.

Round about half past eleven Tom said to me, apparently without thinking: 'D'you mind this?'

I said: 'Not specially. No one loves it, but it's the same for everyone.'

He said: 'Is it?'

After that, it was too noisy to talk for a while, so I thought the more. Is it the same for us all? We know bombs are no respecters of persons, and would as soon fall on the Lord Mayor as on the most insignificant docker. But circumstances are not so impartial, when you come to think about it. If you have money you can reduce the odds against you very considerably. You not only can, you do, in this democratic country. I don't know how it went in Spain, but somehow I think that in Spain practically every soul was at war; and therefore too busy to expend intensive effort on preserving his or her own security. How many people in England, I wonder, are really at war now? Sixty per cent? Perhaps, but I doubt it. The rest, I suppose, are engaged in dodging the war, protecting their personal fortunes from the war, or founding new and very dirty fortunes on the chances thrown up by the war. Something is certainly rotten, even in this fundamentally sound and upright state.

When it was quieter again I said: 'What did you mean by that?' And he said: 'I know an influential family who had a beautiful deep shelter made under their house. Really deep – reinforced and double-reinforced. Cost them several thousand. But the people in those little houses along the side-streets haven't got several thousand.'

I said: 'Almost thou persuadest me.' And he smiled, and said: 'I've never said one thing to you that you haven't been thinking for months. You only use me as a mouthpiece.'

In a way he's right, for I've never been altogether easy about the health of our social system, at least since I joined up. No one can be long in Liverpool and remain complacent about such delicate fictions as 'equality of sacrifice'. But we didn't plunge into any long-winded discussions on democracy just then, because a small bomb chose that moment to come down about a hundred yards from us, tear a ragged hole in the turf, shove two young trees over bodily, and spatter our shelter with soil and splinters of root and bark. I'm not sure whether we threw ourselves or were thrown into the furthest corner of the shelter; but that's where I found myself, flat on my face on a far from clean concrete floor, with Tom holding me down. We stayed there until the reverberations died out of our ears, and then picked ourselves up and brushed each other down in the most matter-of-fact way imaginable. Both knees out of my stockings, of course; what else could I expect with rough-finished concrete? Luckily they were the greenish-black cotton official issue, not silk ones, so precious little loss. My hands were filthy; I suppose my face was, too; but I was still in one piece, not so much as a square inch of skin missing. So much for my first bomb.

We went back to the doorway. A large, leafless branch was propped across it, one side of it neatly flayed of its bark. We could see the irregular rim of the crater, the two trees sagging with their boughs against the ground, and the turf trailing in ribbons from their roots. The sky was now a great mottle of reddish light, uneasy like water in a wind; but apart from an occasional burst the batteries had ceased firing, and a sort of exhausted quiet began to settle upon the night. That was the end of it. Another half-hour passed before the all-clear went, but there was nothing more during that time.

So we finished our walk. On the doorstep at quarters we two grubby mortals kissed each other goodbye; and he walked away again to hop a car to his billet; and I rang the bell, and was presently let in by a Petty Officer who appeared to be walking in her sleep. And early next morning he put himself and his kit into a south-bound train and went away on another phase of his wanderings, leaving me behind.

I could hardly believe, afterwards, that one lets it pass like that. Just a kiss, and 'Well, goodbye!' and 'Goodbye! Don't forget to write.' But that was all, Nick. No high drama. Just as if we should see each other in a few weeks, and know each other stolidly safe in the meantime. I can't bring myself to wish that we had that assurance. I don't want to know what's in store for me; only to be equal to it.

When Owen comes back to the watch – it won't be yet – I shall be able to finish my interrupted leave; and then I shall really see you. When I shall see him again, God knows. But supposing – just supposing – that bomb had fallen just eighty or ninety yards nearer? Supposing the concrete roof of our shelter had come down and put an end to us both, while we were together, before we could gamble and lose any part of what was ours? A few people would have been sorry, I suppose, but it would have been so easy for us, and so final. Perhaps too easy to be satisfying; I don't know. I suppose I should resent having all my problems solved for me, even by fate. But it didn't happen. We go the longer way round, and perhaps to a better end.

I wonder if Tom thought of that, too? Probably not. His mind, from long contention with things as they are, is never greatly concerned with things as they might have been. Besides, he is the one who's going, and I'm the one who's left behind. It makes all the difference.

Since that one isolated raid, all has been quiet here, an unreal quietness. The old routine is getting me. My rut is a highly respectable excavation now; I should very much resent it if I were told to move, especially at short notice, which is the usual disturbing practice. I don't think the service believes in ruts.

I shall never go to the Little House again, Nick, not even with him. Those few days make up a thing completed, rounded, polished and set apart, something unique, never to be discovered again, only to be contemplated in retrospect and experienced in dreams. There may be other times as delightful to come, but never a return of this one. Never, at least, unless time starts flowing backwards over the head of

Your Saxon.

VII. SPRING BLITZ IN THE NORTH-WEST

W.R.N.S. Quarters, Liverpool.
March 24th, 1941.

Dear Nick,

What a week! The middle of Plymouth gone, and half our people here waiting on thorns for each successive post, worried about parents or friends left behind in the south-west. And we thought we were coming into a dangerous zone when we came up here. Scarcely a single siren in all this time, not a single bomb until that isolated raid last week; and there a heavy death-roll, and all the centre of the town smashed or burned to ruin. St. Andrew's gone, and the Guildhall, and most of the big shops; and our old quarters, too. Yes, that house of cards came down at last. It shook right from foundations to roof every time the wind blew; and now it's gone. It wasn't a direct hit, and thank God no one was in it when it collapsed; half the street was down in ruins, and it became clear that the place was not safe for very long. The wonder is that it stood through the vibrations of the first night's bombing. The Wrens were evacuated in a hurry, and the old hotel collapsed next day. Most of them lost half their kit and a good part of their personal possessions. I had a letter from one of the girls down there; she says they went back afterwards and grubbed among the ruins for books and photographs they valued; and one or two of them were lucky, but the great majority lost everything they had of home. Her letter

– she's the most ordinary of mortals – talks brightly of clambering over fences with sandbags and buckets of water and stirrup pumps to put out incendiary bombs, and trotting back to cover through a hail of tiles from a roof twenty yards or so away. And we sit here!

There's nothing new about it, of course. It happened to Coventry, and London, and Manchester, and Clydeside, and it happened here, to some extent, a while ago, and may happen here again any moment. But to think of Plymouth, a town I knew so well and love so much, battered and burned in this deadly methodical way, night after night prompt to an efficient timetable of destruction; to say to oneself: 'The Octagon's just a waste of debris, and —— Street is flat, and I shall never see another flick at the old Electric.' That's peculiarly horrible. Especially at this distance, where we can do nothing, but only listen to the dreadful details of deaths and losses and nightly treks to a gypsy sleep on the moors in the cold, and go to our own beds thinking of them as if they were only the things of a curiously vivid dream.

It sounds completely crazy, and I can't begin to account for it, but I take it very hard, Nick, that the stress came while I was not there. I believed I was entering a danger zone, not leaving one, when I came up north; and here we had almost forgotten a war exists, while there they sleep with it every night and get up to the patient contemplation of its ravages every morning.

My friends from the old, ramshackle home from home I left six weeks ago are dispersed now, about half of them in a big house over the water – lucky people, I know that house and park – and the rest are scattered in twos and threes and half-dozens in lodgings throughout the town, and some even as far afield as Yelverton. Not a soul from quarters was even injured. When I remember how the old place shook and plunged and waved in the wind, I can hardly believe it went out so harmlessly at last. But more than one Wren died in the town during those few nights of concentrated frightfulness. And – I almost wrote 'as usual' – nothing seems to have been done about removing the unnecessary part of the population, even after the trouble began. Something could surely have been done for the schoolchildren; in that uncrowded country there must have been room for them every one; but no, they stayed in Plymouth, many of them to their deaths. I've tried to believe that there must have been insurmountable difficulties, concrete reasons why things had to be left as they were; but, Nick, I can't do it. I see only folly and lethargy there, and these are crimes in a war such as our war should be. The thing could have been foreseen. I remember writing to you myself once, some time ago, a letter full of foreboding for Plymouth. I would have moved the children long ago; and after the first night I would have sent away all other people who could go and could be spared. But no one was sent away out of danger. Those who went, went of their own will and ingenuity. And they were very many, Nick. They packed up their bedding in rolls every night, and somehow by car and lorry and bus and every other conceivable form of conveyance made their way up to the edge of the moors, and there camped through those noisy, fiery nights. And in the morning back again to town, to their work which had to be done. This trek became habit in a few nights. Dockers did it, shop girls did it, office-cleaners did it, business men did it. Children did it. In March weather. Oh, Nick, how can we possibly justify that? If we were a hundred per cent interested in winning the war, even if the majority of us were interested in the welfare of humanity, things like this couldn't happen.

I know I warned you, once, to be sceptical of damage and raid stories from Plymouth or any other town. No one could be more unbelieving than I am; but this is not hearsay, or at least it's the most watertight hearsay imaginable. Johnny Fairmile paid us a visit last night, and we got it all out of him. Johnny was in it, and you know how probable it is that he'd talk about his own part in a thing like that; but in his Titan innocence he's by no means unobservant, and in his own jargon – which would make marvellous journalese – he can paint you comprehensive and vivid pictures of the ordeal of Plymouth. He was shocked by it, too, though he doesn't realise it; because, you see, he never thinks of analysing what goes on inside his own head. He arrived in the middle of one of our quarters parties, and the different atmosphere of the place must have made itself felt, for he came in quite cheerfully and danced, even though Gwyn was not there. I showed him over the place, the garden, too, by moonlight and in the hint of a frost; and it was then that he talked. He stared at the stars, and he said, and it was as childish as profound: 'A chap doesn't mind dying so much if he can see something for it. But nobody wants to sit quietly around under a falling bomb when he might just as well be somewhere else. It's too wasteful.'

He told me how the roads looked every evening, out towards the moors. And he told me how much of the town was smashed, and it was far too much. We've reached the stage when we talk as sound friends; I suppose I am a fairly reassuring sort of shelter for a shy young celebrity, and favoured as having already the favour of Gwyn. And he is a lion, and lions need a keeper. Not everyone here realised who he was, or I think his evening might not have been so happy; for Johnny has now reached the headline stage, in fellowship with Bader, and Tuck, and Eric Locke, having twenty-three planes chalked up to him, besides half a dozen or so doubtfuls. This, of course, we don't talk about. Even *they* don't talk about it, unless in some rare moment or two when they are alone together, which happens less often than you might suppose.

But he'll talk about Gwyn. Oh, yes, as often and as long as you like. About how grand she is, how lovely, how original, what a sport. As openly as I might talk of a rose I'd raised with my own hands. And as merrily as a child vaunting its possessions.

We danced, and we walked in the garden, and it struck me suddenly that for him the future didn't exist. All his talk, all his thought, was of now, of to-day, of the coming meeting with her, of the war as it is, not as it will be. And I said the terrible thing. I said: 'You never think of afterwards, do you?' I hadn't meant to say it; I just thought it, and out it came.

Well, he checked, and stood looking at me uncertainly, and he thought about it then. I saw it strike root in his mind, the thought: 'What about afterwards?' That keen, hard, weatherbeaten face of his softened line by line into doubt, and consternation, and terror. I don't believe he saw ahead; but certainly he looked. He tried to see himself emerging from the war, but I think he saw a blank wall. He has no imagination; the most

163

successful pilots haven't; but when he attempted to visualise 'afterwards', and himself taking part in it, and could conjure up no vision at all – then he was filled with the panic of a child in the dark.

He said: 'I suppose we do get into the habit of living from one patrol to another. It's hard to avoid it.' But he was frightened; and so was I, for I'd started something I knew I couldn't stop, no matter how valiantly he pretended and I played up to him. And I was desperately sorry I'd spoken at all, to turn his eyes to the problems still to come.

And yet he'll have to think about it sometime. I suppose the war will end, some day, and he'll be left with a headline reputation, a body and mind out of tune with the normal cadences of living, a spent splendour of achievement worth nothing at all in bread and butter, and a wife to keep. And when I say keep I'm not thinking of money alone. How are they to live together? And yet how are they to live apart?

If you had seen them meet, as I did late that evening, you would understand. We were dancing, and suddenly he stopped, and looked round, and she had just come into the doorway. I am sure he felt her come; I am convinced she knew he was there. They walked straight to each other, and their eyes kindled, and they forgot the rest of us. And yet the least sentimental of people. I doubt if they often so much as touch each other, but the core of passion is there; and what's to happen to that perilous and imperilled white-heat of love in the anticlimax of 'afterwards', I don't know. Maybe she and I are haunted all for nothing, and this winged thing will settle into repose as softly as a bird lighting, and they put on inaction and security with as good a grace as they now wear danger and excitement. Maybe. But I wish one could know. For the first fatalistic uneasiness came from her, and not from me.

Well, more problems than one will be solved, this way or that, when the war is over. We can none of us expect to live through this time of intense change and not be changed. Unexpected things have happened to me. People who loomed large in my life have dwindled, and strangers – but they are not strangers – have come into the foreground. Perhaps Johnny's right, after all, and the only way to live is from one day to the next.

All I can say is, thank God nothing alters your status. You don't recede.

Lights out again, and I hear steps on the stair – coming down to the cabins, not going up, owing to our peculiar way of living. Goodnight in haste. Perhaps a PS. to-morrow.

Catherine.

W.R.N.S. Quarters, Liverpool.
April 6th, 1941.

Dear Nick,

We seem to have crammed half the war into the past ten days. Yugoslavia, bless her, has come to life at last; too late to save much out of the wreckage, probably, but it's cheering to find one more country with the guts to stick the business out on the side of the angels. We have a Wren here who lived in Yugoslavia for several years, and knows the people well; all along she's been quite positive that they would never give in, and those frightful few days while they played around with Hitler in Vienna had her in a high fever. But even then she swore they'd never stand for it, there'd be a revolution first. Happy the land whose sometime guests speak up so stoutly for her integrity. I wonder what they say of England?

Well, she was right. They've delivered their souls, anyhow, whatever happens to their bodies. They have the honour and the ordeal of providing the left wing to the Greek resistance. Heaven help them both! They've got a very different proposition from the Italians to tackle now. But the help of Heaven seems curiously dilatory in arriving sometimes, even if it arrives in the end. I hope Simovitch and Koryzis don't have to wait for years for the whirligig of time to bring in his revenges, as Haile Selassie did.

All things considered, in this sudden spate of news the good has far out-balanced the bad. We've collected several African aces, Harar, Keren, Diredawa, Asmara, Adowa and Adigrat – you see my geography is improving – besides the terrific moral effect of the entry into Addis. We shall be seeing newsreels of the Emperor's return soon, I expect. I can imagine how he will look, that slight, upright man with the superbly patient and dignified face and the suffering eyes; unsmiling in triumph as he was uncomplaining in adversity, betraying nothing whatever of what goes on in his mind. If ever there was a persecuted being who seemed to suggest by his bearing and his face that he had the secret of overcoming circumstances, it's Haile Selassie. It gives me a warm feeling inside to think of him riding back into his capital on the first full circle of the wheel, quietly magnificent. The civilised conquerors shout and vaunt themselves and beat on their chests after the manner of Tarzan straddling the kill. The savage takes up his purple, as he put it aside, silently, and with an unmoved face. Heaven preserve us from civilisation!

I know nothing about the earlier history of the Emperor; but certainly since the Italian outrage he's behaved like a white man, if ever there was one. At the time some people professed to believe he had run for safety in a way they presumed to despise; all I can say is, if that was the best speed he could make, he wouldn't stand an earthly against the average European monarch.

But I suppose the real plum of the news, from any viewpoint, is the action off Cape Matapan. What I like about the Navy is their refreshing freedom from the national vice of half-heartedness. When they do make a promising contact the fight that follows is a one hundred per cent affair. They never let go. Now if only that action had been in the Atlantic, we should have got a running commentary on it; as it was in the Mediterranean, the news came to us just as it came to you, in a B.B.C. news bulletin. Nothing was said about what business the Italian navy had in those waters; but as we'd already been told that our naval forces in the Mediterranean were squiring our convoys between Libya and Egypt and Greece, we came to the conclusion here that the Italian ships were sailing on German orders to intercept an important convoy, probably of troop transports on their way from Alexandria to Piraeus. That was one ambush that reacted on the designer, anyhow. Scarcely a flake of paint knocked off a British ship, and five of theirs total losses, and others damaged. Yes, that's everyone's idea of a major victory.

Do you know, Nick, Matapan gave me furiously to think, even before the official announcement to-day that we had an expeditionary force in Greece. I've had no word from Tom yet, and didn't expect any. But where is he so likely to be at this time as in Greece? Where would they be sending fresh units except either to Greece or Libya, where the present pressure is heaviest? And although I expect they drew most of their force from the troop reserve in Egypt, yet it seems extremely probable to me that a unit on its way to Libya might be deflected north to Greece. He may have been a little bit of the Italian objective, that day of Matapan. I don't know whether I like the idea or not. Who wouldn't want to be fighting side by side with the Greeks now? But who would want to hear of someone she cared about being sent out there? It's going to be that sort of campaign, whatever the end of it may be.

Of course I've nothing to go upon really, and shall probably be no wiser even when I hear from him. But just in case my hunch happens to be a good one, I have begun to read up Greece and the Greek campaign furiously, raiding all the local libraries, and buying up half a dozen Sunday papers to see what they have to say separately and collectively about the terrain. Greece is going to be a life-and-death affair; you can see that by the painstaking lay-out of the Yugoslav approach (except that the Yugoslavs have altered the pattern considerably) and the synchronised heavy offensive in Libya, which is obviously meant to prevent us from sending any further reserves out of Egypt to the help of the Greeks. I suppose, for the sake of Axis prestige, apart from the continuation of the German highway to the east, the defeat of Greece has become an urgent necessity. The Italians bungled the job. I hope to God the Germans fall down on it, too, but in my contemplative moments I remember and admit the inhuman efficiency of Hitler's war-machine, and I'm frightened.

That's my life just now, burrowing among books and newspapers and trying to imagine what's happening to Tom. Because nothing's happening to me. The anticlimax after his going was as flat as stale beer, and defied anything to leaven it very much, even the new daffodils in the park, even your letter. On nightwatches, when the traffic has petered out around three and four in the morning, and half the watch has gone to bed, I sit concocting letters he'll get some day if all goes well. If they don't grow into volume dimensions before he sends me an address. Together, we were rather taciturn for people in love. Separated, I grow prolific. I say nothing happens, but I find plenty of uncensorable material to write to him. I hope and think he'll find himself productive, too.

I can't say the snap you sent of Billy exactly flatters him. He looks like one of the Dead End kids. For Pete's sake don't tell him I said so, or he'll be cultivating the resemblance for all he's worth, and Mrs. Lane's life won't be worth living. I'm beginning to know your adopted son, Nick Crane.

My love to you all. Next time I'll enclose a letter for Billy, a nice, safe letter; also two or three Brazilian stamps, if I can persuade Dan to part. She has a sort of third or fourth cousin out there.

Yours, as ever,
Catherine.

W.R.N.S. Quarters, Liverpool.
April 21st, 1941.

Dear Nick,

I've heard from Tom at last. An undated letter, from on board ship, and of course quite a minus proposition as far as news is concerned. I wish we'd had time to arrange some sort of code before he went, but there was no time to think of anything so practical. It would have been so easy, too, because the possibilities are not so very numerous that we couldn't have covered them adequately with pre-arranged code words and phrases, or references to a book. We played that sort of game quite successfully in our childish days. School was full of secret societies circulating messages in cypher. Ah well, a little childlike enthusiasm would have helped us in a great many directions in this war, but the only sort of enthusiasm we seem to breed is the stone-blind variety responsible for horse-laughs like the song about hanging the washing on the Siegfried Line. Horse-laughs on us, and of the cheapest.

He's very well, he says. Why wouldn't he be? I never knew him to be anything else. He says, what's obvious, that where he's bound for he won't be able to write me the letters he'd like to; and he says that because of this he'll write, and keep, other letters parallel to the ones he sends by post, the kind of letters one can't send through His Majesty's mails at this time. And if ever an opportunity offers of sending them home to me by some other way, he will send them; and if not, he'll keep them until we meet again.

It sounds to me a major undertaking. By the time I see Tom again he may be carrying the equivalent of a three-volume novel around with him. Once abroad, I'm only too certain that he's liable to stay abroad, in one tight corner or another, for the duration. But I know what he means. If he comes back from Greece, or wherever he's going, as monosyllabic as I've found him about Spain, then I shall need those letters. Because there's an insatiable thirst in me to be in all he thinks, and says, and does, and experiences and I know his conversation afterwards will never let me in, but the reactions of the moment, written down on the spot, and with the fine tongue-loosener of distance co-operating, may open the door.

He writes a curiously cool, detached letter, does Tom. As if his mind was a little sceptical even of its own conclusions, as it may well be; for though he gives the impression of knowing exactly where he's going, and intending to keep on going no matter what stands in his way, yet I feel at times a strain of discouragement in him. Suppressed, yes, and too weak ever to be allowed to interfere with his progress; but still a source of sadness, and disillusionment, and weariness. Why not? I think Spain was a fiery inspiration to him, horrible in effect but unslackening in fervour; but Spain was a defeat. And Britain touched that pinnacle only once, after her allies had fallen away like eroded rocks into the sea of ruin and loss; at Dunkirk we believed utterly in ourselves and our cause, we were one sudden iron island of courage and resolution and defiance. But that lasted only as long as the worst stress, and we settled down comfortably to make the best of the war, instead of winning it. Tom has never doubted, never could be made to doubt, that we're worth fighting for, we and our way of life and our small measure of democracy; but I know that emptiness of disappointment that clouds his mind because we are not better worth it. The Chinese patriots fight with more conviction, more singleness of purpose, than we. So do the Greeks. You will know, you more than anyone, what I mean. Even to think of them, even to read of them, is to feel your heart rise and your nerves grow taut with joy, even now that the Army of the Epirus is broken, even now that the defenders are retreating on Thermopylae. Yes, and even if the Germans march into Athens at last, it will still be one of the grandest things in the world to be Greek. Can you, in spite of all our virtues and heroisms, feel that in the same degree about being British? God help us, I can't.

Wouldn't it be fatal to write to anyone but you in this strain? Mother, to whom Churchill is a demi-god, the accepted order inevitably the only millennium, the government a sort of super-human Brains Trust, and any Britisher equal to five or six foreigners, would be shocked beyond words if I suggested there was or could be anything lacking in our national perfection. But you know and I know that we expect more of England, and hope more for her, than the wishful thinkers who sit down contentedly in the middle of things as they are. And that if this war is won in the end, it is we who will have won it.

But although Greece gives me the complete, single, unique thrill of pride I've missed up to now, how can I be anything but terrified about the way things are going there? The Epirus lost, Thermopylae threatened, Koryzis dead, and all that shining, confident glory of achievement against aggression soiled and turned to loss. What can be done to save Greece now? Is there time left for anything more? And did we do all we could even while there was time? I know Egypt is threatened,

172

and the withdrawal of more troops from there would be a great risk; but are we in this to avoid risks? And here in England there must be thousands upon thousands of men who joined to fight and are still digging sewers. Are we in such a precarious position, here in this island, that we could spare no more from all the regiments we have rusting and rotting here? I know I'm only another arm-chair critic; but they're a symptom of a malignant growth, not the growth itself, which is a thing the government hasn't yet realised. If the people of this country perfectly trusted their leaders to be neither rogues nor fools, there would be no arm-chair critics. If we had not by sad experience found some to be fools, if none were rogues, this distrust would not exist. I suppose we have probably the most incorruptible high public servants in the world, but folly can be as far-reaching a crime as dishonesty.

What will happen in Greece? Will Athens fall? And if it does, what happens to our people there? Will it be another Dunkirk, grown wearisome with repetition? And if so, what will become of Tom? He takes his chance like the rest, I know, and neither of us would have him take a step ahead of them, not for a long life-time of happiness afterwards. But someone must be growing frantic just now about every Tom among them.

I wonder if I'm wrong about all this, and he's really in Egypt or Libya. I wish I could be sure, but until I hear from him again I shall be no nearer a solution and heaven alone knows when that will be. There must be precious little time for writing letters in Greece or Africa these days. Probably all will be over, and the Imperial Force, or some remnants of it, evacuated from the Piraeus long before I so much as know whether he has been there.

There have been times, since we came up here, when I haven't read a newspaper or listened in to a news bulletin for weeks. But now I sit over the wireless anxiously in my off-duty moments, and read all the papers religiously every day.

There is nothing here to distract my mind from him. Spring is with us, and makes a world of difference; life in this house becomes very pleasant now that the garden has snowdrops and crocuses and daffodils all in bloom together, and the park grass under the trees is all a golden sea of daffodils. There was a wood near to us at Hillingham where the ground was blue instead of green in bluebell time. Sefton Park is literally pallid gold, sunshine-colour, with daffodils. So is Thessaly, I expect, Spring being impervious to wars.

Apart from that, not very much is happening to us. A slight feud has broken out between watch-keepers and office-hours workers. The bone of contention is drills, first-aid lectures and various other extra-duty sessions of the same kind, which we do in our free time, and the day-workers in their office hours. Now no one admits more freely than I that we have much more time off than they do, and therefore should be willing to give up a part of it if need be. But our conditions are notably more trying than theirs, and our work while we are on watch is of a more urgent nature; and when this is taken into account I do think that the growing claims on our leisure are becoming a trifle steep. We have said so, but it is hard to make people who have always worked office hours appreciate the rights of watch-keepers. The affair is not very serious, and your Catherine in the presence of preoccupations infinitely more important finds it quite easy to ignore it altogether; but it has caused a slight stiffness between the two factions, we considering ourselves aggrieved and they convinced we're simply shirking. In any case we watch-keepers seem for some reason to be regarded from the administrative angle as a lesser breed without the law. It's just one of those things.

Oh, and one scrap of news; poor little Jean Perris has got a draft. She doesn't want to go at all, and hates the thought of going farther north; her mother, a widow, lives in London; they're sending her to Scotland, which will make weekends impossible from the point of view of time and of money. She has asked to stay, I have asked to keep her, both equally vainly. There's no appeal. She was told yesterday, and she goes to-morrow. Most of last night she spent in tears; whereas Goodwin, of A. Watch, who hates Liverpool and asked for a draft the day after she came here, is biting her nails with jealousy now at what she considers Jean's good fortune. I don't pretend this is the inevitable procedure in the service, but it is one case of undoubted hardship which seems to me quite unnecessary. It will probably mean quicker promotion for Jean up there, but believe me that means nothing to Jean just at present. All she wants is to stay here among her friends, where she knows she's happy.

I shall miss her, too. She's a sweet kid. How I hate to see these little, kind contacts snapped off short like this. But on the whole we've not done so badly, Jean being our very first loss.

It's getting late, and the bath-water will be cold. Oh, hell, there goes the siren! Now I can't have a bath at all. I'll go to bed grubby, and get up betimes and have a really hot soak to-morrow. Goodnight, Nick!

Catherine.

W.R.N.S. Quarters, Liverpool.
May 1st, 1941.

Dear Nick,

I think Walpurgis Night has slipped its moorings and come in twenty-four hours adrift. There's a noise going on just now, at nearly midnight, like a dozen Witches' Sabbaths rolled into one, and certainly all the powers of hell are loose over Merseyside in about fifty German bombers, according to the last estimate. If this isn't the real thing, all I can say is it looks, feels and sounds like it.

Actually I'm seeing nothing of it. We're in the cellars, the very first time we've had to take to them. Which is not bad going for a reputed blitz town.

The siren went earlyish, probably round about ten o'clock. We took no notice. We never do until it gets noisy. Which it did most notably within ten minutes, and those of us who were still upstairs in dressing-rooms and common-rooms were sent down to our cabins. Those who were already in bed had given up by then all hope of sleeping; so Carfrae produced her mandoline, and we set up a healthy row in opposition. We got about halfway through our repertoire of student songs, and then bits of plaster, mere flakes, began to fall on us from the ceiling, and we awoke to the fact that we were losing, hands down, to the hullabaloo outside. And just about then the powers that be decided that we ought to go to earth.

Well, I suppose there was more grumbling over going down into the cellars than there would have been over walking out into the thick of the raid. Garfield, to whom an incendiary is something to be put out with glee, shrinks from touching clammy walls, and fears cockroaches as few sinners fear hell; and the bulk of us have much the same blind spot when looking at danger, and the same sickening, illogical horror of insects and murky places underground. Still, we went, oozing complaint at one step and exuberant song at the next, after the queer fashion of this remarkable people. Our inveterate drippers dripped solidly all down the steps into the dank brick wilderness; but they dripped about mice, and beetles, and the risk of catching cold, not about H.E. and incendiaries and the chance of the house collapsing on top of us. Solid though it is, periodically it rocks to some not-very-distant concussion which is indubitably a bomb, and shivers as if it might come down. Our only nerve-case – not a very bad one, at that – jumps violently at every explosion, and states with satisfaction: *'That was a bomb!'* or *'That was a gun!'* according as a carefully acquired knowledge of which she is inordinately proud distinguishes one from the other. Half the time I believe she's dead wrong, and should dearly love to contradict her; but how to prove it? Lacey, who looks like a Hollywood baby blonde, is getting worried about her insomnia; she says she can't sleep. So much for the panic-stricken women of Britain.

Our cellars are good cellars, a whole series of small brick labyrinths with several exits, reasonably warm and dry as cellars go, but still not very warm nor very dry. The wise have brought their blankets, the beetle-conscious and fastidiously dirt-shy have preferred to be cold. We're nearly all in slacks and sweaters over our pyjamas, most of us have greatcoats or dressing-gowns on top; some – and your Catherine is one – have both dressing-gown and greatcoat, and are rather proud of their foresight, though they look like nothing so much as navy-blue barrels. We have a good large supply of deck-chairs; kept in the cellars they can hardly be expected to remain dry and spotless, but better a head cold any day than a bomb. Those of us who arrived too late for deck-chairs are sitting on (a) boxes, (b) upturned buckets, or (c) earlier comers. Dan, to whom luck adheres as flies do to fly-papers, has penetrated to the farthest cellar, and is cosily curled up in a nest of ground sheet and travelling-rug against the wall of the furnace. Periodically she beckons me wildly. How she supposes I am going to traverse the intervening twenty yards or so of cellar, packed with roughly sixty tangled bodies, is a point I'm much too tired to argue about.

Speaking for myself, I'm not doing so badly. I have a corner of clean new wall to lean against, a large box to sit on, and something to occupy my mind. Very few of us were caught napping. Sometimes in the lulls I can hear the knitting-needles ticking like a clock shop. Gwyn, who is on the other end of my box, is half-way up the front of an Air Force blue pullover. Her face is fixed in a strained expression, and she keeps up a constant mutter of magic formulae to remind herself how many rows she's done, and what's due to happen next. I think it's the first thing she's ever knitted in her life; she holds the needles like a man rather than a woman, and every now and again gets herself into a hopeless mess with the very neat rib pattern she's chosen, and has to call me in to disentangle her. I wish Johnny could see her now. Her dark hair is down over her shoulders and will keep falling forward into the needles, so that I'm sure she'll end by knitting it into Johnny's pullover and having to be cut loose. Her face is puckered like a bulldog puppy's, and she recites the pattern (memorised) in a sort of ecstatic delirium. Dan usually has to stand by to bring off the rescues, Dan being an expert knitter; but to-night

I'm the only one within reach, and any moment I expect to have the wretched masterpiece held out to me suddenly, in a gesture at once imperious and piteous, with a despairing sigh of: 'Oh, Cath, I've gone wrong again!'

Do men find it pleasant when people they're fond of reveal a helpless spot and have to appeal to them? I think they must do. I remember how the fair searchlight boy patronises his pal over money. The dark one has no money sense at all, and the fair one superintends his spending like a cross between a father and a fag-master. Incidentally, isn't it plain hell that I should rake in more than they do, I with my keep assured, and living in conditions of almost fantastic comfort?

My bit of cellar is full of knitters, from a Fair Isle sweater at one end to a khaki sock at the other. I am the sole letter-writer. I often write letters in bed, and therefore had my writing-case to hand when we had to get up and file to the cellars, and here I am on my box, with Gwyn's needle wagging in the region of my left eye, and the bomb-concussions shaking my hand and paper so that my writing wobbles about the page like the wanderings of a drunken fly, and I doubt if even you will be able to decipher all of it. There's light enough for the most intricate bit of knitting, luckily; this is one place where no querulous voices demand that the lights be put out. Darkness in these grimy depths would be a bit too much.

It's a funny sight we make, funny-ha-ha as well as funny-peculiar. Eighty or ninety girls in pyjamas, blankets, travelling-rugs, eiderdowns, greatcoats, scarves, their hair in curlers under giddy chiffon handkerchiefs, their faces greased and glistening with cold cream; and all these girls crammed into two or three small rooms and the wide tunnels between, in deck-chairs, on the floor, on top of one another, entangled in one another's knitting and embarrassed by one another's books. Like a feminine jigsaw puzzle in the box-and-bucket corners, and rather like the deck of a cruising liner on a roughish day in the deck-chair areas. It's so odd, and being a part of it is so difficult, that we forget about the raid, except to long for the all-clear, and an end of this cramp.

In the darkest corner on my right D. Watch, mixed up like a litter of replete puppies before a fire, are being so frightfully and vociferously British that it sounds more like a troop-concert than a heavy raid. But a raid it is, by much the worst I've known, so why blink the fact! The only reason I'm not frightened to death is that from long security through many alarms, I don't think I altogether believe in raids. My intelligence does, but my instincts don't. Or else it's just that we look so damned silly it seems absurd to be frightened.

It seems to have been going on for a long time, steadily, much the same volume of noise all along; being underground dulls it, we get the reverberations like earth tremors, and the impact of each burst like sullen, heavy thunder. If we listened the constant, unwavering pressure of noise would get into our ears and get its nervous effect in the end; but what with the row D. Watch are making of 'Rio Grande' and our own individual preoccupations the rhythmic tension is broken, and we escape without nervous harm. To be sure there was one major panic, a regular screaming-match in one dark corner, half an hour ago; it turned out that one burst of noise had shaken down a shower of dust and cobwebs over the local inhabitants, and the cobwebs were found to contain a large spider. You never saw a corner evacuated so quickly in your life. It just shows how speedily we can disentangle ourselves in an emergency.

Sometimes I love my sex, Nick. I rather like them to-night. They're doing all right.

I have a feeling that this is only the beginning. There's a methodical touch about it. I wonder if they're beginning a systematic flattening-out of Liverpool, a six- or seven-day affair like the one at Plymouth? After one raid night we generally take it for granted there'll be others. Anyhow, my slacks are going to bed with me every night from now on.

Dust keeps rustling down over my paper with every bang, so please treat this epistle indulgently if it turns up looking as if the dog had first walked on it and then chewed it. Anyhow you're helping me to while away a tedious and trying time, so bear with the grubby result.

This quite unexpected outbreak has given me something to think about here at home. For days I've thought of nothing except the way things have gone in Greece. You'd be quite aware of that even if I didn't say so. How can I put that tragedy of tragedies out of my mind? There doesn't seem very much of anything left in the world except the fall of Athens. And Tom, of course. What's become of him? I wish I knew. I wish to God I knew. Our war, which could have been a crusade, has become so commercialised and soiled and hung with bits of dingy jingoism like that nauseous brand of popular song about being on our way to Berchtesgaden that only here and there has some unveiling of glory shown us the things at stake. The martyrdom of Poland, the land of no surrender, was one such moment; the fervour and heroism of Dunkirk was another, our only contribution; and the defiance of

Greece has been another, the most poignant, the most profound of all, the most blinding to the eyes. And all to no purpose, or no present purpose. And yet I find myself wishing I'd been born a Grecian woman, yes, even if I had to kill myself, like poor Koryzis, to avoid seeing the ruin of my country; or even if I had to live through the horror of a German and Italian occupation, which must be infinitely worse than death. If only one could believe that Germany knew how to respect such an enemy! But we know only too well that the measure of Grecian gallantry will be the measure of German hate and cruelty; and the thought of what's to come is beyond bearing.

It makes me mad when half-hearted and imagination-less so-called Christians talk glibly about having no hate for the German people. They can please themselves. Their hate would probably be a poor wishy-washy thing, anyhow. But I have hate, yes, such a load of it that sometimes it all but strangles me. I am not concerned with paper ethics, nor troubled about the welfare of my soul. All I know is this white-hot, angry, inarticulate, unassuageable hate is in me, and feels a good and godly thing to me; and if God thinks other-wise, well, it's up to Him to damn me for it. I don't know that I want any part of the sort of heaven that sort of God would have; the company of Lucifer in his clean old Renaissance hell might easily be preferable.

Sorry if all this sounds a shade hysterical. Believe me – but you will believe me – it isn't. It's quite cool and considered. Conscience seems to me a better guide to right and wrong than all the rigid rules worked out by logic; and my conscience says this hate is right and good; and as far as I'm concerned, the final verdict on that can wait till the Last Judgment, and whatever it is I'll abide by it.

Curse these dust showers. I don't think I've ever felt so dirty, and my hair's full of grit, and itching like the devil. My pen's getting temperamental, too, may be running out of ink soon. It's just flooded. As if you needed to be told!

I had only that one letter from Tom, and now he may be anywhere, and I can do nothing, I can't even project my thoughts after him because I don't know where to send them, so to speak. This uncertainty is beastly. The Germans are in Athens, and thousands of our men are making a precarious way down to the ports of the Peloponnese to embark at intense risk upon an even more hazardous voyage to a destination which seems to me the hottest spot on earth at the moment after Greece itself; and I can only sit here and wonder if he's among them or safe – if anyone is safe – in Egypt. In a way, though I wouldn't have hoped for it, this onslaught here is a relief to me, since it offers me a distant share in the danger they live with day and night. But I fear Liverpool won't look quite the same when we go on duty tomorrow at one o'clock.

Interval. Gwyn has dropped a stitch.

Rescue effected, and she's now safely embarked upon the next row. In moments of exceptional stress she sticks out the tip of her tongue at the corner of her mouth, and breathes hard and earnestly, like an intent small boy. Johnny does a very good imitation of her, which she swears indignantly is a gross libel. There are, I find, masculine points about Gwyn which greatly complicate her already fascinating make-up.

Thank God, even when vaingloriously in love one

goes on being fond of people. Perhaps rather more so than usual. I say thank God because I suppose it might be easy to go mad if no one else mattered in the world but one person, and the one person got killed.

That, however profound the reflection, will be enough of that.

I haven't written to my family about Tom. I don't think I shall now, until there's some prospect of taking him home to see them. There seems no point whatever in drawing them into the same anxiety I feel. One is enough to sit worrying over things she can't help. No, Nick, I forgot that you were in it, too. But I can no more keep you out than I can get out myself. Sorry, but there it is.

I think I'd better close this letter, while parts of it are still legible. There's no slackening of the noise as yet, but I suppose it will end some time and let us crawl away grubbily to bed. The singers have grown tired, and I actually believe one or two of them are asleep. In the opposite direction at least one person is snoring. Such is the sound state of Wren nerves on Merseyside.

Goodnight, Nick. When you get this you will take it as a sign that I am very much alive and at least one post office around here is still functioning. Please don't ever worry about me, you have other and so much better things to worry about, like your next operation and the new treatment they plan to give you. About which, by the way, you've sent no news recently to

Your Catherine.

PS. – All-clear at about twenty to two. And so to bed.

W.R.N.S. Quarters, Liverpool.
May 9th, 1941.

Dear Nick,

The sequence is broken; there was no raid last night. The pause came strangely, as if the world had stopped turning. We were just becoming used to the regular nightly alarm, every night at the same hour, every night of much the same duration; and last night the hour came and passed, and nothing happened. I expect you got much the same pleasant shock, for I remember how, before I joined up, we used to hear the enemy squadrons passing due overhead every time Merseyside was raided. I expect you have lain and listened to them passing over Wastwood all last week. But now we can almost believe it's over; at any rate we know it's possible to have an occasional quiet night. We were on late duty, and it was eerie to find ourselves driving home through the night in peace, after so many chancy journeys with battle bowlers at the ready.

Well, it was pretty bad, and may be as bad again. After that first night the drive into town was through streets which looked for all the world like rows of broken teeth. To me, unused to the worst a blitz can do, it appeared pretty bad. Liverpool seemed more or less blasé about it. The town itself had stood up to it comparatively well, gaps being few; but when we went on duty at one o'clock there were little groups of firemen here and there in the streets, trailing home with tired, grimy faces, with water streaming after their boots from the side streets. One or two shop windows were hanging out in jagged teeth of glass, one or two were clean gone, blown into dust. But for the most part the middle of the town was intact. I think it was over the river the worst of the blow fell that night.

One of our girls, an immobile from Wallasey, came in a little late, and offered in apology the simple excuse that she had been bombed out during the night, and had spent the morning in transferring her mother and all the salvable part of their household goods to her aunt's house. She hadn't had any sleep at all, of course, but even so she turned up for duty only a quarter of an hour late, and took it for granted that she should work her afternoon and night watches as usual. And in spite of the offer of time off, so she did, and went home next morning to grub among the ruins for more portable property.

That night watch seemed almost peaceful to us, with the normal office routine to keep us occupied. We work, as you know, underground and well enclosed, and sounds from the outer world reach us only in a muffled and distant fashion; but we heard the bombs falling all right. Including one which flattened a block of buildings in a back street close beside us.

That was a bang, if you like. Busy about our lawful occasions, we were suddenly struck by what felt like a hammer-blow against both ear-drums. I suppose we all jumped wildly; I know we all stood fixed for a moment afterwards, frozen to the ground, while the first reverberations quitted our ears. Then Seldon, who has nothing even remotely resembling a nerve in her body, remarked complacently: 'That was a bomb.' Curiously enough there was a distinct pause before the block collapsed; we heard that too, a slow, slithering, grinding roar that went on for several minutes in a series of diminuendos. We couldn't tell from which direction it came. From our fastness sounds have no direction at all. But next morning we found a ruin on our back door-step, and the sunlight flooding in at windows which ordinarily it never sees.

We prefer to be on duty, for obvious reasons, if we must have heavy raids. For one thing, since there's no hope of sleep, one may as well be working, and have time for sleep by day, when the skies are quiet and our cabins safe. For another thing, the feeling of smug safety in the office is amazing. Noises are dulled into mere background sound, and actually I suppose we are about as well protected as it's possible to be. And even the most nervous people, we find, are quite matter-of-fact about the blitz when they have plenty of work to do.

It was eerie coming out into daylight next morning, after our reliefs took over. It was a glorious morning, drenched in pale but dazzling sunlight, except that a curious fawn-coloured haze seemed to hang in mid-air over the streets. But if it was sultry overhead it was glitteringly bright underfoot. We walked to our transport over ground white as hoar frost with glass literally blown to powder. Every window was out; we'd expected that, but I for one hadn't dreamed how it would be. There were great glittering slivers lying on top of the frost, but most of the glass was so fine it might never have been glass at all. The street glistened like the whitest mica you ever saw, and rang underfoot.

After that day it grew steadily worse. In the garden at quarters the days were strange islands of sunlight and stillness, warm enough to sit outside if you took your deck-chairs into sheltered spots. The squirrels came out and sat upon the window-sill of the mess waiting to be fed. A funny little moorhen trotted backwards and forwards across the lawn between shrubbery and pond, ceaselessly, shyly, all day long with a small rustling sound in the grass. The girls rowed themselves round and round our very modest lake in a leaky old flat-bottomed, butt-ended wallow of a boat, and sang close-harmony under our one willow-tree in the evenings before the nights closed in. It was all fantastic, like a distant memory of peace coloured with a dream-like light because of the shadow of night which hung always over it. Night was the reality, the only reality.

The nights were hells of thunderous noise and fire. We grew used to that session in the cellars, but there were also the late duty nights when we travelled early so as to escape the siren, but even so didn't always evade it so easily. Once we got in before the worst phase began, once we got stuck at the office and spent the night there; and the other watches had much the same fortune. And every day a bit more of Liverpool was squashed flat, and a bit more went up in smoke.

One gets used to it; that's the amazing thing. By the third night we had the thing organized. Everyone got ready for bed early, tucked herself into layers of surplus clothing, and sat waiting comfortably with a book or knitting, pillow and rugs and gasmask ready, until the sirens began their unalluring song. Then, as if in response to the meal-bell, down the cellar steps we trotted, and filed away into our chosen corners, and settled in. Yes, we even slept. Perhaps it wasn't the most refreshing sleep in the world, but sleep we did, and sometimes without dreams. One becomes inured to noise, and danger isn't nearly so fraying to the nerves as noise can be.

Queer thoughts come into one's mind, Nick, when the thing draws really near, like that. I speak as a fool, for what do I know of danger that you haven't forgotten or discarded long since? But even this touch of the fringe of her garment brings me nearer to you, and some of the thoughts which visit me now must have come to you once, in the last war, when flight was a strange and hazardous adventure with a touch of mystic devotion about it, and fighting was a more or less simple business even in the sky. I think about death sometimes; so must you have done. It doesn't seem to me a terribly final thing, rather a matter for intense curiosity and interest and excitement. No one goes looking for it, but if it comes looking for me I don't see that I shall feel any desperate urge to evade the acquaintance. It has an attraction; I want to know what happens next. And that in turn makes me think how few people, how singularly few, are really capable of being pagans. There's a monstrous innate egoism in most of us which literally cannot conceive of death putting an end to the individual. Do you feel as if you – the inner, unruly, indignant part of you – could be snuffed out like a candle? I'm sure I couldn't. It amounts almost to knowledge, I'm so sure. So why should we mind going on to investigate the next phase? True, as human beings we're suspicious and uneasy of new things, but that vital curiosity has a say in the matter, too.

And I think – who doesn't? – of what my life might have been in other circumstances, and I wouldn't alter it in any detail. I got the one thing I wanted, anyhow. Besides, I feel if I had it over again I should make an even worse mess of the thing, like all second shots. No, I wouldn't go back. Not even to the last years of peace. In those days the misfortunes of Abyssinia and China and Czecho-Slovakia and Spain skidded off the polished surface of my brain and made no impression whatever; but now I think it preferable to go down in such noble company rather than to sit on top of a world of thugs holding diplomatic candles to the arch-devils. No, no going back. Anything's better than that.

And I think of John sometimes. What a waste of my time and his that affair was. Poor John! I wonder if he still holds it against me. I think he does, for he never writes. But what else could he do, poor lad, being John? He takes himself so seriously that it must hurt him horribly to be superseded by a private soldier. Yes, I wrote and told John, though I didn't tell my family. I owed it to him, and whatever he is he's completely reliable. Let me do him justice. No one ever received confidences more faithfully nor kept them more scrupulously than he. He doesn't understand, of course, what more could be offered to any girl than I was offered in him; but he accepts it, and really wants me to be happy. Poor John! He seems a long way off and a long time ago. And would I go back to that neat security? No, never. That's over.

And I thought of you. Often, when the concussions became deafening, so that there was a sort of a physical flinching from them, I hung on to the thought of you, lying on your couch at Wastwood in the quiet and the firelight and thinking about me. It made a sort of sheet-anchor, and kept me content between the crashes. My nerves on their own object to the shocks of noise; but I've become partly acclimatised by now, and can let myself jump and relax without strain. It's a little like getting one's sea-legs.

As for Tom, I think of him all the time. You know that. I've stopped trying to convince myself that he's here, or there; I just let my mind dwell on him, and wherever he is a part of me is with him, and that's all I have or can hope for until I hear from him again.

Well, so we lived through the week. Every night we went to earth, and every morning around three o'clock we shook ourselves fully awake again, gathered up our effects and stumbled up the cellar steps and into our cabins, and there shed our accumulation of clothes and fell into bed for our few hours of sleep. As for the days, the off-duty bits are sunny and smooth as dreams, and the duty bits are, as ever, the one secure link with more normal times. Only when we go into town, now that this blitz week is over and the sequence broken, do we get anything like a just idea of the thing that's happened to Liverpool.

I was in town this morning, and I saw for myself. The abomination of desolation, Nick. There are smoking ruins everywhere. Water runs down from side-streets where firemen have been at work. Several of the biggest shops are burnt-out shells, with concrete piles still supporting upper storeys, and the steel frames of spiral staircases still winding crazily upward into midair at fantastic angles with no steps nor substance left to them, thin black bones with the flesh licked clean off them. The whole of one shopping street is flattened, both sides, simply squashed as if someone had put a foot on a beetle. One square in this area is now the centre of a great open waste of bricks, perhaps two hundred yards or more across. The Museum looks all right from the outside until you catch glimpses of the sky through upper windows, and realise that the roof is gone. Bluecoat Chambers, which housed pleasant little art shows drawn from the permanent collection, is in the same state. The coloured fronts of half the cinemas are sagging in a fashion which suggests collapse, though I think none of them have collapsed yet. The dust of fall upon fall still hangs visibly russet in the primrose-coloured sunlight. Every day an undulating crowd surrounds the heavy casualty lists in front of the Town Hall. Every day in the back streets going down towards the river we meet little processions of people transporting their bedding and the remains of their homes to some new shelter; boys pushing handcarts, women carrying rolled blankets, all so prosaically, as if they have taken in their stride the loss of all their household goods, and if need be will accept a second migration with the same unmoved faces. Every day the mobile canteens race down through such streets as are still open to traffic and dole out hot meals to the people who no longer have the means to cook them for themselves.

If you go over the ferry now – yes, the ferry's open to-day – you don't go directly across, but zig and zag in and out. And at the docks, too, I believe it was pretty bad. It's not for me to speak of the extent of the damage there, even if I certainly knew it.

We have been lucky enough, but we, too, have had personal losses. No less than four of our immobile girls have lost their homes, and one has lost her father into the bargain. And one of our most constant visitors, an old retired sailor of the nicest whose home is only ten minutes' walk from quarters, was buried under the wreckage three nights ago and hasn't yet been dug out. His Sealyham is here with us, he sits by the door all day waiting to make a bolt for home, and nothing can coax him to be comfortable and forget he's in a house of strangers. His mistress is with his master, somewhere under the masonry. Many must have died that way in Liverpool in these last seven days.

If that had been all, if hardship and sorrow had been shared in common among us all, I wouldn't complain. I was taken out to dinner last night, Nick. We fed as if in peace-time, and danced to soft music; and I thought of the mobile canteens doling out soup to the bombed-out women down by the docks, and I felt sick. I was one of the party only by virtue of being a friend of Dan's, but I couldn't stick it even so. I pleaded a headache and went home. The same hotel, one of our biggest and wealthiest, distinguished itself early one blitz-morning by refusing food to a bunch of wet, grimy, smoke-blackened A.F.S. men who'd been fighting fires on the docks all night under heavy bombing. I vouch for this. The firemen were visitors from the Midlands, and the story came to me from Strang, who had it from them. But it's also verified, if Strang's caustic letter needed verification, by an officer of the Merchant Service, one of a party who had seen the Midlanders at work on the docks, and afterwards saw the attempt to frown them out of the hotel. You'll be glad to hear that the Merchant Service boys chipped in, created no end of a scene, and got the firemen the food they wanted. But does that cancel out the crime? I think not. You can't wash out so easily what is all too accurate a sign of the times.

No, Tom was right. Tom and his kind have always been right. I myself know that if you have money enough you can buy, in this town as in all other towns, luxuries the poor have not seen for over a year. I know that if you have money enough you can get a lot of the supposedly impassable barriers of law so bent as to let you through. I know there are ways round food-rationing, ways out of service, ways of evading petrol restrictions, ways of profiting by your fellow's and the world's misfortune, ways of being safe and amassing even more money – if you have money enough. Not that everyone with money enough takes advantage of all these amenities; but very many do, and we all know it – far too many. While the idealists die ungrudgingly in uniform, and the civilian heroes die as blithely without any such stimulant. And this is our warfare.

Well, I suppose my conscience is clear, and that should be the main thing. And yet I begin to think that we shall have to make other people's morals our concern, as well as our own, before this affair is over.

It's late evening again. We can't rely on a quiet night just because we've had one last night; so I must stop writing and get ready for the worst.

Goodnight, Nick. Write again soon, and lengthily, for the comfort of the soul of

Your Catherine.

W.R.N.S. Quarters, Liverpool.
May 15th, 1941.

Dear Nick,

Your letter caught me off-balance, and I had to get up hurriedly from the circle in the commonroom, and go away privately and cry. In one of the lavatories, if you must know; there's nowhere else private, except the bathrooms, which were being scrubbed out at the time.

It's a thing I haven't done for years, and didn't expect

to do again, but it seems there must be some stray bits of base femininity left in your Saxon yet, and you know how to find them – or found them without knowing. The decoration of swear words in the last few paragraphs came too late to save me; in fact it made me cry more than ever because it was you to the life.

What is it about you, Nick Crane? My mother wrote me a dear, anxious, hazy letter full of delightful ignorance of the meaning of the word 'air-raid'; but fond as I am of her, and touching though it was, it only made me laugh and reflect how attractive she was, and how I must write to her at once and tell her that Liverpool was in the pink, and Catherine never better. But suddenly three pages of scribble from you, and on the first one the admission in blasphemous terms of your unsuspected anxiety that Catherine should not collide with a bomb, and my inside turns to water, and I want nothing but to run away and howl my heart out.

Seriously, I never meant to wring your withers, my dear, queer Nick. I've always written to you like that. You've always wanted me to. If I closed up on you now and began considering your feelings to the extent of writing you sweet, soothing letters full of the sort of tongue-in-cheek brightness I keep for mother, you would hate it. What scorching epistles I should get in return! What advanced exercises in profanity! No, it's too late for us to learn new tricks. All I can do is write it down just once, for you to keep if you like, and remember whether you like or not, that I'm glad you feel kindly towards your Catherine, because your Catherine is horribly fond of you.

God knows what you are, but whatever it is it's important. Part father confessor, part salutary elder brother, part disciplinarian schoolmaster, part twin, part Jonathan to my rather unorthodox David – because Jonathan was always the better man – I don't know what you are. But if I hadn't got you, a great part of my life would be cancelled out, Do you think I write such letters to anyone but you? Not on your life! I write the usual sort of gentle drivel, hoping it finds them as it leaves me at present. Except to Tom, and his position is much simpler than yours, of course. But Tom's is a place in my life which you could never covet, and no one but he will ever possess. And yours, no less unique, is yours as long as you live to want it, or I to want you in it.

I wish you two could have met before he went away. Because I'm dead sure you would have known then just how it goes with me.

No more word from him yet, and by now all the expeditionary force from Greece are either in Crete or in captivity. Except for the dead. Nothing has done so much to restore my pride in being English as the attitude of the Greeks to our admittedly brave but certainly unavailing efforts to help them. There must be a good many British bodies now, besides Byron's, to sow a little of home in the soil of Greece. To the Greeks we are faithful and heroes all. What are we to ourselves? Especially in face of their unquestionable splendour.

But I'm not going to talk any more about Tom and the places in which he may or may not be. What you want to know is how I am faring, and so you shall, as well as I can tell you.

We've had, I think, two night sirens and one daylight one since I wrote to you, and they were all of short duration, and nothing was dropped during any of the three alarms. In fact nothing much seems to have been dropped at all lately except Rudolf Hess, in whom I'm interested only to the extent of a firing squad. Still, it was something new to talk about. I expect father has already propounded half a dozen theories to account for the flying visit, and I imagine our local Home Guard are now scanning the skies hopefully for Goering. Only if Goering is so unwise as to land in the territory of *our* Home Guard, he needn't expect to survive to talk to the Prime Minister. The highest he'll ever get will be Corporal Jones.

It's amazingly peaceful and busy and cheerful here. The obstructions still decorate the town to the danger of blackout walkers, but business is going forward much as usual, armies of workmen are busy clearing the closed streets and repairing damaged buildings. One of the burnt-out shops has a small corner of the ground floor still habitable, and is opening up again with a salvage sale next Monday. Trams now start from half-way out of town instead of Pier-head, but that's a very small hardship, and only a temporary one at that. For prosaic, commonsense courage English townspeople take the cake. They wake up, as it were, to find their homes and the organisation of their lives in ruins, they sit back and think it out for a minute or two, decide the thing is a fait accompli and may as well be accepted as such, shake the tiles out of their hair, and proceed to salvage what can be salvaged and shove the rest out of their way while they get the machinery started again. So much for the cherished belief that wars may be won by bombing the civilian population – British or German.

The place looks different, of course, but then it was never a very good-looking spot. And lives have been lost, and that's a thing we shan't forget, but it doesn't intimidate us, far from it.

I'm glad I was here when it happened. In Plymouth somehow it always waited until my back was turned. Being human I always wanted to know how it felt, and now I know, and I'm satisfied. As for taking care of myself, I always do, and always intend to. It's no part of my plan that Catherine Saxon should come to any harm. And you can set your mind at rest about me for this time, because it's pretty evident by now that the immediate pressure has spent itself. Our Spring blitz is over.

Gwyn sends her love. She has a very soft spot for you because Johnny sings your praises so heartily – rather as a pioneer and an ancient of days in the flying line, I'm afraid, but what else can you expect from that adolescent demi-god? Where those light blue eyes admire, Gwyn's green ones adore unquestioningly.

I can't write more just now. I have to go into town and do some shopping before afternoon duty. Owen comes back soon, and then I am going to have the remains of my mutilated leave, and come home and talk the sun down at Wastwood as we used to do in old times. In the meantime you are an idiot, and I dote on you. Which will be no news to you, even coming as it does from the pen of

Your Catherine.

VIII. LETTERS FROM GREECE

W.R.N.S. Quarters, Liverpool.
May 21st, 1941.

Dear Nick,

I've had a letter from him. I was right, he was in Greece. Where he is now God only knows. In Crete, if he's alive at all. I wish I knew, I wish there could be some way of finding out. When things move at the speed of the Greek campaign, letters are so little use. This one is dated April 15th, and there's so little in it, when all's said and done, and all its questions are answered and all its anxieties dead and buried long since. It's Crete we're tearing ourselves apart over now, but Tom writes of Greece as if it could still be saved. It never struck me how dreadful that could be.

I always felt he was there. I don't know why. It was so exactly where he would have wished to be, and so authentically the true place for him. Whatever happens, it must be a deep satisfaction to be able to say, even to oneself: 'I fought with the Greeks.' Well, I was right. He did fight with the Greeks. He had that notable honour. And now, either he's buried in the soil of Greece or he's in Crete, fighting like hell with his back to one defeat and his face to another. But how can I, of all people, wish him out of it, when if he had his choice of all the world I suppose he'd still be in Crete at a time like this. Besides, I have a great deal to thank God for. At least he was alive, and well, and without a scratch, on April 15th; that's so many days nearer to-day, at any rate, than I had news of before. So many days nearer a safe return.

I'm more satisfied now that I know the best and the worst. It's a nice letter, Nick, though he can tell me very little of the situation or how he looked at it then. But after so long, and when the country of which he writes is lost utterly, and his own life all that can be saved for me out of the disaster, it doesn't seem so hard that his letter should be newsless. It helps, if anything. Now that letter is like a few minutes with him, aside from time, and located in some nameless place of olive-trees and rocks and limpid air; as if I were carried to him in the night for a brief interlude, and woke up with something still left of what was certainly more than a dream.

I send you a couple of leaves of his letter. I've always wanted you to know him, and something of him, something of his integrity and detachment, come into this calm bit of writing. And I want to know, too, if you bear out my guess that the place he wrote from was Kalabaka, or near Kalabaka. That reference to the monasteries gave me the clue. I remembered reading about the monasteries of Meteora, years ago, and they seemed to answer the description; so I ransacked the remnants of the city library for a book about Greece, and finally found out that the Meteora rocks were near Kalabaka. I wonder how they came to let that hint through? Perhaps they thought it was too vague to afford much of a clue. I suppose it could hardly do any harm even if it was recognised. At any rate I don't think there can be very much doubt about the locality, do you?

I always want to pin down, in this way, all the details

of his life, so that I can have my part in them. When it's done, I feel I have lost something; until it's done, I feel I am missing something.

Nick, I am terrified for Crete. It isn't inevitable that it should be lost; it shouldn't be necessary to let it go; and yet Greece is gone, and will a few miles of water save Crete, I wonder? Anyhow, the time is gone when it seemed traitorous to foresee failure. We've had so many that by this time it's merely folly not to foresee more. Enough of that 'possibilities of defeat do not exist' complacency. They do. If France could go – though I was never a lover of France – if Holland could be rolled up like a strip of carpet, and Greece brought down to an angry grave, then the pillars of this house can fall too, and if we remain content to trust instead of struggling they will fall, and we shall be engulfed. Works before faith, every time.

Well, the newspapers and wireless bulletins talk and talk and tell us nothing definite. They say that parachute troops landed yesterday in considerable numbers, and that mopping-up operations are in progress, but they don't say who's mopping up who, nor how the process is going forward. They don't say if any precautions are being taken to prevent other similar airborne landings, nor if reinforcements of fighter aircraft, the most precious gold in the world, are being sent from Egypt to strengthen the protection of the airfields. Yes, I know we're frightened for Egypt, but my God, aren't we frightened for Crete? Unless we begin to stake something soon we shall lose all our possessions one by one for fear of losing them.

But maybe I'm crazy, and Crete will be held. Maybe they're doing all human beings can do, and more. I wish I knew. They have a heavy stake belonging to me, and I was never a cool bidder.

The hell of it is, I doubt if any of my letters ever reached him at all. The more recent ones in particular must have been wasted, for the troops in Greece were constantly on the move, and Crete was invested from the moment the last boatload of rescued troops touched land in Suda Bay. Nothing can keep up with the speed of this war. Even one's thoughts are too slow and lame to hold the pace. And friendships and loves make no haste.

Johnny Fairmile came up last night on a flying visit. Gwyn is confined to quarters in her off-time at the moment owing to a slight difference of opinion with our unit officer on the question of the proper time for a respectable Wren to come home from a visit to Cousin Robbie's dilapidated corvette; and the proper state in which she should return, too, though Gwyn was not more than a shade elated. Anyhow, she can't go out, so Johnny had to come in. There was only the garden for it, and the garden is populous just now, and as luck would have it, I happened to be rowing up and down in the boat, which alone offers a suggestion of privacy. I pulled in and took them aboard, and made an attempt to leave them to it, but they wouldn't have that, so off we sailed all three.

Well, a child could have told you there was something wrong with Johnny. It was a sober Titan who sat trailing his fingers in the slimy water and splashing with the toes of his shoes in the bottom of the boat. We got it out of him easily because he'd run to us to get rid of it. I say 'us' because I believe I am admitted into a sort of staccato, sexless friendship. He treats me much as he might treat his fellow-pilots; I never saw him with them, you see, except for one. Sergeant-Pilot Bill, the silent one who climbed Sheepstor with us, back in that other life.

He'd just been helping to bury Bill. They were out on one of their usual sweeps, I gather, and Bill came limping back slightly damaged, with one oil-pipe leaking, and couldn't make his own 'drome. He reached another one, but there were several new bombers out on the landing-ground, and they wirelessed him frantically to stay up while they cleared the flying field. And he did. But his fuel gave out before he could make a landing. Bill didn't want to fold up a bomber, so when he knew he was damned, he glided her off and smashed her and himself against the far hedge. And what was left of him they buried yesterday.

All this Johnny told us in the boat. In his own fashion. You know? In little snatches of two or three words, with long pauses between, and his voice all the while a dead monotone, but as hurt as it was hurtful. Johnny in his generosity loves very readily. All the worse for him, in a fighter squadron with a high record of kills and losses both.

I was thinking all the while: 'So that's the look, so that's the voice, of somebody who's recently been bereaved by the war.' Johnny is changed. His confidence, which is heaven-high, is not in any way shaken; only, as simply as in peacetime, he has suddenly been robbed of a close friend and his equilibrium is broken up as if he had been lopped of a limb.

It made me think how little I'd had to give up, how little of all the anxiety and pain and loss had fallen on me. My will was good, but – I haven't ever been asked for any of the things I offered. Comfort – no, I live in very considerable comfort here. Safety – well, there isn't any safety anywhere, so what? Leisure – I do very well for leisure. I have lost not one person from my life until now. Bill is my first deprivation; and I met him only three times. My God, Nick, it frightens me. I preen myself I'm ready to pay whatever price may be required for freedom, but how do I know how ready I am until the payment has to be made? How if the price demanded of me should be Tom Lyddon?

We talked it out between us, once, in a very few words. He always chooses his words, because that is his nature; and I, instead of talking promiscuously as I used to do, found myself dealing the bare bones of speech in talking to him. We said that the death of either one of us would be accepted with dignity because we had staked each other as well as ourselves. That, but I think in even fewer words. But now, seeing Johnny's face, I wonder if it's as easy to carry out that resolution as it was to make it. Friendships and loves, as I said, perhaps not very clearly, make no haste. No haste to bow to logic or yield gracefully to circumstance. No haste to relinquish lover and friend when the irresistible separation comes. So that a bit of the heart gets plucked out, too, rather than leave its hold.

Why did I drag poor Johnny into this? The problem and the self-doubt were always there, but I suppose it was through him that I turned and looked at it so narrowly. Theories of conduct fall down rather before the actual sight of him with the shock still new on him, that brown face dazed and subdued for once, and those bright eyes wide and bewildered and hurt, and a shade scared, like a child's after an unexpected and unaccountable blow. He was the first touch of the real thing, and he made me wonder if I was so all-fired self-sacrificing, so ready to be bloody and remain unbowed. And I'm still wondering, Nick.

But Johnny has lost other friends before now, not so close as Bill, but still fellows he knew and had worked and played with, and bought drinks for, and been used to seeing around. And I suppose he'll have to put Bill by with the rest, and if he has to he can; and if he can, so can I.

We are not over-cheerful, Nick, but this is not an over-cheerful time, and to tell the truth I am worried stiff over Tom. I've just been thinking there are none of those little diversions in my letters recently, they read like chapters of the history of an obsession, hag-ridden documents one and all. And yet I think people here find little change in me. I fight with the machines just as usual, and my leisure is as well-filled as ever. There are things I could be telling you, just as I used to tell you the amusing detail of my life before I knew Tom Lyddon. For instance, we have recently been allowed to visit some of the escort vessels in harbour, destroyers and sloops. They were man-handling our destroyer with sky-blue paint when we went aboard, and she was so small that every step on her deck took us brushing into some sky-blue obstacle. With that, and the grease we managed to accumulate in the engine-room, we ended the trip as dirty as happy. It was fun, and once I could have made a good story of it for you; but now, though I enjoy the immediate experience, I can raise no interest in it afterwards. No, my life has become an intensive affair, narrow and deep and virtually without ornament.

Don't despair of me. Even that will probably pass.

Read these pages of Tom's letter in the evening, without interruption. They deserve that, if only for my sake.

Ever yours,
Catherine.

[The enclosure follows.]

'Nothing I remember seeing in England looked half so peaceful as this little shallow valley falling away in front of me. The season is Spring as you will not meet with it in our island, a lucid, shining time of clear cold air sharpened with the last breath of the snow, with which the mountains are still blazing white, and softened with the sweetness of the almond trees in bloom. The farm, which is on my right hand where I sit, is a long, low house of stone seated in a niche of the hill, among the pink clouds of almond blossom. There is a slim black cypress tree by the gate, and a sort of placid activity of soldiers all around it. A few of the forward Armoured Brigade, at whose skirts we drag along like a small boy after his mother, are sitting on the running board of a lorry smoking a passing fag with the P.B.I. They look happy. Who am I to pretend to know what goes on in the minds of my fellow-men? But they look happy, and at ease.

'The villagers and hillmen of these parts, like us an undemonstrative people, still have not that look. Their faces are grave and hard and scornful of personal and national danger, their lack of fear, or mastery of fear, is thoughtful and not thoughtless. But they don't look happy. How could they, with the good soil under their feet growing shaky?

'You'd like them. People of strong personality,

dignified, very self-contained, not given to making a fuss about things, not capable of panic. There'll never be a refugee problem here such as there was in France. They remember other wars. They know how to sustain conquest, and in the end how to digest the conqueror. But they don't remember any surrenders.

'I feel a bit of a humbug here. The old man and his daughters treat us like princes; not for the help we may be to them if all goes well, but for the help we've wished to be; and just because we came here, if not of our own individual wills, then of a national will unforced for once by expediency or hope of profit. Because I tell you frankly, if ever there was a forlorn hope this is it. We know it, and so do they, and they welcome us all the more because of it.

'So far, of course, no action, no contact of any kind with the Germans. We go probing north, a day here, two days there, with everywhere this quietly royal welcome; and every day I feel the moment a little nearer. The touch-off should be soon, and by God's grace we shall be in it, up to the neck. But just at this moment I sit in the middle of this shining Spring picture of almonds and anemones, with the hills patched dark mauve on either side with Judas-trees in flower, and the sky empty of planes; writing a letter which possibly may reach you some day, and quite possibly may not. I've seen a good many things you'd like to see, and presently I hope to live through a good many things you'd wish to live through if there was any good in wishing. As for what goes on along the battlefront, we're as ignorant as you, probably rather more so; a thing I don't like and never shall get used to. In Spain I fought my way, with a handful of companions, a speedy pair of legs, a straight face and one ear to the ground. Now I do what I'm told, when I'm told, no matter how idiotic it is; and believe me, it goes against the grain. But the fact remains that I'm not going my own way now; we're infantrymen, not guerillas. I'll go on digging metaphorical sewers. At least they're better than the real thing. And to-morrow, or the next day, our advanced units will touch the enemy spearheads, and the contact will come back to us; and I for one shall be almighty glad.

'In the meantime, we look north, the way we're heading, into a land of fantastic rocks and valleys growing harsh and deep. Plenty to see, plenty to wonder at. On our way to this lull we passed not far from the homes of the original "folks who live on the hill". Freak hills, sheer pillars of rock three hundred feet high and more, with monasteries – several, I believe – perched on top. How the masons got their materials up there in the first place is more than I can guess. How they got up there themselves before there was anyone on top to haul is a bit of a puzzle. But what you can see of the buildings from below looks remarkably solid and sound. I don't know how strong the communities are now; but I imagine they house a considerable number of brothers even to-day.

'Well, that's one way of staying unspotted from the world. Not a way I fancy. Where's the sense in elevating yourself above the slings and arrows unless you can also blind yourself to their ravages among ordinarymortals?Whereastheygavethemselvesagrand-stand seat on every successive catastrophe that rolled over this country through century upon century. To see chaos but remain outside it is not my idea of peace. Nor yours, I know. All the trouble in the world belongs to us.

'They never come down. Stylites, every man jack of them, living on top of geological pillars and going the wrong way about making themselves into gods. Not that I imagine God gets much comfort out of His elevation. And, at that, they must depend for the bulk of their food on the people below; and who's to fill their baskets at the foot of the rocks, when the Germans are streaming over this bit of country in heavy tanks? No, better by far come down and handle a rifle with the rest.

'To-morrow we go north again, and bring up in due course heaven knows where, but as safe as the sun rises we shall be standing on some old battlefield fought over and over centuries ago. Belgium has its claim, but I rather think I'm standing on the bloodiest soil in the world. Which is why the people, civilians as well as soldiers, are so accomplished in endurance, and so methodical in resistance. Heroism is their national profession.'

W.R.N.S. Quarters, Liverpool.
May 27th, 1941.

Dear Nick,

I've just come back from town with Dan. On Lime Street we saw the posters and heard the newsboys shouting. So we did it in the end. We sank the *Bismarck*.

Now that it's over, and the public knows all the bones of the story, surely there's no harm in my crowing a little. Because in my small way I had a finger in that pie. A very small way, perhaps, but you can guess how satisfying. My service existence is justified once for all.

There have been periods of excitement before. I remember an anxious night-watch, punctuated by emergency signals, when the *Empress of Britain* was lost. All the SOS calls, all the orders to tugs, and reports of progress came through our hands; and it was as if they'd taken away something of ours when she foundered in the end, after all our pains. It's a little hard to realise at first that a minute or two lost in cyphering or routeing and entering, or teleprinting an immediate signal may lose us a ship and a host of lives which need not have been lost. How we sweated and rushed to make absolutely sure that if the 'Empress' went down she went down through no fault of ours. And how we pounced on the signals relating to the *Bismarck*, these last few days, and pushed them out over the cables just as fast as was humanly possible. And we got her in the end, if it took us nearly four days.

There's a sort of deprecating attitude spreading among some people with regard to this encounter, as if there was something to be ashamed of in hunting one enemy ship with everything we had, day after day and night after night, until we dragged her down. Why? We've fought them where they outnumbered us, and have they drawn off or shown us any quarter? And are we fighting for glory, or for existence? The same people would hunt a berserk animal with as many guns as they could muster, yet they want to apply the standards of chivalry to the extermination of the most malignant beast that ever mauled the world's humanity. No, me, I was altogether glad, and grateful, and content. I remembered the *Hood,* yes, and the *City of Benares*, too, and a host of other murdered ships whose distress signals I've handled on their way inward from shore W/T stations; and I thought to myself: 'There's a little off the score, anyhow, and the odds look better for it.'

It started while we were off duty. We went on at six o'clock and found the hunt in progress; and the first news was the bad news of the *Hood*. Not an auspicious start, and the next watch and most of the next trailed along in a style ominously familiar. We chased her, we lost her, we spotted her again, we picked her up again, we lost her again; it began to be exasperatingly monotonous, besides the doubt of which way it was to end. But the first thing each watch asked as they came in to take over was: 'How are they getting on with the *Bismarck* business?' And if any *Bismarck* traffic, in or out, happened to be on hand at the time, it was seized upon immediately and hastened on its way with enthusiasm. We wanted her under. So many promising little victories have got away from us.

During our afternoon watch she was damaged by *Ark Royal*'s torpedo-bombers, as this evening's papers will certainly tell you. That was yesterday. Oh, Nick, I felt my fingers on the button that launched the torpedo. Matapan, you see, was not our action, but something we read about afterwards. This was in our own waters; we had a part in the progress of the battle, we helped to speed the hunting ships. Minor and downstage as our part was, we were in it up to the neck.

We handed her over damaged to the evening watch, and during their five-hour watch she was hit again, and again. But she was still afloat, still making steam, and still too fast for our comfort, when we came on duty again at eleven for the night watch. All night we hung on the affair, and in the early hours of the morning we heard that she was afire, and losing speed. And I thought: 'We've got her, we've got her, we can finish her by eight.' But we didn't; that was left for the morning watch. We hated leaving the last of it for them, as if that was exclusively our pidgin. Still, the *Bismarck* sank. Am I to care if I failed to be in at the death?

So she's gone, and my heart is eased once for all of any doubts I had about my usefulness here. And they were few and far between, Nick, for this life has deep and constant satisfactions if only it could be trimmed of all its niggling little kitty bows of tradition and bunches of red tape and 'service' frilling. Then we could get on with the job as adults – as please God we are – with adult minds. The discipline we really need, the only discipline I believe in, is the discipline which comes from within, dictated by good taste, by consideration for others, by respect for oneself, and above all by devotion to a duty shouldered voluntarily and eagerly. But however far conditions here fall short of what I would have them as regards the freedom of the individual mind, still I would not for the world be out of uniform again until the job's finished. The job is real, and vital, and pays for all the temperamental agonies of adjustment and follies of regimentation with considerable interest. For they are small, except when one's mood exaggerates them. But the job is big, and the only really important thing left in the world.

I've no heart now to amuse myself. I don't know why. From the beginning the war should have possessed us all, to the exclusion of all other interests. But it didn't. In my own case the demoniacal possession has been a gradual thing, but it has me now, and I shall never get away again. I go about as usual, with Gwyn or Dan or other of my friends, I eat well, I sleep well, I fill my leisure with walks, and books, and film shows; but I tell you seriously, Nick Crane, I live only to finish the war, and whatever I do that has no direct bearing on that aim is irrelevant, a mere filling up of time.

It isn't only because of Tom, though naturally he's a part of it. In our serenity we've let so many opportunities get away from us, and the accumulation of failure becomes so noticeable that surely all but the blindest of us must be getting seriously worried. The reversal of fortune in Libya was an eye-opener, the loss of Greece was a thing hard to believe, and harder to accept. Impossible to accept without hate and the necessity of revenge. If only they had had the decency to keep the Italians, at least – the creatures who ran from the Greeks among the Albanian hills – from swaggering through Athens as conquerors now! But what could one hope from Germans? No vileness is too vile. Again and again they've proved it, until now even we believe it.

Did you see in the papers yesterday that strange little story about the women of Athens? How, when the Italians attempted to humiliate the British prisoners by marching them out to sweep the streets, the Grecian women ran forward and snatched the brooms from their hands, saying they'd die before they'd see the heroes made into menials. And how they did die, shot down by the Italian soldiers of the escort. I believe so little of what the papers say, but I believe that. Because it sounds so true. I've never been to Greece, but I have very clear ideas now of what can and what cannot be true of the Greeks.

I tried to make a sonnet out of it. That Spartan form is the only one for a subject so awful and so simple. 'The Grecian Women.' But I couldn't do it. I've written nothing since I came here. I find that poetry, as far as I'm concerned, is good as a vehicle for spurious passion, but no good at all for the real thing. I've burned until I've burned myself dry.

And apart from Greece, apart – and yet not apart – even from Tom, there's another troubling in me. Did it really take a war to open our eyes to the shortcomings of peace? Was it really necessary that half the world should be overwhelmed in the most obscure misery, in order that we should suddenly become aware of the inequality and exploitations, the abuse and inhumanity which deface our prized constitution? Because I see them very clearly now. As he did and does; but through my own eyes, not through his.

I had another letter from him yesterday. Still from Greece, but what part exactly I don't know, except that he says his battalion has been withdrawn from the advanced line for re-forming, which gives me hope that they may have been sent out of the country intact instead of going back into the line. Because his letter is dated the nineteenth of April, the day after M. Koryzis committed suicide, and eight days before the evacuation began. Surely they wouldn't at such a time, when it was clear that nothing could be saved, send them back to the attack? *Or would they?* I wish I knew how far I could trust them with my valuables.

Most of Tom's letter – it's quite short – you can read for yourself, but I've kept the first and the last sheets, because I am answering it just as soon as I end this to you, whether he ever receives the answer or no; and those are the personal parts I have to keep before me as I write. In the circumstances, with Maleme and most of Western Crete lost, and the Greek Government already in Egypt, writing letters to one of the Imperial Expeditionary Force may seem rather like throwing one's efforts and emotions to the winds; but I always do it; and send them by air to make more sure; and God knows whether he gets them or not, but it's almost as if he were sitting by me while I write, so somebody is the gainer.

I suppose in a few days now they'll be evacuating Crete. If that was the best effort we could make at holding it, wouldn't it have been better to by-pass it in the first place, and disembark the remnant of the B. & I.E.F. in Egypt? But my knowledge of the circumstances, after all, is nil. Perhaps they did the best anyone could have done. Perhaps it's just the breaks. Or perhaps if we sit here much longer with our eyes shut, convincing ourselves that it's just the breaks, and our right to criticise is nil – well, presently there may be nothing left to save. I hover between the two opinions, and therefore am no use either way.

Owen comes back to work next week, and if she's fit to take over from me I intend to take that odd week-end of mine. I've been promising it to you so long that I've almost ceased to believe in it at all, but I really think it will materialise this time; and until then, think of me, but don't worry about me.

Ever your
Saxon.

[The enclosure follows.]

'We've been in our present home, in the nearest thing to rest-billets we shall see again in this country, for two days now. After the cold uplands we've become accustomed to, this is a sort of paradise, a place of grass and flowers and olive-trees, sheltered from the worst winds, and offering exceptionally good concealment from the air. Not that we're worth bombing, but our air cover just now is nil, and some stray Dornier may come over and take a fancy to us any moment. Then we take to the olives, which are jolly good cover. One of the chief drawbacks of this country, from the point of view of modern war, is the vulnerability of all the strong points to air attack. Only these softer valleys offer sporting cover.

'We've been in considerable action, as you won't need to be told. It's getting pretty obvious that our numbers here are not so copious as to let any of us stay in reserve. We're only out of the line to re-form, having lost quite a few of our numbers. I wonder if they'll let this come through to you untouched? I should think so. None of it is any news to anybody by now, surely. But the idiocy of the censoring system is incalculable. Maybe they think everyone in England thinks everything in this garden is still lovely, in which case you may expect a large black smudge for a letter.

'So far I am in incredible health, and without a scratch, apart from an excavation in one shin from falling over a rock during one particularly active and dark night up-country. How long we shall be allowed to stay here patching up our ranks I don't know, but I should think no more than another two days or so, and after that no one knows where we shall be sent. So the boys are making the most of their time. Who knows when we shall sit down and rest again? If I complained of inaction in England, by heck, I've paid for the grumble since. Thank God I was always a good walker. Quite a bit of our extensive travelling was done by lorry, but there are places where lorries decline to go, and it seems to me that we've been in most of 'em.

'Well, here's to this interlude. It has everything, even to a hot spring, very welcome to army feet. The days already seem long and sunny, though we have snow all round us still on the higher slopes. The air of this everlasting land is clearer than any air I've ever seen or breathed, colours are brighter in it, lines are sharper, distances are more limpid, and seas and skies have a more lucid radiance. God forbid that Germans should ever breathe it as conquerors. But you and I know that if we fail to forbid it God won't interfere. I don't pretend to know why.

'I don't suppose you are any happier about the way things are going than I am; perhaps rather less so, being better informed. We know nothing about any part of the line except our own. We do what we're told, and someone else thinks for us. Except in emergencies. There have been emergencies, and there'll certainly be others. It seems to me, when I sit still for a while like this and begin to do my own thinking, that the final epitaph on this adventure, as on almost every episode of this war of ours, will be: "Too little, and too late." Don't, on that account, worry at all about me. The main thing is that I am here. I wouldn't have been out of it for anything short of the peace you and I hope for. Not for anything less would I come out of it until the end, whatever the end may be. I like to finish a job. Until it's finished, who's to know if it's success or failure?

'There's a little girl at the small white house by the spring. She must be about seven now, and small for her age, and not pretty, but she has odd, attractive ways and two or three words of English. She brings us milk, I think as much for an excuse to be among us as because she's sent with it. The boys have made a pet of her. When the Dorniers come over they carry her off into the olives and keep her amused there until the sound and sight of the things have passed. Her mother never worries about her, simply comes out and calls at mealtimes and bedtime. I don't know. Maybe there's a good deal in being English. But what's going to happen to people like these when the English have to go? As they will. Whether we like it or not, our usual method of progression these days is walking backwards, and our most expert evolution is the fighting retreat.

'Still and all, it was well worth it for me. But the future of our little girl and her mother doesn't bear thinking of. That's the worst of it. In war the only tolerable thing is to be a soldier. For civilians the whole thing is plain hell.'

W.R.N.S. Quarters, Liverpool.
June 1st, 1941.

Dear Nick,

Something awful has happened. I don't know how to tell you, and yet nothing could be simpler. Johnny Fairmile is dead. He was killed early yesterday morning.

I don't know why I never thought of it. It happens to so many of them. One after another they go the same way, all those young creatures with wings. But somehow

I never thought of it happening to Johnny. Knowing him took him out of that fellowship. And yet no-one ever was more clearly marked for that ending than he was. I don't know why I didn't think of it. I suppose he was one of the three foremost fighter pilots of the R.A.F., because he had thirty-two German planes to his credit. Thirty-three. I forgot the last one, the one that killed him.

Gwyn had been out to a cinema during the afternoon, and I, going on watch at six o'clock, took her mail down to her, as she was going straight to the office. That was yesterday. There was a telegram. I didn't think anything of it. He sent her telegrams all the time, just to amuse himself and her. But he didn't send her this one.

She was in the middle of a biggish typing job when I took them into her office, and she saw the telegram, and smiled, and leaned back at her ease and opened it. I never knew there was anything wrong. No-one could have known. She folded it up quietly, and put it back in its envelope, and turned up her paper in the machine and went on with the minute she was typing. Perhaps I ought to have seen. Perhaps there was something I should have noticed, an unusual deliberation about her fingers, or some rigidity of her face, or some little thing to give away the truth of it, that her life was suddenly lopped clean in half. But I don't know. I never had a qualm about her. It didn't seem to me that there was anything changed about her. And I went off and left her there quite happily, and never knew anything had happened that shouldn't have happened.

She was waiting for me in the airlock when we both finished duty at eleven. She looked much as usual, only perhaps rather drawn and tired, but after late duty there's nothing remarkable in that. And she slipped her hand in my arm just as usual as we went out to board the transport, and her touch was quite light and tranquil. Only she never said a word. But she was never talkative.

I usually wander into her dressing-room on my way downstairs; I'm always ready for bed before she is. Last night I took rather longer over getting ready than perhaps I usually do, and when I went in to her she was by herself, everyone else had already gone down.

I shall never forget how she looked. She was standing there in front of the mirror, staring at her own face, and her eyes were very wide open, and as green as emeralds, and quite fixed with staring, as if she was looking for something which wasn't there any longer. She hadn't fastened her dressing-gown and there was a gold cross on a chain between her breasts. Her dark red hair was down over her shoulders in a cloud, and in the shadow of it her face was motionless. Her feet were bare on the cold linoleum, but she didn't seem to know.

She heard me come in. She turned and looked at me with the same look, and she said: 'Close the door!'

I suppose I knew then there was something in the air, but I didn't know what. I went up to her, and said: 'What's the matter? Is anything wrong?'

She said: 'Wrong? I don't know.' Her voice was a monotone. She put up her hands quite slowly, and pushed back her hair from her temples, and standing there with her hands full of copper hair, stared insatiably at her own reflected face. She said, and suddenly it was like a famished, muted howl in her throat: 'Johnny's dead!'

As God sees me, I couldn't find a word to say to her. There wasn't anything. She didn't want sympathy, and sentimental consolations would have killed her. I stood by her and watched her and didn't speak.

She said: 'It's all right. I'm not going to make a fuss. What's the use? I couldn't bring him back. And he's not the only one who's died, and I'm not the only one who's gone on living.' She grew very quiet again as she went on talking, in that slow, level voice people use when they talk to themselves, with an awful reasonableness about it. 'He rammed an Me. 109, and came down with it in the North Sea. In the small hours of the morning. He came down in flames. It's odd, isn't it? He used to say he was born to be hanged, but he burned in the end.'

I thought of that resplendent flesh marred by pain and fire and oil and blood, brought down like a falling star out of the zenith of fame to a death as frightful as brief. Cometwise, drawing his glories after him into the sea. What passed in her mind no-one could guess, but I think there was nothing he suffered that she didn't share.

She went on talking, still in that soft, dry voice, and as much to herself as to me, and perhaps most of all to Johnny who was dead. She said: 'He never thought of dying. It's queer, isn't it? He knew it was possible, I expect he knew it was probable, but it never worried him. He never lived even an hour ahead of time, you see. The present was always enough for him. That was why I had to do the thinking for both of us.'

I saw then what had kept her so calm. I said to her: 'You've thought often, haven't you, of this happening?'

'I've thought of it all the time,' she said. 'I don't know if I'm a coward, but I've died a good many times. Sometimes I've almost wished it would happen, because that would have settled everything. And now everything is settled.' That note of horror and unbelief came into her voice again. She said: 'But I always saw it as coming like a lightning flash – the 'plane blowing up, or some German gunner getting him full. I never thought of the fire.' And suddenly she clenched her hands on the edge of the dressing-table and said: 'Johnny!' in a way I'd never before heard and wish to God I could forget now, as if the mind and the heart and the life were gone out of her after him.

How well do you remember Gwyn? How well have I described her? If I had touched her then, as heaven knows I wanted to, she might have broken, and it might have been better for her. But I knew she'd hold it against me, and I hadn't the courage to do it. So she had her own way about it all.

I said: 'You shouldn't have put yourself under such a strain to-night. There was no earthly need for you to stay on duty, in the circumstances. That job could very well have waited until to-morrow.'

She said indifferently: 'What's the odds? To-morrow's the same as to-day now.'

Well, I suppose hers is the sanest view, but it isn't so easy to begin a new life, an empty life, at a moment's notice, without even a pause for revolt or grief or adjustment. I said so, and she said: 'Loving him wasn't an easy thing. This is much simpler. Besides, there's nothing they can do to me any more now he's gone. There's nothing to worry about any more. No problems to lie awake over, nothing. I think it's very easy.'

Is that why they die? Some are not so blessed. There have been men before now who reached their glory too early, at twenty-five or so, and spent the rest of their long embittered lives trailing the rags of old splendour diminuendo down years and years of aimless existence to an insignificant grave, when their right was to the exit of a hero, in a blaze of magnificence and a noise of mourning. Nelson knew when to die. So did Cobber Kain. So, it seems, did Johnny Fairmile.

I said, almost without meaning to: 'No, there won't be any decline and fall.'

And at that, quite suddenly she turned and smiled at me, and I saw that I'd said the right thing. She knew that I knew exactly how things were with her, how she could be glad as well as sorry that Johnny was dead, how the love she had feared to see despoiled was preserved for ever by his death in the full pride and triumph of its beauty. The afterwards of which she had thought with fear and he had feared to think was not a bogey any longer. There was no afterwards.

She shook back her hair. She said: 'Well, I suppose one still goes to bed.' And she gathered up her gas-mask, and thrust her feet into her slippers, and turned towards the door. Seeing that I looked at her perhaps rather dubiously she said: 'It's all right. There's not going to be any reaction. I know what I'm doing. Don't worry about me.'

So we went down together in the dark, and as we reached the foot of the stairs we seemed to pause instinctively before we separated. And I said: 'Gwyn!' And she said: 'I know. You don't have to say it. But this is as good an ending as any, and maybe better than most.' And she went away to her own cabin, and I went away to mine. And that's probably the only intimate talk we shall ever have on the subject.

But I don't pretend that I slept much that night. I kept hearing her breath groan in her throat as she cried out: 'Johnny!' That was the only glimpse she's given me of the fire that burned her, and I think no-one will see it again. Perhaps if I hadn't been with her that day at Polhawn, a long time ago, when she opened her mind suddenly to the sea and the loneliness about Johnny Fairmile, I should never have been allowed to see her guard slip now. For no-one else has, and no-one else will.

How could she, you may think, have leisure to see the other side of the picture yet? But you have to know Gwyn to realise how genuine her preoccupation with that other side has been all along. I think you have to know Johnny too; the part of him that expanded with power, and the part that stopped expanding. And though you do know him, I think it has to be as a woman knows a man. He was child and brother and friend to her as well as lover, you see. There will be people ready to say now, because she's so calm, that she can't have loved him so terribly much, after all. She won't care about that. Why should we?

Even now I can hardly realise it. He wasn't a person in whose death you could believe easily. Even now it doesn't seem possible that so much vitality and beauty and gusto would be snuffed out like that, though the end was an explosion of glory that fixes him like a star in the minds of men, and will keep him star-like in the zenith of their memories as long as a man would wish to be kept. I suppose the first thing I felt, when she told me he was gone, and the way of his going, was the snapping of a tension in which he and she and all those who were fond of them were strung like beads. That's over. He's dead, and safe. So is she, from any sort of disillusionment or loss or separation of minds. She has him fast and for ever, the same identical Johnny she loved from the beginning; and the continuity of their love is preserved from all the little accidents and degradations of ordinary life. There'll be no finger-marks. That soaring falcon will never have to fold its wings and come down to earth; it can go on soaring now as long as she lives and other people remember his name.

Is it so odd that she should be capable of seeing, even now, that he did well to die?

There are people who may regard that as a sentimental view. But I think not. I've tried to be realistic about it. I've thought, God knows, of the actual apparatus of that death, of the fire scarring him as he fought it, his hands first, and afterwards his body and his face; I've thought of him blackened and stifled, and burned blind; and of the awful pain of that plunge through the air, and the last half-conscious struggling in the sea among blazing oil and smouldering wreckage; and the appalling loneliness and forsakenness of dying that way, without a hand to touch you or a voice to speak to you. I know imagination must fall short of the truth, but I think I've always seen the reality of pain very much more clearly than the possibility of glory. And still, with all that concentrated hell to pass through, I can't help feeling that he did well to die.

All the same, it isn't going to be easy for her to go on living. All those who knew him are going to find a blank wall in their lives now, and I think in her house all the walls are empty, and all the windows darkened, and all the lamps out. I don't know what she will do. For the moment the war remains, his war and hers, and in any case the one preoccupation of every sane man and woman in the country until it's won. And after that there's a long, aimless life to be endured. No, perhaps not aimless. She has too much force and decision to let it be aimless, but inexpressibly wearisome. If Johnny burned for maybe a quarter of an hour, she has years of life to walk through in an even greater loneliness.

I hope to God that her people will have the wit to realise that young as she is she's finished with all that now he's gone. I know she's young, and has a whole future before her, but when the bowl is empty no-one can hope to drink from it again. She has nothing left now to give to any man, and she never will find anything in her worth giving again. I have very little faith in the capacity of most women to adhere to one man for better or worse, living or dead, all their lives; but then, I never knew but one Gwyn, and never but one Johnny, and I am very well aware how they stood.

I expected him to be in the headlines this morning, but he wasn't. Perhaps by the time you read this the news of his death will be common property, and the list of his exploits will decorate the front page; and his photograph will look at you with those long-sighted bright-blue eyes, and that brown, boy's face will smile foursquare out at you under that bleached flaxen hair; and by that time you will have read all about his death, from the outside, as the small hero-worshipping boys will get it, and the A.T.C. youths to whom he was a sort of god. I believe all ace pilots have their following of ardent worshippers. There was one child who wrote to Johnny regularly; and Johnny wrote back to him, too, bald but bright little letters from one boy to another. Poor kid, he'll see no more of his lion's letters now.

I hadn't meant to make such a lengthy business of telling you the news; but somehow my pen has gone on and on, elaborating a thing that was so simple, for ease to me, and not so that you would understand. I have to talk about it to someone because periodically it takes me with horror that he's gone, that he'll never come here dancing any more; and now and again I lose the contact of reality so that I begin to doubt if it's really true, and hope, as I am condemned to hope to madness on every issue, that we shall have better news. Which would only be to delude myself and her, and confuse what is now crystal clear. He's dead, and who am I to want to bring him to life again? He'll never be anything but young, and loved, and splendid now, and God forbid he should.

I want to take her away. She doesn't want to go home yet, she won't go away alone; but I think if only we could get leave together she would come away with me. I believe she would like to come to Wastwood. She has a very real fondness for you because you had a part in the last war parallel to his in this, and understood the wild joys of flight as he did; and she is drawn to you all the more now because you survived to a more awful grief (as she thinks) than his death. There was one thing she said to me that I hadn't meant to pass on to you; but I see now that you wouldn't mind it in the least, coming from her, and in these circumstances. She said:

'He crashed twice before, and they patched him up; this time, if he'd lived, it would have been as a cripple. He might have lived another twenty-five years of a life not worth living, like Nick.'

You see how little she knows of you yet. But perhaps she's not so foolish, for Johnny could never have taken circumstances by the throat as you have done, Nick Crane, and trampled them underfoot. But she would come with me, if you'll have us, and I know you will. I hope it may be soon, but all things wait on the war. Wastwood will be good for her, and you will be infinitely good, as you have always been for

Your Catherine.

W.R.N.S. Quarters, Liverpool.
June 4th, 1941.

Dear Nick,

Your letter was timely, and adequate, and everything it should have been, even from you of whom I expect so much. I'd give a good deal for your gift of going to a delicate point so straightly and with such judgement that no-one is hurt. She read it through, and seemed pleased, and I think she intends to write to you; but for the moment she just asked me to thank you, and said she would like to come. She remarked in a thoughtful way that Wastwood was the quietest place she'd ever been in, and it sounded as if that was an attraction to her. And no wonder, for she's swamped with sympathy here, and she was never civil to sympathisers. His photograph, of course, has appeared in every newspaper we have here, and probably all the rest besides. She never confided in a soul, after that night; but everyone was romantically as well as genuinely sorry, and it was difficult not to force one's pity upon her. She for her part walks straight ahead, not evading or encouraging them, meeting their careful kindness with a forbidding stare, and shutting herself up into a frigid solitude, with, I suppose, the constant lameness of his loss crippling her.

But that, at any rate, will pass in time. She will re-orientate herself to a world without a pole.

Owen is back, and astonishingly well, and if a little out of practice is still quite competent to take over my job. So we are coming to you, Gwyn and I, the day after to-morrow. It's a rushed business, but they were reasonable about it, as they always are over personal issues, and all's arranged for us, and we have a whole week of quietness and your company to look forward to.

Johnny's C.O. wrote to Gwyn. It was a very careful and brief letter, but rather a remarkable one, all the same. Letters to people you've never seen and probably never will see are much the easiest kind to write, and perhaps he did himself better than justice. He told her that Johnny would almost certainly be given a second, posthumous bar to his D.F.C. I don't know that these decorations after death do anything to reduce the feeling of loss; but this one will at least add a ray to his radiance, and the brighter he shines now the more fitting is it he should be perpetuated so, before any cloud can obscure him or any mist dim his magnificence. So, I think, she felt, and she was glad and grateful.

I've done a good deal of thinking – who wouldn't? – about the way things might have turned out, and didn't. And I'm more convinced than ever that Johnny was meant to be loved, not married. He was twenty-three when war broke out, and he joined the R.A.F. almost at once. I have a very clear impression of the sort of boy Johnny was, young for his age, intelligent but not thoughtful, enthusiastic but not profound, of limitless, unsounded potentialities, but quite unformed. And in that state power came to him, the wild power of flight, and of life and death in flight. He discovered things about himself; he found himself, for one thing, quite without fear and that in itself must be an intoxicating thing; he found himself master of the air; his hands had power over the machine, power over guns, as his mind had over fear and stress. The only part of him that ever grew up at all grew up to the stormy, stimulating, violent accomplishments of war, the only profession, the only rounded and assured life he knew. It was not his fault. If he had developed enough roots beforehand they would have held him firmly to earth through all this fire and terror. But he had none. He became a skilled tradesman, and his tools were daring, and heroism, and combat, and death. So he soared out of reach, and to bring him to earth again for life would have been a process of peculiar cruelty. However, it won't be necessary now.

I have a feeling that she was always, from the very beginning, sceptical about that marriage. That question of hers: 'What's to become of us?' was behind every moment they spent together. She could not imagine him settling down again to some office job, coming home at night to a fireside and slippers, like ordinary mortals, procreating children and helping to bring them up, growing grey beside her like a dutiful husband. No, that was not for Johnny. She wanted it for herself, I suppose. What woman doesn't? But not for that changeling, never for him. Better by far he should die than be shut into those four domestic walls of the commonplace. Better by far she should live without him than see him squeezed and compressed by alien circumstances into a shape not his own.

Well, he is dead. Horribly and piteously and resplendently dead. At his bravest, and loveliest, and most formidable. And I think in her heart of hearts she is at rest but you will see how forsaken she is.

Now that summer has really begun, at least it's possible to be solitary here. The garden is large, and full of quiet corners, and just now is foaming with rhododendrons. We spend our free time lying in the grass, reading or writing letters, and hardly speaking at all. We don't walk, because we should have to walk in uniform unless we went miles out of port, and to walk in uniform just now would be a minor hell. But once let me get her into the wilds of Wastwood, and we'll walk ourselves into exhaustion, and in more appropriate clothes. I long for those piny hill-woods, the scent and the silence and darkness of them, and the gloss of the needles underfoot. The only trouble is that I should ever have to take her away again. But the war disposes of us all.

Just at the moment I see everything through a mist of Gwyn, as it were. My own affairs have slipped into the background, but they're still very much in the picture, for all that. All's well at home, and my mind's quite easy about them all at Hillingham, where the war is a sort of Home Guard frolic and A.R.P. parade. No, all the anxiety I have to spare for my own concerns is directed towards Tom. Surely all those who will get out of Crete are out by now. Letters, cables, all possible means of communication are always so far behind the event in this too-rapid war. I know I can't hope to hear if he reached Egypt safely for a long time. So many will be left behind to add to the cumulative wasteful loss of men in evacuation after evacuation. This unfortunate body may well be getting exhausted. And armchair critic that I am, I say clearly that Crete could have been held. I am sure of it. If we had learned fast enough from experience we shouldn't now be still in the stage of despising air power and airborne warfare, trying to combat a sky full of 'planes with a handful of A.A. guns and a host of helpless infantry. No, it's hard to understand Crete, and harder to forgive it. Especially since Tom is there. I mean everybody's Tom, not only mine.

I had another letter from him this morning, and will copy out a little of it here for you. I think he must have written it shortly before leaving Greece, when the evacuation had become an obvious necessity.

'Don't be uneasy,' he says, 'if you don't hear from me for some time after this. You will understand, for by the time this reaches you what is now imminent news will be ancient history, and you will already have lived through my ordeals of the next few days; probably lived through them over and over, which is bad, for I want you to be happy for me, not anxious, and I have to go through every hot spot only once.

'I am not satisfied with what we've done here. Who could be? But with what we had, and in the lamentable circumstances which hampered us at every turn, I don't see that we could have done more. And at least we did what no one else in the world did. We came here with nothing to gain and everything to lose, and deliberately submitted ourselves to the flames. As it turned out, merely a form of grandiloquent suicide, but if luck had turned even a little the other way it might so easily have been a triumph.

'Well, what's done's done. What remains to do, and how we do it, will be knowledge to you by now. At the moment all I have to do is keep the pad steady on my knee against the motion of an overcrowded lorry moving incautiously along a shored-up hill-road in the very uncertain dusk. It requires concentration, and so will the deciphering at your end.'

He was right, it took me ages to disentangle his scrawl; that's why I keep back the actual letter, which would be Greek to you, I know.

And then he says: 'If anything should happen to me, you will already have heard of it. This is like one of those novels on the convention that all time is concurrent. If you've not yet received any official intimation that I'm dead, or captured, or missing, or wounded, then I am going to survive untouched. So you see you can afford to wait a long time for the next letter.'

That's not particularly like him, that dabbling of his toes in paradox. I suppose it isn't easy to project one's mind overseas and over time with a letter; and at any rate he made his point, and he was right to make it, for I hadn't thought of it. If anything had happened to him in the evacuation of Greece I should already have heard the news officially. He must have survived untouched. And perhaps I can afford to wait for his next letter, but at a time like this how hard it is to wait.

It was very short, that note. It was like him and yet not like him. I think he was under a double strain, the pressure of failure, and dangerous failure at that, and the constraint of the censorship; though always his letters seem to stare the censor in the eye and dare him to black out a word. Even Tom may well have owned himself tired and disappointed and frayed under that inexplicable disaster that happened to Greece. And letters are very revealing things; as I think you must have discovered long since. In two short days I shall see you again, and for a week you won't be rid of me. Even now I don't believe you realise what that means to

Your Catherine.

IX. AFTERTHOUGHTS ON DEMOCRACY

W.R.N.S. Quarters, Liverpool.
June 14th, 1941.

Dear Nick,

Back to the grindstone, this morning at eight, and the whole business looks more distasteful than ever to me. I suppose after a whole week of being a private individual again that's only natural, and I'm prepared to wait for it to pass. But there is a great difference, somehow, in the way I look at the service now. When I first entered I believe I was quite prepared, allergic to discipline though I was, to accept the standing order complete, traditions, shibboleths, conventions, spit-and-polish, and all. Yes, without question. I suppose the war hadn't then revealed itself as the urgent, spare, intense thing it is, demanding the abandonment of all amusements, all trimmings, all non-essentials. If it did occur to me that this custom or that habit was silly and wasteful, I soothed myself with the reflection that possibly the powers that be knew better than I did. No more of that now. I stand on my own feet; I think with my own brain. I question everything. Everything! Regimentation has made an individual of me, for better or worse.

Well, that's no note on which to begin a letter, especially after you've listened to similar diatribes in the flesh for a week. What I really wanted to say was a small thank-you, for everything. Gwyn, I know, will write to you for herself, but it's for me to tell you how clearly I feel the new cohesion and form in her now. Wastwood gave her what she wanted, what The Little House once gave to me; a pause in which to reassemble, and master all over again in their new pattern, the dispersed details of her life. She has re-formed herself now, to cope with a world lacking Johnny. I think you felt, in those quiet evenings in the dusk, how the process went on ceaselessly within her. She made no attempt to hide it; I think she set about it deliberately, seeing that it had to be done. Whatever her decision, she has it clear now. She can and will go on living with all her heart, and mind and energy, and intelligence. I am much easier about her.

We had rather an interesting journey back yesterday, as things turned out. The morning train was pleasantly full, but only pleasantly so, and we found ourselves in company with a Dutch soldier and an airman who turned out, after puzzling us for some time, to be a Czech. The poor lad had no cigarettes, and we opened the ball by offering him one. After that he was Gwyn's child. It was because he was a pilot, of course. She set herself to draw him out, as if the Johnny motif had become a sort of sublimated love and kindness for all young men with wings. He didn't need much drawing. His English was not good, but it was graphic, and he had a great sense of humour, sharper perhaps than the English, but remarkably similar. A shrewd, formidable, quiet, long-memoried people, the Czechs. I think there must be something in what Strang told me when I saw him last week. He said the Germans fear the Czechs more than any other nation, because they mix ridicule with their hate. This boy was in the true lineal descent from Schweik, and escaped from Moravia just after the outbreak of war after serving in a German labour battalion for four months; during which time, I wouldn't mind betting, he had the same demoralising effect on that labour battalion as Schweik had on the Austrian army. More power to him and all his kind.

He was travelling to Liverpool, as we were. I don't know where he's stationed, but he now has a standing invitation to quarters, and we shall look forward to seeing him. I think Gwyn can be trusted to make it clear to all susceptible young men that her friendship is to be accepted impersonally or not at all. I should hate to think that he or any other boy like him might be broken against the memory of Johnny; and believe me, there's no hope of anything else.

Well, the week passed much too quickly, and yet it seems much more than a week since I had anything to do with teleprinters. The noise and heat of the place are quite unfamiliar, and throw me off balance. But that phase is always dazzlingly brief, and by to-morrow it will feel to me as if I have never been out of the place; and from then on until my next release, the unreality will be Wastwood.

I never saw the woods looking quite so lovely, or the trees at their fullest in quite such abundant leaf. And I don't believe I've ever seen you look so well. I can't tell you what a marvellous moment it was, Nick, when you wheeled yourself out in the new chair to meet us. I'd always – yes, always without exception – seen you flat on your back, and the sight of you propped half-upright with pillows and propelling yourself down the garden path towards me, between the roses – well, it made my heart turn over. I know it was meant as a

wonderful surprise, and so it was, utterly wonderful.
But you should have told me. You should have warned
me, Nick Crane. It was a shock in its way; I wanted to
scream first, because I thought you were venturing
something you shouldn't have attempted, just to please
me; and then I wanted to howl because it was so marvellous.
Oh, Nick, we shall do it yet, I know we shall. You
shall sit upright again. You shall walk again. I shall
show you Cawsand, and Meavy, and Polhawn. You
shall walk along the sea with me on that cliff path,
with the spray beating up over us, and Kingsand clock-
tower red in the distance above the rocks all purple and
green. It must be possible. It shall be possible. Having
submitted to so much in these twenty years past, there
must be some worthwhile answer to it all.

It doesn't sound so great an advance, does it, for
twenty-odd years and about twelve operations? Just
the difference between lying flat and and being
propped up at an angle of forty-five degrees, but it
gives you a quarter of the world back again. It was
grand to be able to take you with us into the woods; and
how grand it must be for you to be able to take yourself
there alone, as with the new chair you can. Like coming
to life again. But no, that's not just to you. No one ever
was more acutely alive than you, and this return to
independent activity enlarges only your resources, not
your scope. Isn't it odd, after all this time, to see
Saxon's face at a normal angle? I wish it was better
worth looking at, for your sake.

I didn't tell you, because I was a shade startled
myself, and had to think it out – I didn't tell you about
that last week-end at home. I know I've changed, I
know my ideas have changed during the past six

months or so; but nothing had happened to make me take stock of my attitude to things. And in those two days at home it did happen.

You know our M.P. was lost at sea very early in the war. They've just concluded the necessary arrangements for presuming his death, and are busy filling his seat. There's an official candidate, of course, with the blessing of the electoral truce on his head. Probably quite a good man, but certainly one never heard of in the division until now. We know nothing about him, nothing at all. But just because another man, whose name at any rate we know, has chosen to present himself in opposition, with a more vigorous prosecution of the war as his programme – well, you'd think hell itself had been busy in Hillingham breathing out contagion to the world. The press was full of letters of support from influential – or once-influential – conservatives; and the hoardings were covered with a liberal splashing of the cause of the paper shortage. Good books are failing to reach the public because the publishers simply can't get the paper to print them on; but our candidate has his photograph, in good rich sepia on two-colour posters four feet by three, on every spare bit of board in Hillingham, with the extraordinary caption: 'The Man Churchill wants'.

Now ordinary people like you and I may think that the other ordinary people should cast their vote – the one sole voice they have in the disposal of their ideals and their lives – for the man *they* want. We may even think that they should do some hard considering before they choose him, too. But to suggest, in that singularly simple way, that they should hand their ballot papers to Churchill to fill in for them, because he is all-wise and they fools and sons of fools, is a thing so patently anti-democratic that it knocked the breath out of me. Have I really changed so much? Should I, once upon a time and not so many months ago, have accepted that argument as a legitimate one? I have only one voice, and it speaks for me, for me, not Churchill nor any other person outside me. He can be an influence; he is an influence, but no more. I vote as my intelligence and my perceptions advise me, and my errors and my triumphs are alike mine.

Well, I saw red. I cried up Churchill, heaven knows, when he was outside the pale, a sort of Parliamentary Cassandra, own brother to the writing on the wall. But those posters and that abominable slogan stank of a curious kind of political blackmail, and some new sensibility in me was mortally offended. So I went to see Strang.

Polling day is next Friday. I wish I could be there, but I can't, and at any rate I left a shout behind. I said: 'For the love of heaven, Gil, let me have one third of a column in Wednesday evening's issue, when it's too late for anybody to get my arguments completely out of their heads before the poll.' He said: 'There'll still be time for the other side to get their case in at the end.' I said: 'Who's trying to stop them? All I want is a hearing for mine.'

So he said: 'Go ahead.' And I wrote him a new sort of electioneering manifesto. I told them that the party truce was being used as an asbestos blanket to stifle the first spark of individual thought or criticism. I said that the greater part of government of the people by the people and for the people was condensed into one small vote per person; that this was the ordinary man's sole voice, nationally speaking, and that if he gave it away to Churchill or anyone else he was cutting out his own tongue; that a nation could not grow to maturity except by the growth of its individuals, by their assumption of responsibility for their own actions and their selection of their own courses. I said that the implication that the collective will should submit itself in blind faith to one man's idea of what was good for it was an evasion of duty and a betrayal of democracy. I didn't tell them to vote either this way or that way to please me, but to make up their own minds and vote accordingly.

But the devil of it is I know they won't. The fact is we are not yet an adult people. We like to think we have the right to grumble, and say what we choose about our public figures, but for all that we've allowed ourselves to be kept in the pockets of mistaken leaders for twenty-five years. We like to find a superman; it gives us an excuse to close our eyes and fold our hands and be carried. But supermen being far to seek, we're beginning to see the stature of our leaders through magnifying lenses, so that our consciences may be soothed, and we ride easy. But we're waking up, Nick, we are waking up. I climbed out of the political pocket somewhere between my joining-up and now. Others, I know, have found their eyes opening in the same way. Only not enough of us. Not yet.

Did it take a war, then, to draw this people to its full stature? Did there have to be a war to make us stand up and open our eyes and see how we're being cheated? Could only this unbelievable disaster make socialists out of people like me? Oh, Nick, is that what it's for?

There are times when I could almost believe it. If you could witness, as I have, the appalling ignorance of some of the girls here – the very small minority, let me say at once, but oh, so unavoidable – their utter lack of consideration for other people, their pre-feudal ideals of class distinction, you would know how I feel. Let me quote you a few of their choicer remarks. On the occasion of Warships Week here, when we were asked for volunteers to recruit Wrens in the town, one of us – I am generous, and she is nameless – protested: 'But we don't *want* to recruit Lancashire girls.' Or try and think how it felt to hear another one say: 'Isn't it disgusting to think that these niggers walk about actually on the same pavement as you! In India they wouldn't even be allowed to walk on the same side of the street.' How many centuries back would you expect to have to look for a remark like that? I heard it last night.

Admittedly these are fools, who don't even think when they speak; but that unthinking speech should take such a form is the symptom of their disease. That they take such remarks for granted, instead of uttering them with deliberate malice, makes the crime more horrible and the disease less curable. Can you wonder that France tore the well-meaning aristocrats in pieces? To change them was impossible. They did not understand, they were incapable of learning. They could only be destroyed.

I am standing well back, and looking at our democracy. And a poor half-hearted thing it is, though it means so universally well. What have we of equality? Equal opportunity? Rubbish, and we all know it. Equal circumstances? Oh, God, even the complacent don't suggest that. Instead they argue against the attempt, saying that slum-dwellers will make slums wherever they go. As if the hopeless can learn in one generation to reject the squalor urged upon them for centuries. Do you know, Nick, our democracy is a bit of a mirage, after all; nice to look at, but it won't stand wear and tear. It's a free country, ours, a humane country; provided you keep your hands off the sacred person of Property, the chief of our household gods.

And yet if that was all of it I should go out and shoot myself or something. It isn't all. There's a sort of blundering, tenacious, patient greatness about the people of this odd country; even their tolerance of things as they are has been formed not quite from lethargy, but from a monumental slow devotion to justice, and a resolve not to entertain anger until they know every facet of every side of the case. The body of Britain is a chained Prometheus, and certainly vultures devour its liver unceasingly. But oh, let me live to see it unbound!

Yes, I have changed. Once I thought everything perfect in our perfect country, and I really don't think I loved it very much. Now I see it diseased and wronged and struggling and foolish, and I love it quite terribly. It's easy to say one would die for a thing, and not so easy to do the dying. But I do believe one could love this incredibly blind, insufferably long-suffering England enough to die without regret in its name. Dulce et decorum, etc. You can't get away from it. It *is* a sweet and seemly thing.

But there are people, I expect, who will say I have thrown my weight into a movement to hamper the war effort. I've done my level best to create – not the notorious 'alarm and despondency', perhaps, but certainly argument and anger. And to them that will be the act of a traitor; because the state in which they believe is the old state, the established Britain as She Was. But my loyalty is paid to quite a different person, the new state, Britain as, by God, She Shall Be.

Yes, Nick Crane, I have changed. Service life is a queer affair, full of happy companionships salted with a few wild antipathies. It is any other communal life condensed, deepened and aggravated, and much of what I've learned came to me with the way of it; and much more with Tom Lyddon. And I think it was from him I learned that patriotism has nothing to do with national pride, any more than love has to do with approval of the beloved. But it has a great deal to do with the insatiable longing to do away with all unworthiness in one's country, to have the beloved admirable and admired. It needs a lover's eyes, keener and more jealous than a friend's, to see the blemishes in England's face.

At home they wouldn't understand that attitude. To them, quite simply, the loved thing must be lovely. As for me, I am an unaccountable being, allowed by my profession to indulge a temperament which faintly disquiets but at the same time pleases them. Bless them both, who wants to spoil things for them?

Write soon, and don't be afraid to slate my third of a column. It was rushed, and not written as I would have liked; but I mean it every word. And now, for the good of my body, not my soul, I am going out gardening, and down comes the curtain for an hour or so on politics, and parties, and classes, and all the petty divisions between man and man which so plague

Your adolescent Saxon

PS. – Yes, you're right. The voice is the voice of

Catherine, but the vision is the vision of Tom Lyddon, feminised and robbed of half its generosity, but still Tom's. You see it isn't always blind; sometimes it cures blindness.

W.R.N.S. Quarters, Liverpool.
June 18th, 1941.

My dear Nick,

Your letter reached me yesterday afternoon. It was nice of you to send on the snapshots. They're very good, and he would have liked them. But of course it's no use now.

I meant to write to you last night, but I sat and sat with the pen in my hand, and nothing would come. It's silly to let myself be numbed like this by something I always knew might happen to me at any moment; and it isn't as if we hadn't talked about it, even, and agreed between us that it couldn't do a thing against us. Only just now that seems a long way off and a long while ago. And it can, and does, do something very dreadful to me. But that's all over now. I've thought about it all night, and I'm getting the hang of it. Like learning to live without eyes; because blindness doesn't kill, and no more can I expect to die of it just because he's dead.

He is dead, you see. He must have been dead for nearly three weeks, and I didn't know. You wouldn't think it possible, would you, to love anybody that much and yet not feel anything wrong when he died? It proves all the romantics are liars. There wasn't any moment when I felt him go. There wasn't any moment when my thoughts left him, either. Even when I slept and didn't dream the very drifting into sleep was a sort of journey to him. I shall have a long way to go now, sleeping or waking, before I come in sight and sound and touch of Tom Lyddon again.

The official notification was waiting for me when I came off duty at midday yesterday. Just the usual sort of thing, so brief it didn't seem to mean anything, only some bit of office formula. Regret to inform you Private T. Lyddon missing, believed killed. I couldn't expect more, and yet what there was didn't seem to get home. I don't know why. I suppose it's human nature to shut up one's wits against bad news. I went on reading and reading it for a long time before it sank in. I wasn't so clear-headed about it as Gwyn, but then it was no young war-god who was taken away from me, it was plain Tom Lyddon, an ordinary man to anyone but me.

Well, the curtain's shut down now. I know what it means, very well I know it. I haven't told a soul, not even Gwyn, until this moment when I tell you; because no one but you has ever been told his significance living, and no one would understand how much of me dies with his death. I guaranteed myself privacy, anyway. No one will come sympathising with me, no one will know I've graduated as an object for sympathy. As far as the people here are concerned nothing at all has happened, and I haven't any dead to cry over. Not that I've wanted to cry. It hasn't taken me in those inadequate ways. It's no trouble to keep my face straight before the watch, no trouble to go on with my work. Only I don't seem to be quite awake or alive, somehow. I suppose that passes over, too. Everything does.

If my friends here knew the facts I suppose they would try to comfort me by saying that he may not be dead, that missing men often come back, that while there's life there's hope. Do you see much hope for the few British soldiers left alive in Crete? No, that's not for me. They waited long enough, God knows, before telling me he was lost. No more of our men will get out of Crete, unless as prisoners of war. And Tom will never be made a prisoner. I know him well enough for that. No, they don't say 'believed killed' unless they're pretty sure about it. They don't say 'killed' unless they have indisputable proof. Do them justice, they're very scrupulous about raising false hopes or killing legitimate ones. No, I know men believed dead have survived before now, I know missing men have come home. But not from Crete.

Isn't it odd that I, who have spent my life shutting my eyes to probabilities and wrestling with accomplished facts, optimist to the point of lunacy, and sometimes with justification in the end, should be so realistic in accepting this worst blow of all? But I do accept it. There's nothing else to do, and I prefer to do it now, quietly, with dignity, rather than wait until I'm battered into acquiescence by the accumulation of despair. I don't expect that any miracles will be worked for me. I don't think I believe in miracles.

He's dead. That's all about it. Tom's dead. I've got to do without him; I shall never see him again.

Well, Gwyn said all there is to be said. He's not the only one who's dead, and I'm not the only one who's got to go on living. It's a fairly common problem, these days, how to get along without the main pillar of your life. Lots of people have solved it. Some, a great many,

I think, by closing the door on what's past and starting from the beginning again. But I wouldn't want to do that, even if I could. I don't want ever to forget one moment of the time we had together, nor one word of all we said to each other. As for ever feeling about any one else as I did and do about him, the mere idea is ridiculous. No, there's no solution that way. I'm twenty-eight. I know my own mind. There'll be no second Tom Lyddon.

Besides, I can't and don't believe that I've altogether lost him. I've never been a religious person, Nick, but I can't help having a strong faith in individual survival after death. And then, knowing him – oh, no, he couldn't be extinguished like a candle, his ideas couldn't be quenched all in a moment, like that. Tom could only be killed, not silenced. So I'll wait. I think I shall meet him again. Yes, even now I do believe that. The difficulty is to believe that I've seen my last of him in the flesh. And yet every leave-taking may turn out to be a final one; how many millions are dead by now, in how many countries, and every one leaves someone trying to understand, trying to realise that he's gone, that he'll never come back. Never in this world.

I have so much to thank God for. I might so easily never have met him. I might so easily have been married to John before I met him. Or even meeting as we did, we might have felt about each other in a different way. There are so many ways of loving people, so many ways of being loved. There are men who have to be loved to the exclusion of everyone and everything else, so that your world narrows to the width of their shoulders; and there are men who have to be loved blindly and abjectly, with your eyes covered and your ears stopped.

But Tom wasn't like that. No, you couldn't be in love with him without feeling and sharing the currents that moved him, until your heart and your intellect expanded to take in all the best hopes of humanity. You couldn't love him without loving your fellow men, you couldn't love him and remain undeveloped and indifferent. Something he wrote in one of his letters from Greece keeps running and running through my head. 'To see chaos but remain outside it is not my idea of peace, nor yours, I know. All the trouble in the world belongs to us.'

I am not much. But such as I am, I am because I knew him; and I know it's better worth being by far than the person I used to be.

So you see, death to either of us was logical and acceptable. We were responsible people, with our eyes wide open, and the stake we placed, which was our own and each other's lives and all the promise of our mutual happiness, we placed deliberately, knowing very well what its loss would mean. Well, we have lost. His debt is paid, and mine is being paid now. We're not going to cry over it. Gamblers might, but an act as purposeful as ours is no gamble. We offered a price for the thing we wanted for the world, and the price has been claimed. That's that. I find no regret in my mind. I've no complaint to make. We knew what we were about.

Yes, that's the secret of it. We were no conscripts for freedom, but volunteers. Tom offered to die, if need arose. It isn't easy to try and formulate now what was never said, even between us two. But I think there was only one condition made to that offer. He stipulated that he should receive full value for his life; that he should die to the world's advantage, usefully, every ounce of his strength, every drop of his blood, spent by a wise bargainer towards the purchase of justice and liberty. Yes, that was implicit. Money given for a considered purpose must in fairness to the giver be competently administered. When lives are given, the responsibility of the administrator is so much greater; and if he misappropriates those lives, his guilt is so much the darker, and so much more widely divorced from all possible forgiveness.

And I have had qualms. Why deny it? Do you remember I once wrote: 'I wish I knew how far I could trust them with my valuables'? That sticks in my mind, too, for no very clear reason that I can see. Yes, I have had doubts. I have been afraid. I have found myself wishing that someone else had the using of Tom, someone who carried more conviction than any of the present High Command, someone who inspired more trust than any of the present government. But now that the fund has run out, now that he's dead, I think I'm easier about that than ever I've been. I'm not looking for scapegoats. Mistakes there have been, but mistakes are human. And the great point is that he had no complaints. He did, now and again, express misgivings about the outcome, but he said also that in the circumstances everything man could do had been done. He knew how he was being used, and he has never in his letters to me uttered either accusation or reproach. And until he cries out I will be mute.

So there's no bitterness, you see, none at all. I don't know how he died, and it will always be hurtful to me that I was shut out of that part of his experience; I don't know, and no agonies of imagination can ever help me to understand, what he had to bear. But I know he never grudged either effort or pain, the wounds or the dying, the farewell to the past or the loss of the future, as part of the price of freedom. What he could accept gladly, so can I.

I never thought what a difference that could make. Even having that peace in me, sometimes while the pain is new I seem to turn round and look at it again, and see it for the first time, and it's like having the cold of the sea break over me. It comes back just as before, just as when it first took me and stopped my breath; and I think: 'He's gone. He's dead. You'll never see him again. He's not coming back.' If I couldn't answer myself then that he set out on that journey prepared for no return, that I saw him depart knowing and not complaining that I might see no more of him in this world, I think I should drown in that sea. As things are I know that I shall weather it. So much and a great deal more is due to Tom Lyddon. He is my disease and he is the cure, the cavern of longing and the core of content both. Yes, I have a great deal to thank God for.

But if you knew how I want him, if you only knew. It doesn't take very long for a person like Tom to take hold of one's life and wrap it round himself like a cloak, so that the warmth of him touches every fold of it. That makes my life now just a cast-off garment, already growing cold. Oh, Nick, never love anyone this way unless you're willing to lose them this way, too. For if I were a shade less sure of what we wanted in our union and want now even more insatiably in our separation I couldn't go on living. But I am quite sure.

Once they cried out against the suggestion that war has grandeur. But it has, and who will deny it now? Dulce et decorum est—— That was no mawkish attitude struck by an immature schoolboy, but one of

251

those tremendous utterances which only great men can frame so simply, and only men in their greatness can fully understand. And Tom died for a bigger thing by far than his native land; he died for the liberty and dignity and brotherhood of man.

Have I made him into a giant? I didn't mean that. He was only a man like other men, though like no other man to me. He wouldn't want to be set aside from them by even one pace. He was just a private soldier who happened to believe in the things he was fighting for. There must be a great many of him in the British Army. A great many of him, too, left to root or rot in the soil of Crete.

Death, even with a war prodding at its elbow, is very impartial. First Johnny, you see, then Tom. Johnny dead in good time, before his improbable excellence was diminished by being brought down to earth; and Tom taken out of time, strong because his feet were firmly planted on the ground, and his friends saw him not through a glass darkly, but face to face. The legend, and the reality. Well, they've both gone. Her Johnny in a blaze of glory and a frenzy of applause; and my Tom just quietly, with his tools in his hands and no one looking on. Well, that's it. They went their several ways about it, but they both knew where they were going.

Nick, some day I shall go back to The Little House. I said once that I should never go there again, but I think that I shall; after the war is over, by myself, at the same time of the year, to see if he left something there which I can't find. I mean his youth. He will always be about me, wherever I go, so vividly that sometimes in the dusk I shall almost be willing to believe I see him, and his arm brushes mine. But he comes very sombrely now, very darkly, perhaps because the world is so far from being the world he wants it to be. When I first knew him he laughed, and had leisure sometimes to play with squirrels. In The Little House, when the war is over, perhaps I shall find the echo of his laugh left from the happy time. If he had lived we could never have found our way back into that timeless island; alone, I may be admitted, and if God is very good I shall find him there.

It's growing dusk, and in the corner of the garden there's a small cold wind stirring. I'd better go in. Life goes on; and I must sleep, or how can I work? He hadn't much to leave me, I think, but he left me his part of the war, to finish for him. And so I will finish it, or die fighting.

Don't worry about me, I am going to be all right. And please don't write to me yet. Leave me alone for a little while, and I shall get it straightened out once for all. I don't want you to be anxious about me; nothing is going to happen that shouldn't happen. I know what I'm doing. But just now I have to keep myself apart from everyone until I find out how best to carry this pain; even from you, my dear, dear Nick, for the first time in my life. I promise to write to you again before too long, and until then I shall know and be glad that you think often of

Your Catherine.

X. LETTERS FROM CRETE

W.R.N.S. Quarters, Liverpool.
June 23rd, 1941.

Dear Nick,

Just as I was getting things straight something happens that puts me right back to the beginning again. I'm all confused in my mind, and so I'm not going to try and tell you anything of my own thoughts; only to send you these, and explain how I came by them, and leave you to discover in yourself the stages of my confusion, and to come to some conclusion, perhaps mine, perhaps not mine. No comment from me. Not yet. Not until I know how the gale sets that blows me.

Don't untie the green string yet. Let me tell you first how this packet came to me. And then, when Catherine has been read, begin the reading of Tom Lyddon.

I was beginning to settle down; and if it wasn't easy it wasn't so difficult as I expected it to be. And then yesterday morning, when I was tired and haggard and altogether unpresentable after a night-watch, not bathed nor rested, a man came and rang our front-door bell and asked for me. I couldn't think who it could be; no one I knew was in these parts. And when I went out to him it was someone I didn't know, someone I'd never seen before in my life. He was American, a big lanky person somewhere in the thirties, and he said his name was Lee Wallace, and he was war correspondent for some U.S. syndicate. He'd just got out of Crete by one of the last boats, and made his way back from Egypt by air. He said he'd met Tom in Crete, and Tom had given him a packet to bring home to me; because, you see, Tom and his unit were left behind with the rearguard. And then he fished this same little bundle out of his pocket and gave it to me. I've done it up again just as it was, in its oilskin envelope and green string; I don't know why, but it seemed a natural thing to do. So you see it just as I saw it.

I told him that Tom was officially dead, and he said what I've thought all along, that there was hardly a hope in the world of his being anything else. You can't think how strange it seemed to be sitting there in the hall at quarters, with the sun just coming in at the windows, and to talk about Tom to someone who had been with him so short a time ago. I'm afraid he was awfully sorry for me, and I don't want anyone to feel that way; but he praised Tom, and no one who does that can stay out of my favour. And he told me a little of his own travels, how he'd had to run from Belgrade after the bombing, turning his back on the indescribable confusion of Yugo-Slavia for the comparative calm and order of Greece; and how in turn he'd had to leave Greece in the evacuation from Rafti, attaching himself to a New Zealand battalion; and then the run continuing with Crete, until he was hustled away from Tom and his friends for his own safety's sake, and pushed thankfully into an Egypt which didn't interest him very much. He told me that he was going home now by way of Lisbon, to render account of himself and do some retrospect writing; because few correspondents had his opportunity of seeing the holocaust of Crete at first hand. I asked him, after that what? And he said after that Russia, if he had his way.

There's no lack of material, at any rate, for war correspondents. The whole world seems to be their stamping-ground. Now if Japan takes fire, as it seems she must do sooner or later, Lee Wallace and his kind will be in their native element clean round the globe. But I think if I were in his place I should want to make for Russia, too. There's the unknown quantity. All the ordinary man's views of the new order there have been purveyed views, carefully sifted through a sieve of the prejudice of the British governing body. We've been neither encouraged nor allowed to investigate more closely. There was the alien race, the destroyers, the enemy of all order and law. Now that veil will have to be raised, since they are in the fight with us shoulder to shoulder. Unless we are to believe ourselves wholly malignant we cannot believe them so. What will follow the gradual filling in of that abyss of ignorance with regard to Russia remains to be seen; but I have a feeling it will turn out to be one of the widest and wildest steps from the past world to the future world. But let that go. The fog has only just begun to lift; time enough to see the horizon clearly when it has all blown away.

But although this man talked freely about most aspects of this awful business, he was quiet about Crete. I feel that all those who survived that hottest corner of hell will freeze into silence over the things they saw. As the Poles close their wounds over Warsaw and will not bleed. Oh, Nick, I am so tired, so very tired. I want it to end.

He was very kind about Tom. He had business in Liverpool, as it happened, and so preferred to deliver his trust in person rather than risk it even in the English post, which was all Tom had asked. He says that Tom knew he was going to stay behind, that he would have no other opportunity of reaching me; and that he spent the last quiet hour before the final detachment left writing a letter to me. The last one of these and of all his letters. The summing-up, if you like.

I've read them through only once, and it's as if every word is cut into my mind, so that wherever I turn my eyes I see his scrawl on that thin, soiled paper, saying terrible things. Terrible as an army without banners is a better simile than the one in the Bible. Tom's army – not the khaki one, but the other, the one he was in at Barcelona, as at Thermopylae – waves no flags, but some day those who stand in its path will say to the mountains, fall on us, and to the rocks, cover us.

There are passages I can't get out of my mind. You will read them, and know why. The dead do speak, after all, you see, so loud that I shall never be able to stop hearing as long as I live.

I said there should be no comment from me, and this is comment, so no more of it. I want you to read these few letters from Greece and Crete as coming from him, not from me. Only send them back to me soon. I can't bear to let them go far away from me, or stay away long. They are the only part of Tom Lyddon that he could leave with

Catherine.

(The enclosures follow.)

Thermopylae.
April 23rd, 1941.

My dearest Catherine,

I have just been up to the summit of the Hill of Leonidas, where they say the Spartans made their stand against Persia. The place can't have changed very greatly since that day. There are even bits of a barrier wall here which may be almost old enough to have sheltered the Spartans in that onset when the Persian arrows darkened the sun. It's the Dorniers that darken the sun now.

Just now everything is quiet and curiously still. This is a beautiful place, a space between salt marsh and sea on one hand and sheer cliffs on the other. The narrow plain runs all up the coast, and shrinks here to its narrowest. There are hot springs that break out from under the rocks, and wander steamily down into the marshes and the sea. Fringes of pines dip towards the water here and there, leaning over narrow beaches where the hardiest of us bathe in our few leisure moments. Once we were machine-gunned in the water, and one of the fellows was killed. Imagine coming so far to die naked, playing in the surf. As yet it's cold sport, but at midday the sun on the water gives it a suggestion of warmth, and from the monotony of being hunted this interlude of staying put gives at least an illusion of relief.

Once, when Leonidas was alive, no doubt this strong point in the hands of determined men was practically invulnerable. So it would be now if only we had something in the air to cover us; but the plain truth is we haven't, and the enemy dive-bombers and machine-gunners do what they like with us. We've given up looking for any support in the air, having looked so long and so vainly. But what's become of all that rising flood of war material the workmen at home are being urged to turn out? Where are the 'planes and the tanks which we are told so endlessly are 'rolling in ever-increasing numbers off the assembly lines'? Not here, I take my oath on that. Not in Libya, surely, or why that recoil back to the Egyptian frontier and beyond? Where do they go? If they're being stored in England against a hypothetical day when it shall rain Jerries, I can only say the rain has already washed the heart out of Athens. And if those ever-increasing numbers are merely a figment of somebody's comfortable imagination, then the sooner somebody is shot the more hope for us all.

We've no need to be ashamed of the way we've fought here in Greece. Man against man, no-one could have done more. But if we had had the air strength they would never have taken the northern passes; and surely somewhere in the world there must be a man or a group of men who know *why* we didn't get it. I wish to God I knew where to look for the answer, but it's a thing no-one seems to know.

Yet it hasn't been all our fault. Yugo-Slavia, on whom the Greek left rested implicitly, melted away like snow in front of the Germans. They were not ready, either in equipment or positions, to withstand that pressure, for the powers that were had dispersed them according to their own plans of non-resistance; and like many another country, they found one day long enough to save their souls, but nowhere near long enough to go any appreciable way towards saving their lives. So they were driven harder than they could bear, and they broke, and they broke us too. Our northern positions were good enough for a frontal attack, but they came at us front and flank, and hit the join of Greek and British forces like a steam hammer, and the joint gave.

I was on the Haliakmon for one day. I saw the New Zealanders at work on the south bank of the river, gunning the German assault boats as they came over. The Haliakmon ran red and black instead of silver, and its sand wasn't white any more. We killed and killed them, and still they came. Fragments of boats and bodies washed up along the sands at the borders of the gorge, until we grew sick and tired of killing, from the very monotony of it. And they never did force that passage. But a few New Zealanders sitting in the steep crannies of the Haliakmon pass couldn't hold the line balanced, and we were withdrawn gradually southward to make our main stand there. By that time, though we had no means of knowing it, our line to the left of the Haliakmon positions was bent back into Thessaly, and the enemy were pouring in three streams southward, the centre column rushing through the Monastir Gap, the right advancing from Kleisura upon the western part of Thessaly, and the left creeping down from Salonica along the coastal plain, aiming at the Vale of Tempe. At least that's how I read the general lay-out from what accounts have reached us up to now; for generally speaking we, who do the dying, are the great uninformed, inevitably so because we exist where news can scarcely penetrate.

We had some bad moments on that withdrawal. It isn't easy to quit unforced positions, even with an eye to the larger strategy. After that we were pretty well aware that anything could happen to the campaign. I wrote to you from Kalabaka on our way north, though God alone knows if you got my letter. That was in the midst of it, with everything still smooth and easy. Believe me, Kalabaka wasn't like that on the return journey. We had a bad day there, and a worse night, in a rocky valley without a patch of cover, with mountain batteries moving up to our range and the sky alive with Dorniers; but we held our position while the bulk of the supporting infantry were extricated behind us, and the line moved back contracting on Pharsalus. I don't think I expected to write to you again after that night; but in the early hours of the morning the pressure eased and a part of the air cover was deflected eastward, and what was left of us, only the rags of a battalion, scuttled after the main body and came safely to our new positions, north of Pharsalus. We fight backwards and forwards over old battlefields – chiefly backwards – with every move we make here; and something primitive clings to the whole style of our warfare. Positions are chosen purely from a land-fighting point of view; ours because we have virtually no air strength to be considered, theirs because having all the air strength there is they don't have to consider it. Thermopylae has held, in its day, Turks as well as Persians; and again it will be held as long as flesh and blood stand the strain; but if you could see how this historical fortress of nature lies open and naked to assault from the air I believe you would even venture to pity us. We are doing exactly what the Greeks did in the fifth century B.C., and the Germans are behaving much as the Persians did then. History repeats itself, but with a difference. Impassable barriers no longer exist. If you cannot climb Kallidromos you can fly over it.

Actually we have been lucky here. We were drawn back here three days ago, before the general trek south began on those devastated Greek roads. We, and the poor remnants of several other units as battered as ourselves, were pushed together into a composite battalion, and given a breather to get ourselves into shape for the last stand. For the first day it was wonderfully peaceful, for the German air force was still occupying itself with

Yugo-Slavia, in its usual deadly methodical way of doing one job at a time, and the skies were clear, fitfully sunny and grey, and there was a wonderful quietness about this piney place that made us silent in our turn. We bathed in the hot springs, and walked along the edges of the marsh, and the war receded wildly out of our knowledge, so that it seemed lunatic, as well as shameful, to be digging slit trenches in the slopes of anemones and moving up our few guns to positions commanding the Gates beyond the belts of black pine. But on the second and third days the dive-bombing and machine-gunning began, gathering way gradually until now they all but fill the days for us; the night they never loved, especially in these deceptive airy regions, with the slopes of Kallidromos ready and waiting to crumple their noses at any miscalculation. We've made the best of the cover the pines give, and our desperately inadequate anti-aircraft armament is disposed to the best advantage, and has discouraged them from pressing too closely home upon our particular spot. But the convoys coming southward tell us the main roads are hell, crowded as they are with lorries and tanks and gun carriers and men, and absolutely uncovered to air attack. English, Australians, New Zealanders, Greek and a few Yugo-Slavs all share between them the two or three workable roads. How long we can keep them open is a gambler's guess. What happens to us when we can no longer keep them open is no guess at all, but a certainty.

So it seems pretty clear that Yugo-Slavia is dead and done for. The vultures wouldn't leave that corpse while there was a twitch left in it. They're inhumanly consistent, the Germans. They believe in finishing one job – yes, to the last nail in the coffin – before they turn their hands to another. But they have finished it. In a few days now I think the total weight of their Luftwaffe will be deflected on to our position here, and particularly on to the roads which make it tenable. Those roads will be swept incessantly by the Spring rains of the new order, machine-gun bullets and bombs; only in the night, which oddly enough is the only time the powers of darkness cease to be omnipotent, will there be any respite; and we, like moles and other shy creatures, shall emerge from our earths only by night. What a world!

So the next coffin will be for Greece, if any tomb can contain so much beauty and gallantry and grief. There's no shadow of doubt of the outcome now. Koryzis saw it coming, and couldn't bear to live through it; the army of the Epirus is gone; our line across the narrow neck defending Athens, from Thermopylae round Mount Oeta and Parnassus to the Gulf of Corinth, is in action at almost every yard, but unbroken. I think it cannot be broken, and God knows that is a lot to say; but I know that with transport crippled and reserves non-existent it can be rendered useless, an isolated, wonderful, dreadful gesture, like the Westerplatte at Danzig. Heroism without hope or aim but death is surely the last, most frightful renunciation of the world; a turning of one's face to the wall, a shaking off from one's feet of the dust of the earth for an accusation against it. To live is to be useful again. We as a nation are not given to these savage, magnificent suicides; but there, we live on an island, where so far there have been no Westerplattes.

No, I don't think they will leave us here to write another chapter in the history of despair. I have a feeling that there will soon be what the Nazis have always boasted they would give us, a second Dunkirk. Better to retrieve what can be used again. Already there's talk of embarkation ports in the Peloponnese, Nauplia and Megara and Kalumata. They say the Piraeus is totally unusable from raids; it must have been quite an easy place to destroy. Athens has suffered, too; better bombs on the Acropolis than Germans, God knows, but I fail to see how anything human can save that glorious city now.

What tanks we have left are in action now north of the pass. To-morrow the shock will come back to us. Catherine, if these letters should ever reach you, remember when you read them that I love you, for it will not be said very often. I have been writing of Greece, not of Catherine, and I know women who would find that no compliment. But to you it won't seem strange that I should be haunted by the ghost of this country, and talk to you about the Acropolis instead of about your eyes. Nor very strange that I should be unable, even if I believed you wanted it, to soothe you by making the dangers less than they are, or shutting them out altogether. If I loved you even a little less I should not tell you the half. What I have I neither can nor will hold you back from sharing, even if it's a slow bleeding to death over failures and losses. My mind, and all that's in it, is open for you to go in and out as you please. That's what you want of me, I know. That's what I want you to have.

My ghosts accumulate. Poland, Czecho-Slovakia, Spain, Abyssinia, China, Greece – and as yet only Abyssinia laid. Others have gone down, but these are my dead. Catherine, my heart, we have a long way to go.

On board the transport 'Berenice',
two hours out from Monemvasia.
0600 hours, April 30th, 1941.

It's light enough now to write, and quiet enough, so at last I can tell you something of what's happening to us here. For the past five days I've been aching to get back to you, and never a moment's leisure day or night from fighting and running and running and fighting. In every half hour of lull we fell instantly asleep where we lay, but it never lasted long, the pressure was too great for that. Now that I could sleep I don't want to. Most of the other fellows have found corners for themselves and passed clean out. I couldn't sleep now if I tried.

I'm sitting on the deck of the 'Berenice', with my back against a bulkhead and my feet propped against our piled rifles. The whole deck is littered with soldiers, and their equipment. The crew pick their way up and down between the sleepers silently. Everything about our passage is singularly silent and quick, and wisely so, for we are still within very easy range of aircraft from Greece, though less prone to attack, I imagine, than the main convoys from Rafti and Rafina and Nauplia. So far, at any rate, we have sailed in comparative peace. The stars are pale almost to invisibility now; while we lay there under the cliffs waiting for the transports they were brilliant, and more, or seemed more, than ever the skies at home could hold. We had nothing to do but to watch them, and try to pick out various constellations. Vickers and Hale started a heated argument over the position of Orion. It was wonderfully warm – even the nights are warm now – and we were visited only once by a few isolated dive-bombers in all the hours we waited, though the town bore marks of earlier visits.

We quitted our positions at Thermopylae two days after I last wrote to you, on the twenty-fifth. Certain units were drawn away on the night of the twenty-fourth, and left us open next day to the worst and most prolonged air attacks we had during the whole campaign. We lost a great many men, and almost all the tanks we had left. We were dead sure by then that we should be withdrawn almost at once, but it looked as if the rearguard would have a desperate time of it. I expect they did. There'll be thousands of prisoners; I see no way of avoiding it. However, we were among the lucky ones, for our notice to quit came on the following night, while the line was still rigid. Some of the fellows we left behind will be brought off safely, I hope, but a great many won't. Well, I suppose that's the luck of the draw.

That night we went no further than Athens, the first lorries of our column coming into the city about five o'clock in the morning. There was some delay there, and no wonder, for the road from Thebes to Eleusis was solid with transports taking men south and lorries rushing supplies north. Pretty well all the provisioning was being done by night, the days being absolutely impossible. I suppose we met on that journey some of the last supply lorries that ever did go north, for we heard from the crew here when we came aboard tonight that the Germans entered Athens on April 27th. Why our exit was so little hampered in the end is more than I know, except that Monemvasia is only a subsidiary embarkation port, the main flow being from Nauplia and the Attic ports.

The road into Athens was alive with Greek soldiers in

that dawn. We had little room, but such as we could we picked up and carried along with us, for they were in the last stages of tiredness and marched like sleepwalkers. I had a Greek boy – twenty at the most – wedged tight against my shoulder as we came over the last ridge and saw Athens in the dawn, a clean, gracious, shining whiteness in the plain, with Hymettus soaring behind it. He said something in his own language which no one dared asked him to translate though he had English; and I shall never forget the look on his face. Except for his eyes he might have been already dead. By now I expect he is.

He told us that he had been at Rupel. He said that most of his friends had died there, but that he would die nearer home. He was from a village near Marathon. He said that he thought it would have been better to die at Rupel, which is a frontier fort, rather than live to see the same pollution contaminate Athens. I said to him that so far from being violated, Greece had given herself a new crown; and I believe I also said what one seldom says; I quoted the Bible. Even agnostics may do that; almost everything that needs to be said has been said there first and best. I said: 'Fear not them that kill the body, and after have no more that they can do.' And he smiled, and his face was alive again for a moment; but he said that was not much help to a man in love with the dead body. So I left him alone. He knew what it was in him to do, and if he prefers to die who am I to try and dissuade him? In the outskirts of the city he hopped off and left us, and the rest of our Greek passengers went with him.

The streets and squares of the town were crowded with traffic; but it was all orderly and controlled. We were diverted into a quiet square where our particular convoy for the next night's journey was massing, had been massing indeed for some time, ever since the former night's convoy had moved out. No one knew where we were headed for, but they said our predecessors left from Megara.

We spent the whole of that day in Athens. We did a little work, and got some sleep, and some news, all bad. The Germans were in Janina in force, and had pushed some advance units even beyond, on the road to Missolonghi; which boded ill for any convoys we might send over to the ports in the Peloponnese. It was evidently their object to cut us off from any way of escape. Fortunately for us the Greeks are still fighting strongly in those parts.

The middle of the day grew intolerably hot, there between the white pavements and white buildings, and even before the first flight of bombers visited the city we had all gone to earth. It was well to sleep, for we were all half way to exhaustion, and no one knew when we should sleep again. We began the second night's trek almost as soon as it was fully dark, and glad we were to go, for Athens is the last place in the world just now to look for happiness or peace of mind. The faces of the people, quiet as they are, are not to be looked at for long if you want to sleep easy again.

So we left in the moonless night, and drove back through Eleusis as part of a very large, very slow convoy, crawling painfully up the Scironian Cliffs, where the road hangs over a sheer drop, and the darkness becomes a treacherous friend. Most of the time we moved so slowly we could have travelled faster by leaving the lorries behind. Besides the natural hazards the road had been methodically bombed during the day, and the craters filled in too hurriedly, so that the heavy transports and the guns moving up to protect the Isthmus of Corinth had crushed awkward hollows in the softer earth, and our progress was a series of jerks and plunges. Twice we had to dig ourselves out, and once we were brought to a total stop by a commotion ahead, and walking forward found that the lorry in front of us had sunk heavily over to the left and capsized, throwing overboard and pinning down several of its load. Luckily the earth was too soft to afford a dangerous resistance, and the worst-injured was only bruised and half-smothered. Further on we saw the crew of a gun carrying up bodies from a lorry which had driven clean over the edge. There must have been more than one such accident.

The road across the isthmus to the bridges was much easier, and we made good time over it; but in all, the forty miles or so from Athens to Corinth took us eight hours. As an obvious target the canal bridges had been given as strong a guard as was possible with our worn-out forces, and a continual watch was being kept for enemy parachutists. It would have needed only one well-aimed bomb to wreck both the road and rail bridges and repairs would have held up our movements for a day or two at least. No more would have been needed. But so far in a dozen or so daylight attacks, no hit had been made. We swopped greetings with some of the fellows stationed along the the isthmus, and they told us the roads ahead had been badly blasted, and hundreds of transports burned out, with the result that all considerable convoys such as ours were permitted to move on only at night, and must lie up for the day in cover where they could find it. We asked them what were the prospects of air cover, for there was talk of new landing grounds down here in the Peloponnese; but they warned us to expect nothing. The landing ground near Argos had been ploughed up with bombs and a great many newly arrived British planes shot to pieces on the ground. How this could happen no one seemed to know, but happen it had. So we and they were in the same old position, minus any sort of fighter protection. Well, we were all getting used to that.

We moved out of Corinth on the road to Argos, and found ourselves a convenient olive grove, and fell out for the day, for by then it was growing very faintly light. There was plenty of speculation as to where we were going, as we were then on the road to Nauplia; but finally Sergeant Wills told us that we were making further south, for Monemvasia where we should be embarked the following night. That was the intention, but it didn't work out that way.

In view of what followed, that day in the olives was by way of being a blessing. We went a fair way towards catching up with our sleep; but in the dusk, as we were mustering again for the road, the day's last flight of bombers came over later than we'd expected, and got almost half of our transport with a couple of bombs which weren't even aimed. I swear they never saw us; it was simply the careless jettisoning of the last of the load.

We recovered five bodies and three men injured, but not too desperately to travel; and these wounded and our weariest we started off in the lorries which were still serviceable, keeping back only one light lorry, in which the Sergeant and Vickers were to go back into Corinth to commandeer what transport they could for the rest of us. But that wasn't the end of the hitches. The next came while they were away, in the person of a Greek motorcyclist from the nearest village, who told us in amazing English that German parachutists had landed in the low hills just south of Corinth. He was cut off from Corinth by this force, and had made for the Argos road in the hope of picking up English help at once. How Wills and Vickers in the light lorry would fare we couldn't hope to guess; but though parachutists attacking the bridges from the south would have all Corinth between them and their objective, we seemed to be cast for an active part in the business, if only as an extra insurance. Hale went off by motorcycle after the lorry, and the Greek took the rest of us cross country towards the village where the Germans had been sighted. By that time it was just fully dusk, but not so pitch-black as the night before, and going was not too bad.

Luckily for us this parachute raid was on a very small scale. We found one dazed Jerry dragging himself along among the anemones still in his harness, his right leg broken below the knee. He was quite young and very frightened, and talked freely. There was a faint sort of starlight to which I think we were more accustomed than they, for most of the encounters that night went our way purely because we seemed to see them better than they could see us. Once we walked slam into the middle of a machine-gun crew who had gone to earth in a hill position overlooking the road; but they were taken even more completely by surprise than we were, and we got both the gun and the crew for only one man killed and one slightly wounded. The village was very much awake, alive with men and women standing to what arms they could find. They were perfectly calm and quiet, and with our Greek as interpreter helped us considerably. We spent the entire night combing the hills and beating the olive groves for Germans, and rounded up fifty-odd before morning. We had a sentry watching the narrow road for Wills and his lorry – or lorries, as we hoped it would be by this time – though we had no means of knowing whether Hale had overtaken them in time, or whether even so they had got safely through to Corinth. But two or three hours before dawn they came, sure enough, guided by one of the Greek garrison from the city. Hale had overtaken them before they reached the town, and they had driven on, notified the authorities at Corinth, borrowed three or four trucks and a handful of New Zealanders, and made straight for our friend's village. As for trouble, they had had none except one German parachute patrol which had tried to stop them a mile out of the city on their way inward. Vickers drove over them. They smashed the door of the lorry with machine-gun bullets, but missed Vickers. He says one of them leaped aside at the last moment, but one was certainly run down, for they felt the jolt. However, we found no body on the road afterwards, though there was certainly blood on his tyres. I fancy one or two miserable survivors from that raid are still at large around that mile of road. The wounded can't hope to hide for long, but the others may well stay at liberty until their friends come in force to take over the Peloponnese. Thank God I shan't see that day.

Well, so we used up the night of the twenty-seventh, and our timetable went to blazes. The next day was raid after raid, so that it was madness to think of moving by

273

full light. The morning we spent in Corinth, getting rid of our prisoners, hearing a few details of the night's activities north of the bridges, where it seemed much the same sort of thing had been going on. In the afternoon heat we dropped into the grass under the olives again, and slept like the dead. And at night we lined up our borrowed transport and set off on the last lap to Monemvasia.

Well, the rest was fairly uneventful. After Argos, where we turned aside from the road to Nauplia, there was considerably less traffic on the road, but at the same time the road was very much more difficult in itself. There was the fragment of a moon, which helped us, and we made fairly good time down the coastal roads of the eastern prong of the Peloponnese, through Astra and Leonidion, with the Gulf of Nauplia widening on our left hand, until with the dawn we found ourselves driving alongside the open Aegean, and the nearest land on our left was the Cyclades, eighty or ninety miles away.

We came down into Monemvasia about nine o'clock in the morning of a brilliant day. There was little shipping in the bay and little life in the town, though the place had obviously been bombed fairly recently. But as far as the British evacuation was concerned, Monemvasia was smallish fry, and we had an easy time there. We did not go right into the town, but parked our transports on top of an isolated stretch of cliff, and made our camp underneath in the shadow and shelter of overhanging rock, of which there was no lack. Wills went into the town to find out what was to happen to us, and came back with word that we should be taken off around three the next morning, from the beaches.

So we slept most of the day, and in the evening we got up and set about putting our lorries out of action, which we did very simply by running them over the cliff into the rocks below, and afterwards smashing whatever vital parts survived. Then we lined up and made ourselves as comfortable as possible under the cliffs again, and lay and watched the stars come out. In the last light a stray flight of dive-bombers came over, but failed to do more than raise flurries of water among the rocks. A battalion of Maoris waiting with us sang Poi songs as it grew dark; and the mountainous promontory of rock on our left, jutting far out into the sea, threw back an echo. All excitement seemed to have receded out of our lives. An old fisherman in a tasselled cap, with the head of a patriarch and a saint rolled into one, brought us a bowl of milk and sat with us for an hour, not speaking, since he had no English and we no Greek, not even smiling, for by then no one in Greece smiled, but obviously our friend and worshipper far above our deserts. If only we could get rid of this awful and illogical feeling that we've let them down, it wouldn't be quite so heartbreaking. But at least, thank God, they, who have seen us fight, have no such feeling towards us. We are heroes to them. They are heroes and martyrs both to us. Well, if this war has done nothing else, it's taught us to know our fellow-men. Now's the time to note down our findings, before they wrangle out another miserable unstable peace full of injustice to the staunch and pity for the perjured. As they will if they have half a chance.

Around half-past two in the morning we began to see furtive pencils of searchlight feeling their way here and there along the water. It was intensely dark, the stars seeming for all their brilliance to have no effect upon the blackness. Presently barges began to sidle up to the beach, and we were taken aboard and brought off to transports we could hardly see until we were under their sides. The Navy was dead on time, and the embarkation went off like a drill to numbers.

So here we are, nearly three hours out from Greece, in a delicious soft morning in a heavenly Spring. We have three or four small transports like this one, and four destroyers shepherding us, and Crete is already in sight ahead as a snowy ridge above a violet haze lying along the shining sea. It's hard to believe that we've said good-bye to Greece. Harder to conceive of what follows for her. I can see nothing of the Greek coast now; even Cape Malea, the last headland, has sunk into the sea. I shall see no more of her until the war is over, and even then the slime of the German will spoil her beauty in my memory. What must they be feeling? The swastika floats over the Acropolis now, and the boy from Rupel and his kind will be expected to salute it. And if he spits instead, as I think he will, they'll kill him. Better to have died at Rupel, while Greece still spurned aside the filthy German hand from the hem of her skirt, than to live to see the same hand make free of her breasts. Oh, Catherine, I know what he meant, and he was right. At our own peril, at the risk of our own national existence, I wish to God we could have done more.

But that chapter is finished, and we're still at war. No rest, no pausing even to digest failure, which is a very bitter meal indeed.

I am very tired. Once they get us ashore, I think I'll find me a quiet place somewhere under the trees and sleep until they make me get up and march again. Which won't be very long, if we're to avoid being slung out of Crete as we were slung out of Greece.

I wonder if I shall ever get these letters home to you, Catherine. By the time I see you again all this will be so distant, and so changed, please God, that we shall feel differently about it; but I think you will want to know, all the same, how it looked to me when I was too near to it to get it in focus. Why not? Let's have no endless shelving of everything until we've ceased to care about any of the issues involved. I want you to know everything I feel, even if I'm to regret feeling it when the smoke clears. But in this case I see no probability of change in me. Greece, 1941, has been the most shattering, the most stupendous tragedy in modern history, perhaps in all history; and in time to come no reparation exacted for it can be too high. That's my opinion now, and I want to set it down while it's white-hot. I wonder how you feel about it? Some day you shall compare notes with me about this whole horrible business, at home, after it's all over and the repairs are in hand. But God alone knows when that will be.

The sun's closing my eyes; I'm falling asleep even over your name. Catherine, good-morning and good-night!

Near Maleme Aerodrome,
Bay of Canea, Crete.
May 11th, 1941.

They told me the name of the village, but it was long, and I've forgotten it. Let it go. The above is all the address that matters, for unless I miss my guess Maleme will be in the headlines soon. It's the biggest 'drome on the island, and almost the only one. I'm told there are one or two auxiliary stations and an emergency landing ground, but it seems to me that once again we have only the slenderest of links with our fighter cover, and that link is Maleme. And a disquietingly vulnerable spot it is, placed beside the main road from Canea westward, and about three miles from the junction with the road which turns southward into the mountains. A nice focal point in the alluvial plain which runs all along the northern coast of Crete. Actually this village is on somewhat higher ground, and has a very respectable crop of trees, good for shade and cover.

Why our air power should still be resting on such a flimsy foundation after we have occupied the island unmolested for six months is more than I can guess. To my mind there should have been, as soon as Greece began to be over-run, an intensive labour campaign to turn this place into one great fighter base, from which we could have made the concentration of Nazi air strength in Southern Greece at least a damned uncomfortable business, and at best impossible. True, about two-thirds of Crete consists of mountain ridges which offer no landing-ground to anything less expert than a bird; but I bet what I have, which at the moment is nil, that the Germans could and would have raised a series of flourishing bases along the plain if they had had the place in their hands even half as long as we have.

What are we doing all these past ten days? I think we're considered to be preparing for either siege or seaborne attack. Now I know a very little of Crete, and have managed to learn in Greece a thing or two about the Germans. Once, long before the war – I mean before even the first campaign of the war, which opened in Manchukuo – I spent a blissful holiday coasting round Crete and the Aegean islands in a caique. I know the south coast is as good as invulnerable; a few mountaineers sitting on top of the cliffs with a machine gun could hold it against all comers from the sea; so it must be quite obvious to the Germans, who always take the trouble to know the lie of the land before they begin working over it, that we shall be sitting in good numbers along the north coast, watching the sea, and that the Navy will also be cruising along the coastal waters to the north, ready and able to deal with a sufficient percentage of their convoys to make our job easy afterwards.

So naturally the main attack won't come that way. They'll certainly make a feint at us by sea. They may even make a serious attempt to complicate our position by landing attacking forces along the plain. But I have very little doubt in my own mind that the main assault force will be airborne.

I know there still exists a tendency to pooh-pooh the effectiveness of parachute troops. Why, after their devastating effect in Holland, is more than I can say. Two days after our embarkation from Monemvasia the last of our fellows were brought off, among them some of the men who were holding the Isthmus of Corinth. They landed at Suda Bay on the third of the month, and we heard something of what happened after we left. There was a very heavy air attack, and then round about a thousand parachutists were dropped. No more British troops crossed safely into the Peloponnese. Yet we're still discouraged from taking parachutist attacks too seriously. Seems to me that's impossible, anyhow.

Still, we've dug some very neat slit trenches, and our

anti-aircraft guns are ready for action at any moment. Most people seem quite happy about it all. Maybe I'm the crazy one.

It's been so quiet it's almost eerie. The last few days one or two enemy 'planes have made what I take to be preliminary reconnaissance flights along the coast, very tentative affairs, sheering off when fighters went up after them. One or two have been fetched down into the sea. In this particular position we haven't been attacked at all. After Greece this has been like a holiday, an interlude of sleeping in the sun. If only we could be sure there was no sting in its tail.

Behind our position a small valley goes down between meadowy hills, and a thread of stream with yellow flowers starring its sides slips along under plane trees just coming into full leaf. In our off-duty time we lie down there in the grass and sleep. There's nothing else to do. We could lie and think, but when you are a mere private soldier thinking doesn't pay. You may begin to think too closely about the way things are going, which would be bad for your peace of mind. Ah well, I took on the job of obeying orders, and I shall have to abide by it now, whatever the outcome.

The truth is, Catherine, that I am not at all content with myself. I think perhaps this is a sort of green sickness all on its own. Probably every man who went through that fire and came through it into this pause has left his peace of mind in Greece. There's no cure for it. Nothing will be right for me, no one will be fully trusted, until we've wiped out that memory, the latest and the worst of many. Which can only be done by restoring the whole world to its keel again. So you see there's only one way to go, and that's ahead. No short cuts to peace. No short cuts to happiness. No short cuts even to death in this world, Catherine. However tired you are you have to keep moving. And just now I'm deathly tired, and sick to hell of it all. It comes, now and again. It goes, too, praise be. But just now I am at the point where I should like to drop into the grass and fold my arms over the indifference of defeat, and let the world skid back into hell.

That phase, not very obviously, usually arises from an obscure dissatisfaction with one's own deeds. We sicken of the fight because we've not fought well enough; never because we've fought too well.

We haven't fought well enough. I haven't fought well enough, to my own mind, either as an individual or a member of an army. Did we set ourselves so impossibly high a standard, Catherine? Is that why we seem now to fall so far short? In the beginning, when we first put our hands to the work, our war was such a crusade, such a blazingly clear issue between right and wrong, that we naturally wanted our conduct of it to shine with the same radiance. Instead we've been at every turn complacent, timorous, long-winded, selfish, blind, undecided. Heroes, too, in the extremities to which we successively brought ourselves, but our heroism should have been used with the clean urgency of a well-directed bullet going home, not at every last instant as a life-line to get us out of the mud and back to the path again. No, Catherine, my heart, we've been neither inspired nor inspiring, though we had the most overwhelmingly right and clean and piteous cause any army ever had. That's what makes you sicken suddenly of yourself and the whole palaver, and think all at once: 'What good are we, after all? To hell with us!'

Fortunately it isn't in most of us to remain for long thinking so poorly of ourselves. Besides, it's so obvious that someone has to do something about it, however inexpertly. So back we come to the charge again, without even the stimulus of self-admiration to buoy us up. We despise our own muddled efforts, but we go on making them. Is that a very special, a very English, a very perverse sort of heroism? Or only a criminal squandering of valuable blood and idealism and a forespoiling even of the victory we shall almost certainly come by at the end of our blunderings? Catherine, I wish I knew. Is it both? Sometimes I think it must be. But if both, then the heroism and the guilt belong to different men, or at least to us all in very different proportions. Who's going to do the judging? And when?

Once, when I was very young, I believed in all the traditional English virtues. But now I've lost all the legends long ago, and being a champion of Christendom without them is a dreary business.

I am lying on my face by the brook as I write this, my dear, with the pad pressed into the warm grass, and away on my right hand the slow lift of the hill to a shining white cottage with a roof of red wavy tiles, and three tooth-brush trees in between the cottage and me. At least they look like tooth-brush trees, every limb dead straight and bearing a close tuft of foliage on the end. I don't know the name of them. The smell of the grass is sweet and strong and spicy in the sun. I wonder if it will cling about this letter and reach you in England, when, if ever, the letter reaches you. I should have liked you to see this part of the world. I should dearly have liked to bring you away with me on another caique holiday. Who knows? Some day we may do it yet, and there'll be no ghosts of this present time to bother us, either. The white cottage will be a white cottage to me then, not Battalion H.Q. and trees and bushes will be trees and bushes, not cover, and our caique will be just a Greek coastal boat suited to the holiday requirements of married lovers, not a hypothetical transport for Nazi assault troops. And then you will remain with me even when I open my eyes.

Catherine, I love you very dearly.

Somewhere in the Bay of Canea.
May 19th, 1941.

This unsteadily, in haste and in the dark, by the light of a very small torch. I have perhaps half an hour off, not long enough for sleeping. Something is happening outside, something we don't understand. The storm we expected is blowing up now with a vengeance, but how it will break is anyone's guess. It's nearly midnight, and very dark, and yet the skies are full of activity; and German pilots are not fond of the dark, as I know.

All day since early dawn there have been fitful attacks on our positions by dive-bombers, and fighters feeling at the seams of our defence with machine-guns. We've had no rest at all. We went to earth early, and have had no option but to stay there. Fighters from Maleme, heavily outnumbered, have brought down a number of German 'planes, and we've reaped quite a gang of prisoners. Young, sullen, arrogant and speechless every one. No help in 'em.

All this air activity, of course, originates from Greek aerodromes, which the Germans have occupied from the end of April only. What we could destroy there we destroyed. They must have started from zero. What have we done here in the same time?

According to tales from Canea and the sea-front, which come in to us only by word of mouth, destroyers of the Royal Navy have also been having a busy day. There seems to have been some sort of attempt at a small-scale landing. Not one man came ashore alive, not even into captivity. They say fragments of caiques and bodies of men are being cast up on the beaches now. I knew our danger wouldn't be from there.

All we see of the sea from here is the pale threads of searchlights wavering about by night, and occasional gun-flashes. They at least are in action. As for us, all we have been able to do for our cause so far is dig ourselves in and dodge the dive-bombers, to keep ourselves alive for to-morrow and whatever comes after to-morrow. In the meantime we are not doing even that with complete success. During the day we've lost more men killed than I like to think about, Sergeant Wills among them. Canea, they say, is a shambles, and there are civilians in Canea. I shall be glad when this whole mismanaged chapter is over. It can't, however bad it may be, go on very long.

Only one possibly good thing happened to-day. An American newspaper-man turned up unexpectedly from Heraklion. Name of Lee Wallace. It seems he came here on the run with an evacuation convoy from Rafti, having had some of his papers stolen in Athens, and preferring not to stay and explain matters to the Germans. The intention was to send him on to Alexandria by the first boat, but in the meantime they made the mistake of taking their eyes off him for a moment, and he set off for Retimo and points east, taking a comprehensive look at Crete. The authorities have been looking for him for days. Now to-day in the middle of a bad strafe he tumbles in on the top of me, apparently rather surprised at all the fuss his comings and goings have caused. He spent an hour or so with us before the attack slackened enough for us to get him back to H.Q.; and as they'll certainly ship him off to Egypt at the first opportunity I asked him if he'd take my letters off with him, and somehow send them on to you from Egypt. He's agreeable enough; the only doubtful thing is whether they'll be able to get rid of him. For it looks as if no more ships will leave Canea and Suda Bay until after the battle. In the meantime he's sticking around at H.Q., and unless they keep an eagle eye on him, he will be down here with us again before long.

It's perhaps not a very strong chance; but it is at least a slender sort of bridge to you, for an American journalist is an embarrassment they can't afford, and they'll certainly strain every nerve to get him away safely to Egypt. He's promised not to leave without letting me know, and I'm satisfied he won't; so for the moment I can go on writing to you with some hope that in the end you'll receive my letters. Wallace hopes, so he says, to be in England himself before very long, in which case there'll be no difficulty in reaching you; but in any case he commands ways of getting things done, once he's well out of Crete. Things have reached the pass when I prefer to get something of me home to you now, rather than take a long chance on getting everything home to you in the very far-distant end.

Through the wooden walls of this goat-shed I can see

the glimmer of flares. Another wave of activity beginning. I think I'd better go down and see what's happening to Hale and his fellows. I forgot to tell you that I've been acting as a corporal ever since Barclay was killed in the first outbreak of dive-bombing, five days ago, and shall probably find myself acting as a sergeant now Wills is gone. It's a thing I didn't want. The strategy is not mine, and the tactics are not mine, and I'm in the unfortunate position of being unable to close my eyes to all that and concentrate on my particular outer ripple of the cycle. Still, we have to do what we can with what we have. No time now to argue about methods. Not until Crete is over.

My torch is giving out. I can almost see by the flares now, and the searchlights are busy again. I must go back. Any moment now it comes. I kiss you, Catherine. God bless you!

South-east of Maleme.
May 24th, 1941.

So much to say, and so little time to say any of it. Maleme is two days gone, and our air cover is gone with it. We've seen not one British 'plane to-day, not one. The sky is thick with German troop-carriers. This can go on very little longer.

Almost all the people you knew in this outfit, even by name, are dead. Hale was killed yesterday, in that impossible confusion before we crawled back as best we could to this position. I tried to bring his body back with me. I should have liked to see him buried. But he was a heavy man, and the ground was alive with Germans, and I had other fellows to look after. I couldn't make it, I had to leave him. He was the one I knew best. We'd been together eight months in all; that's long enough to make you miss a man when he goes. And Vickers is gone, too, and Taylor, and Stevens, and Reid. Only the younger men left. And me. I wonder how I come to be here? It doesn't make sense. I suppose I ought to call it an act of God, but it doesn't seem too easy just now to believe in acts of God. Only hell is active in Crete.

We are all either dead or so changed that wives and mothers wouldn't know us. Since this thing began, we've had no sleep, except now and again five minutes on our feet, as we stumbled along, or lying in the grass with the sights of our rifles the only world we knew; and I'm not sure if my date is right, but I think this must have been going on for four days and four nights, and when it will stop, short of the time when none of us remain alive to care, God only knows. It seems a hundred years since I did anything but kill and fight and run. Even this precious pause, into which most of us have fallen headlong as into an abyss of sleep, comes only because we've drawn back to new positions, and it's night, and they prefer to do their most dangerous probing by daylight. Not that we shall have a quiet night, but we may at least have a night at arm's length, instead of breast to breast.

It began four days ago, the day after my last letter was written, in the cool of the dawn at Maleme, with an appalling air attack that blew holes clean through our lines, and then low-flying aircraft laying screens of acrid smoke along the beaches to cover disembarkations from barges that never came to shore; and then like a new sort of delayed-action snowstorm the

parachutists came floating down out of the blown
smoke, by hundreds, by thousands, among us and in
between us so that we had to fight every way at once,
whirling like dervishes. It was like a nightmare, fantastic; even the horror and the danger were like two more
facets of a shiny thing not altogether real. That was the
first day. They came down like queer black-and-white
flowers, and folded on themselves slowly, and dropped
a dark, hard, horny fruit that killed. They had tommy-
guns; some of them were firing before they even
reached the ground. One came down into our arms
firing. He got Vickers before we could even reach him,
and then I got my arms round his knees and dragged
him down into the grass where a tommy-gun was no use,
and somehow, though I don't know how, I killed him. I
think it was done with my hands, for there was no blood
on my bayonet.

It went on all day long. The skies dropped men until
dusk, and even into the night. There was so much smoke
that it was difficult to see even while the daylight lasted.
We drew beads on them as best we could while they were
in mid-air, and hundreds of them were dead before they
ever touched the ground, hanging in their straps and
being drawn along the ground by the wind. We killed
and killed, but they were so many. Besides, they dropped
among us. We turned and twisted and tried to see
every way at once, and still they came up at our shoulders. Reid was bayoneted from his left as he sprang
round to face an attack from the right. We shouted
warnings to one another, and turned to find ourselves
jaw to jaw with the enemy, and embraced him and fell
down with him until one of us died. We were separated
man from man, and in that mad business to be alone

was to be dead. We fought towards each other as few men would fight for paradise. But we couldn't shorten our line and shut the invaders off in one force before us, because that would have been to lose touch with our corner of Maleme aerodrome, and there wasn't a man among us who didn't know that to lose contact there was just another, more lengthy way of dying.

As for the few 'planes we had – few by comparison with theirs, which they threw at us in flights, as thick as confetti – well, they did what they could. Their time began when the long comets of troop transports began to come down the sky, 'planes towing eight, ten, twelve matchwood gliders overloaded with men. The fighters shot them down by scores. They flashed along the beaches burning and splintering and spitting out bodies, they crashed and broke apart among the rocks and spilled bodies like blood, they flew too low and flapped their tails upon the sea and split, and men strangled with equipment struggled into the tide and tried to swim ashore. It was horrible, crazy, like a devilish dream. One undamaged 'plane soared over us with ten gliders blazing in an arc of crimson behind it, and men leaping out one after another with their clothes afire. The beaches beyond Maleme were littered with wreckage of men and 'planes, and the fields around us were withered brown with smoke and flames. But they kept on coming. Our pilots went on shooting them down until they were sick and drunk with excess; and we on the ground killed and killed and killed until from simple monotony the muscles of our bodies ached and our minds screamed for release from doing the one useless, helpless, unavoidable action. There was nothing else to do; and even that had no effect. It was like trying to stamp out a swarm of locusts by killing them one by one as they fell. There was no sense nor reason in it, and yet what else could we do?

It went on and on. At night it was even more fantastic than by day. The skies were full of flares and tracer shell and burning 'planes turning and plunging downward and pouring smoke along the wind in ribbons. Searchlights from the destroyers covering the north shore, and our own searchlights around Maleme, wavered about the sky and picked out here and there the white parachutes swaying gently to earth like monstrous flowers. We followed the beams, and waited, and often killed, but we knew there were more and more of them on their way down, more than we had time or strength or weapons to kill. Before morning we were fighting in isolated groups again. We couldn't see where our friends were. There was no way of finding them. All we could do was weld a little group together and fight in a circle, covering one another's flanks. Hale was with me then.

The second day was like the first, but worse, for we were reeling sick with the fever of killing, and they grew in numbers every hour, and nothing we did could limit them. But at least while there was daylight we drew together, and found such officers as were still alive, and made ourselves some sort of a stable position. Maleme was no aerodrome that day, it was a battlefield. But we held it all day, God knows how. We held it with our hands. There was precious little besides to defend it with. And the third day we couldn't hold on to it, even with our teeth and nails, any longer. I suppose the papers will tell you the Maleme position was abandoned. Don't believe it. We no more abandoned it than I could abandon you if you were here in this inferno. If it had been a choice between dying and leaving it, we should have died, but there was no question of choice. We were swept out of it like a leaf on a tide. For two days and nights they had been continuously reinforced, and we continuously depleted. It was like trying to stop a whirlwind with a fan. But we never drew back, we were thrust back, body to body, by a weight ten times greater than our own. All we could do was stick together in our going, so that something like a defensive line was presented, even though more of the locusts fell behind us and hacked and machine-gunned us as we went.

Oh, Catherine, my life, did I say I wanted you to have everything? If I could keep back anything from you now, I would, but you are in me, and there's no way of covering my mind from you. It was no shame that we lost Maleme, God knows – but why did we lose it in working order? Why wasn't it mined? Did they honestly believe that we could hold it against all comers? That there was never any question of losing it? What we foresaw, what Hale talked out with me the second day after we landed in Crete, were *they* incapable of seeing? No one was ever told to mine Maleme. They took it from us damaged only by their own bombs. Who's going to answer for that in the day of judgment? Or for the lives we lost yesterday trying to do from outside what should have been done from within before ever we faced the first attack?

Yes, we attacked Maleme yesterday. We shall attack it again to-day, I expect as soon as dawn comes. A handful of infantry with bayonets and hand grenades and a few tommy-guns. We attacked before it was fully light, and worked up an impetus that carried us right on to the flying field. We did what damage we could, and tried to keep what order we could, but my section penetrated ahead, and were cut off. So I imagine was many another group, for we're still looking for many a man who hasn't rejoined yet, and our escape was a freakish business. We couldn't get back, and we had some weight unexhausted from our advance, so we went ahead and through them. By mid afternoon we were among the rocks between Maleme and the sea, with a machine gun we'd captured from among the debris of parachute descents. Half its crew, I think, had smashed among the rocks as they came down, for the gun still trailed torn ribbons of parachute, and had never been fitted together. We cleared the immediate ground about us, and drew gradually in again towards the main road to Kastili, but by then it was easy to see that the attack had broken apart into a frightful confused hand-to-hand fight, in which our people were outnumbered, God knows how many to one. We made another swathe into it, and got across the road with our gun, and were in the thick of it, but the tide had flowed towards us, and we couldn't fight our way through to our own fellows again. The only way we could get out of it was towards the sea, and we drew off to the rocks again, but when we reached them Hale wasn't with us.

I went back. I knew he'd started towards the road with us. I knew he hadn't a scratch then. I found him in the grass on the Maleme side of the road, where the turf was ploughed up by a grenade. He was groping round and round in circles with his arms, dragging the rest of him; and when I took hold of him he knew me, though he was stone blind. He wanted to talk – Jim always was talking – but it wasn't so good. He said: 'I'm all finished, Tom,' and 'We made a bloody mess of it'; and he tried to say something about what had happened to him, but in the middle of it he coughed and blood gushed out of his mouth, and he died.

I didn't want to leave him there. I got his body over my shoulder and ran for it, back to our machine-gun post among the rocks. It was as good a spot as any for the moment, so I laid him down there. He was dead. He was too smashed up to have lived long even if we could have got him to a surgeon at once. We stayed there until the first dusk, and then we had little ammunition left, and knew that we should have our work cut out to get the living back to our own forces, let alone the dead. So we left him there among the rocks, with his eyes closed, finished with killing and being killed.

It wasn't easy getting back. We had to work round by the shore. The beaches were littered with burning shells of aircraft, and bodies; and washed-up broken bits of caiques and drowned men lay along the fringes of the tide. We made a wide detour, wading at one point through the phosphorescent shallows, and in the dark we worked round the outskirts of Maleme and came off very lightly with only a few hand-to-hand encounters. But only by sheer luck did we join up at last, after six hours of wandering in the moonless night and steering by searchlights and guesswork, with our friends. We stumbled on a patrol, and they fired on us. The bullets tore my left shirt-sleeve and cut a furrow in my arm. But we are back where we began. So much for yesterday. As for to-day, it will be all the same story, except that every day is bloodier than the last. And for the love of God, what has happened to our 'planes? Have they gone altogether, and left us here without even the suggestion of cover? They were outnumbered ten times over, we know. So are we. Their maintenance was being made precarious. So are our lives. They were not many three days ago, but yesterday we never saw one. We knew nothing except the progress of our own few square miles of indescribable chaos and desolation. I've never been so cut off from the world, nor distrusted the world so much. This is not how the battle of Crete should have been fought. The end, if it ends as it goes now, is not as it should have been. He was right. We've made a bloody mess of it.

Perhaps three hours till dawn yet. The searchlights are still uneasy, but not so frequent now because much of our equipment is back in that shambles at Maleme. There are still parachutists coming down, but they are fewer, for they hate the night. There is still continuous noise, from 'planes and bombs and ack-ack guns, but compared with what we've known this is almost peace. And precarious as it is we welcome it. Time – between struggle and firing and ducking to earth – time now at least to send a thought or two back to our own people. We, as witness this letter, though I could never under any other circumstances have written so much in so short a time, and even this has been many times broken – we have kept the quietest and most retired corner of an eccentric line. Even between the sentences of this letter, Catherine, I have killed one man. A searchlight held and blinded him as he fell, and I shot him dead in his harness, with a tommy gun in his hands. And then came back to you, and can you find the blot he made between us? Oh, Catherine, I am sick of myself, but I am sicker by far of the disgusting shadow of that disgusting people, and their toothmarks in this savaged continent's throat. As long as I have a rifle and can get a German in my sights I will go on killing. So much quicker an end to it all.

In the hills of Western Crete,
travelling south-east.
May 27th.

We're on our way to the sea. Not the Aegean, but the Mediterranean. We've been on the march now for nearly twelve hours, and going is getting difficult, I mean in its own right; it's been hampered from the beginning by every possible means the enemy have at their disposal. Their 'planes follow us constantly, and the hill tracks we have to use are wild and bare of cover. Their advance units are not so far from our heels with guns and grenades. Every hour our numbers are less. Such wounded as we can possibly handle we carry with us, and our pace has to be their pace. We halt only for periodical rests during the night wherever cover offers itself and a rearguard can hold off the pursuers. As we are halted now, and I am lying along a cranny in the rocks over the butt of my rifle, waiting for the first movement along the dark crotch of the sky between the slopes of this V-shaped cleft we travel; waiting, and writing to you by guesswork and the last of the daylight.

Yes, it's all to do again. Dunkirk, Monemvasia, Sphakia – if we ever reach Sphakia, and if there is anything there to meet us when we do – are successive high spots of my non-stop retreat round the world. Why should we, having done as individuals more than it is possible for flesh and blood to do, and borne more than it is possible for flesh and blood to bear, be thrust out of every bit of country we try to hold inviolate? And what will the next evacuation be, after Crete? Cyprus, perhaps. I doubt if Cyprus will learn anything from Crete, or get its learning in time to make any use of it. But a lot of us will not live to see that following chapter.

We got our orders to get out last night, and but for the difficulty of drawing together all our wounded, should have been further on our way now, and further ahead of the pursuit. It came as no surprise to any of us that the soil we stood on was become German under us. We knew, none better, that Crete had been lost for days. All the fighter 'planes were withdrawn to Egypt two days after Maleme fell; withdrawn by order, because their position was no longer tenable. Neither was ours, but we held it. We're still an army, and like them we go only because we are ordered to go; but so much later and less intact. I tell you no more than we all think, Catherine, when I say that they should not have been taken from us; and the answer that it was impossible to maintain them here any longer is no answer at all; it should never, if our time in this island had not been wasted, have become impossible. Crete should have been an armed fighter camp from east to west; as it will be in a few months, after we are out of it, or prisoners, or dead.

No use now going over that waste ground. Except that if we cry out loud enough other future Cretes may be saved from this humiliation, and other armies from such a march as ours.

To order our removal was easy, but to carry it out

isn't so easy. Retimo, they say, is still workable by naval vessels, and Heraklion; but the Germans in overwhelming force are between us and Retimo, and Canea and Suda Bay have been in their hands for days. There's only one way to get us out, and that's from the south coast; which has no harbours, and only two or three workable embarking places, and is fifty hours or so away beyond a mountain ridge. All the same, southeastwards into the mountains we go; there's no other way we can go.

We're already well up into the foothills, and except for a four-hour halt in the midday heat, which was terrific, we've been on the move since just before four o'clock in the morning. After this break we shall go on again at as fast a pace as we can make, hoping to gain on the pursuers, though I fancy we shall be hard put to it even to hold them off, let alone gain on them. To a man we are exhausted. We sleep as we climb, and shake ourselves awake again by falling against the stones. We have fought day and night almost without pause since the twentieth of the month, sleeping only by snatches that did no more than whet our appetites. We carry little food and less water. We are hungry and thirsty, and wounded, and ragged, and by turns we burn and freeze as the sun multiplies itself by every facet of rock and beats back upon our bodies, and the mountain hail and rain blast us. The tracks we walk on are goat paths, and we have left trees behind us, except here and there a clump where soil clings in a cranny of the rocks. Fired on from behind, bombed and machine-gunned from the air, as often on our faces as on our feet, so we climb the mountains. We are very feeble, and sweat easily and copiously. Fifty per cent of us have fever, and a queer light-headed mountain sickness possesses many more, so that we walk in a shivering daze, like sleepwalkers or imbeciles. But we are still an army. We are not broken, we shall not break. More than we can endure cannot be done to us; because there is nothing we cannot endure, except the loss of our self-respect; and we know now that after all we've survived we can afford to spit upon any attempt the Germans may make to damage that precious thing.

The weather is ghastly. Rain, hail and blazing sun followed us up the foothills taking turns to batter and burn us. Now, in the heights, we move in scurries of frozen snow, though the rocky ground is bare. Our boots are pulp. We carry the accumulation of exhaustion like a weight on us, and struggle to lighten it by throwing away everything we can live without, spare clothing, any books which have survived so long, anything but our rifles and vital kit. The weight grows all the time. But I think during the night we shall reach the crest of the island, and if need be we can crawl on all fours down the other side.

The wounded are heroes. None of them has complained, not one. They tear their hearts out in silence to keep our pace, and are bitter with themselves when they fail. As for us, the rearguard, we like our job as well as any. At least we have something to do to keep us awake, and something worth doing, too.

The light is almost gone, and the usual evening's hate diminishing gradually. We are not so persistently bombed and machine-gunned during the night; no one would voluntarily fly by dark among these broken jagged slopes. In half an hour more the column will re-form and move on, crawling back to the track from whatever holes and corners they found for themselves against the storm. Many of those who lay down will be dead asleep, but they'll wake at the signal and drag themselves to their feet and go on. I shall stay in my hollow of rock; after the column has moved the pursuers will draw in a little closer; as they do at every halt, optimistic to the end that we shall turn our retreat into a flight, and quit our rearward watch. So with our two or three tommy guns and a handful of rifles we shall cut another swathe and leave another reminder for the ones who follow. They never learn sense. We have the advantage of them here, for we choose our positions, and are motionless and invisible, while they must advance by the only practicable path in this cramped gulley, which we cover carefully before ever we lie down; and they must move, and movement is visible even in the dark when your life depends on seeing it. So a number of them, as many as we dare wait to reap, will die between the walls of rock, and the rest will draw off and hesitate before they come on again; and having stood them off like this for a little while we shall remove ourselves quietly in the track of the column, and find another position, and wait and kill again. After each blow they recoil like a hedgehog curling up from a touch of the finger. And we breathe again.

The column is on the move behind us. God knows when next I shall write to you, Catherine. This pause is over. Perhaps I shall be safe in Alexandria before I write your name again. A few more days will see it ended.

In the hills, inland of Sphakia.
May 30th.

Catherine, my love, my heart, this is goodbye. I shall never see you again. Some of us are to go, and some to stay, and I am among those who stay. It's hard, but it had to be hard on someone, and why not on us?

In a little while Lee Wallace will be coming back for my letters, the only part of me I can send home to you. He made that awful march with us, and was a tower of strength to the wounded, and to me. He swears you shall receive this safely, and I know that unless he dies on the way to you he'll keep his word.

It is all over, this appalling tragedy, all the waste, and complacency, and disquiet, and heroism. Some time during the night they'll send up to us from the sea, four miles away, the signal that the cruiser is ready to take us off; and those who are to be embarked will come out silently in the darkness from caves and gullies, and begin the last long trek down the cliffs to the sea. Here in the caves we can hear the sighing of the water dragging at the cliffs. The nearest I shall ever hear it, I think. For one thing there are too many of us; one ship can't possibly take us all aboard. For another thing we are the rearguard, and by the time they've got the wounded down the cliffs, and the whole body after them, it will be too late for us to withdraw. We know it. Every man of us knows it. We're going to die where we are.

Well, better this way than for us all to stand and fight and be slowly killed off together. We shall not have died for nothing, though we shall have died for something which need never have happened; and they will live to fight again, for us as well as for themselves. For me this last rest by a fire in the warm, dry cave, with the survivors of the march dead asleep all round me; and then back to the position we've chosen to hold, and unless the millionth chance comes I shall never leave it again.

We lost a good many men on the way over the mountains. We marched for forty-nine hours before we came to the welcome caves, high above the last lap to the sea at Sphakia. We brought the wounded in here, and then we fell, and lay, and wanted nothing but to sleep. Well, soon some of us will have our fill of sleep.

But oh, Catherine, Catherine, what am I to say to you? With so short a time left, and so much to say, so much I've never said to you, even when time was. And now time's gone by us, and all I can give you is this hasty goodbye from the last halt in my last march, by a campfire half the world away from you. And then no more letters, no coming home, no re-entry into your senses, no taking you back into mine. Only these final words crying to you wildly at the last moment, I love you, I love you in all the ways there are, with all the intricacies and pains and delights of which we never spoke once together, because they seemed then so unimportant. Now, with all Europe between us, I see you very clearly through all the smoke and the burning, your dark eyes that looked so straight at me the first day we met, and your wry smile, and your strong, indignant face. I never saw you without being intensely aware of the urgency of this struggle for the world's life, an urgency I always knew, but felt at its most passionate and angry when you were with me. I never saw you without the thunder and lightning in your eyes and the vaulting of the storms over your head. There's no life left for us; but there never could have been any life for us until this tornado had passed, and the world grown sane again; and we knew from the beginning that we might be among the debris. As we are, my dear love, now, at this moment, you in England, and I here in the ashes of this burnt-out bonfire.

But no lies between us. Neither then nor now. I am not satisfied. If I die here, as I believe, I die an angry man; and if the last improbability should happen, and I live through it, I live in anger, no less. I don't complain of death. I didn't go to Spain in 1936 to keep my body safe, I didn't join up in London in 1939 to ensure that I should live to enjoy peace again. Only that there should be a peace for someone to enjoy. If this had happened as some unavoidable incident in a coherent plan of campaign, as God sees me I should never have grudged it, no, not even with you at my heart, not even with you to be lost with the lost future, Catherine Saxon. But it happens as one involuntary blind blow in a sorry tale of muddle and half-measures. And I do complain, I do begrudge it, not only my own life, not even chiefly mine, but every life thrown away in the defence of this island, which we, tired men from Greece, undertook with our hands bound by conventionalism and our eyes bandaged with complacency. To die in front of the enemy's guns is war, but to die strangled by the ideas of your own leaders is murder; and I do accuse Britain, I do reproach her, for the blood of Jim Hale and many another like him; yes, and for mine.

What am I dying for? To save the lives of all those who will presently go aboard the cruiser at Sphakia? Very well so, if the sheer weight of circumstances had brought them into this extremity. Very well so even now, except that they should never have been reduced to this. We were swept out of Greece, and I felt none of this anger then. Mistakes were made there, too, but the tide had us and carried us, and from the first we knew we were fighting against the odds. But here in Crete, where we sat down in our slit trenches and looked at the sea, our battle was against the stupidity and arrogance and lack of imagination of our own strategy as truly as against the German attack.

They did not foresee the possibility of intensive air attack. Why not? We, the private soldiers of their army, knew from the first day that our death would come that way. God knows we had warning enough. The Germans have used the air with genius from the beginning, and their preoccupation with its development as a weapon of offence has been obvious. They did not take parachute troops seriously. Why not? Parachute troops destroyed Holland in five days. They did not believe in the usefulness of the aeroplane as a troop-carrier. Why not? In Norway the German front line was constantly reinforced by means of troop-carrying aircraft; and in Norway as elsewhere we, the common stuff of England, fought magnificently, aimlessly and hopelessly, and were driven into the sea.

Why have we been quiet, then, we who stood to lose lives and all by a sickness which was not ours? Why? If we knew that, we should be halfway to our proper greatness. Is it because we're too lazy and indifferent to rise up and denounce the incompetence that kills us? Or because we're too prone to trust, too patient, too ready to do more than justice to a man on trial, and give him the benefit of the doubt even where there is no doubt? Or because we're afraid of responsibility and terrified of the guilt of commission. The guilt of omission is a thing we never seem to see. Or is it that we're not yet out of the shadow of the idea that government should be left to the elect by birth and training, still bound hand and foot by a theory of social discipline which died long ago and will never carry us through any ordeal again? Well, I don't profess to know. I was not always silent. From Spain I wrote certain articles I am glad now to remember, the only utterance I leave behind me, except these letters to you. But when Britain went to war it was as if I closed my mouth on criticism because that country was mine, because I valued her so, because she was so much greater than I was, and I was jealous for her, and believed in her, and awaited her lightnings with the most profound faith. My mountain laboured with what should have been a new Prometheus, but was only another mouse.

It was not we who failed Britain; it was she – some rottenness in the present form of her – that failed us. And we, who make up the sound heart of her, how can we forgive those who cheapened and despoiled our enthusiasm, and squandered her proper splendour and our lives, which are her life-blood? Oh, no, there can be no forgetting and no forgiving. It's time to cut out the diseased part of Britain's body, before the whole body dies.

Because I believe more passionately now than ever before in the beauty of her, in the patience and goodness and enduring heroism of her ordinary people, their cheerfulness and modesty and goodwill towards the whole world. And I know you share that faith. Continue, for the love of God, to believe in these things, and for the love of God and them, Catherine, cry havoc on the other part of her. In my name, as well as your own, for after this I shall be silenced. Cry havoc on the indifferent, the half-hearted, the selfish, the incompetent, the opportunists who make nests for themselves with the debris of other people's lives, the profiteers who traffic in other people's disaster, the enemy wherever you find him, in cars at the races, behind desks in Whitehall, propping up money markets, in uniform and out of uniform. My death and all these deaths come home to their door. I want no revenge, I want no reckoning; only that there shall be no more Cretes, no more breaking of our ranks from within, no more wilful or involuntary betrayals, no more empty optimism and costly, maddening binding of our hands. No more destroying of everything we build with our blood and bone, no more looting of the house of our integrity while we are away dying.

This is not only a war, but a revolution, too. If God is good we shall hold the sky up, and the world will not die, but it will be changed; and those who cling to the old order because their interests lie there will go down with it. The process may be slow; we do things slowly; but the mechanism is under way, and nothing can stop it now.

Catherine, my dear love, the time runs out so fast, and even what we had I've spent. You know, better than I can ever say, how I have loved you. You know how my heart builded on the life which would be ours together. That's all lost now. There can be no long good-byes, thank God, for how could you or I bear to begin remembering, or thinking of what might have been? You have to live with what is, and to help to make the things that shall be. And I——

If I told you there was a chance for me, I should be

lying. The truth is we have been hard put to it to hold them off for the past twelve hours, and when the first detachment leaves the rearguard the remnant of us will be over-run. The last of us cannot hope to get aboard. No use playing with impossible dreams.

They are moving the wounded now. I can hear their lame feet going softly on the track outside the mouth of the cave, and their breath coming heavy and hard. The time is up. Lee Wallace goes with the wounded. He is here beside me, and I must end this now.

Goodbye. It's easy to say when one has no choice. That's one advantage of being a private soldier, I have no choice about anything. What can I say to you? I believe in you, and in your country, and in your country's victory; and I love you more with every moment until the moment I die. And after, if there is anything after.

I kiss you, Catherine. God bless you, my heart's heart. Goodbye.

[The enclosures end.]

XI. SHE GOES TO WAR

W.R.N.S. Quarters, Liverpool.
July 1st, 1941.

Dear Nick,

Many thanks for returning the letters so quickly. They came back to me safely yesterday morning, and I have them in my hands now, though I haven't yet tried to read them again. No need, I remember every one of them with some special side of my memory which pushes away everything but Tom Lyddon, and functions with a desperate certainty where he is concerned. Even that, of course, will fail in time. Love him as I may, love him as I do, I can't keep the manner of his face and speech and movement before me so clearly through the years of a life which I fear may be all too long. For I'm very strong, and I doubt very much whether the bombs will do anything about me. I wish I had a photograph of him, but he never gave me one, not so much as a snapshot or an army group. Do you realise that the time will come when I shall no longer be able to recall just how he looked? I'm going to need these letters then. They're all I have, these and his seal ring. And his anger and his love. Because I'm in the same boat with Gwyn. Done with that way of loving, once for all. The spring is quite dry, Nick.

I was very tired yesterday, I don't know why. It was hot in the teleprinter room, and we were busy all morning, but not busier than we've often been without harm. But I think I've used up a good deal of my body's energy in my mind, and having reached the end of that march with Tom at last had no strength left to do my own walking. That passes, too. To-day is quite another day.

I went out into the garden with your letter, and lay under the flowering lime-tree, and read it there. You never put a foot wrong with me. You didn't try to be comforting, you didn't urge me to fight against the bitterness you know I must feel. Even Gwyn, if she had known of it, might have made those mistakes, for she's not always wise, and she for her part has no bitterness, and no need of any. Johnny died justifiably and deliberately, destroying an enemy bomber, died effective and formidable, a polished tool. But Tom was a good weapon shamefully mishandled, and the seeds of his warfare never even came to leaf. One was used, the other was wasted. And there can never be very many Johnnies, but there are thousands upon thousands, dead and living, in the same case with Tom.

Once, after we came back from Wastwood, Gwyn opened her mind to me again, I think involuntarily. Dan had brought back a new boy-friend, a Pilot Officer in a fighter group somewhere around here, very young, scarcely older than Dan herself, and still at the pink-and-white stage fair young men seem to go through. Gwyn said afterwards that it was hard to keep from screaming at Dan what a fool she was to give her heart to a pilot to smash with his own body, but she remembered in time that with Dan the heart was not involved in these affairs. And again, one day when she was tidying her drawers, she happened upon a half-finished Air Force blue pullover, the one she was knitting in the cellar during the blitz; she sat and looked at it, and her face broke up suddenly, and she dropped her head and arms into the open drawer upon the poor curling bits of her masterpiece and cried for a long time.

For me there's nothing like that. I don't want it. I reject it. No one knows I have anything to cry about, and myself I don't think I have. My composure has never halted since the first news came, and will not be shaken now. I stand aside and examine from outside, as it were, the thoughts passing through my own mind.

It is not that I follow him blindly. He wouldn't have wanted that. What is it that burns me, then? A cold burning, but steady, one that doesn't consume its fuel and die. I told you that I had changed, but until he took me aside in dying, and showed me the Catherine I had become, I didn't know how much. What do I want for him, now that he's dead? The blood that cost his blood? No, that's irrelevant now; and I've never for one moment lost my grip of the main issue, from which I could no more turn aside to left or right than I could drop it and go back in my tracks. No, no vengeances. Only to take up his quarrel where he left it, and carry it as far as I can in my lifetime; for it won't be ended, I think, in one generation.

I've been at war, according to my service papers, for nearly eleven months, Nick. At war with Hitler and Germany, with Mussolini and Italy. When I began my war it was a national business, and I began it because the fathers of my country, the architects of Munich, made patriotic appeals to me in speeches and posters and newspaper statements, telling me that this quarrel was mine. It is mine. It belongs to me and to many like me, people whose sense of personal responsibility was in the embryo stage then, who accepted what their political and social leaders told them without question. Well, they told me the quarrel was mine, and I accepted it, and it is mine. The day may yet come when they will try to arrest the tide they themselves launched, to take my weapons away from me, to tell me I have accomplished my warfare. Those who unleashed an idea to serve their own purposes will try and put it back in its cage then. Let them try. They will find the tide swollen beyond their power to dam; the idea will have outgrown both their control and the cage they kept it in. I shall keep my quarrel. I shall continue to wage my war. They have begun something which will mean at last the end of them.

I am not the only sleeper to awaken. There's a thing no one, as far as I know, has remembered to say about war. It's a great educator. Before I became involved in it I was content to keep my interests within the country, if not within the parish; I conceived that most things in England, if not in the world, were very well managed, and that the method of management was no affair of mine. I even believed our scheme of living was a true democracy. Well, I've learned a great many things: always to distrust, always to question, always to turn the stones of our neat national paving, and look underneath for the unlovely creatures who dislike the light. I've learned that we are not such wise or humane administrators as we thought, that our prized democracy is a half-hearted and inefficient business, our equality of sacrifice a euphemism for the most blatant exploitation of the great underdog, and our concern for life much less than our concern for property, since one may be commandeered wholesale and the other may not be so much as breathed upon. Not a pleasant education, but an essential one. They called me to war; I obeyed the call, and learned in consequence all those things which certainly they never meant me to learn. And I am one of very many, all full to the heart of new and bitter knowledge; one drop in the ocean which in the fullness of time will rise and sweep the old order away.

But I've learned other things, too. I've learned that my country, the Britain I hardly knew, is very much greater than I thought her, as well as very much less. I've discovered that the virtue and kindness and courage and constancy of her common people are beyond all praise, that they are the salt of her earth; that because they are what they are we cannot fail to reach our victory in the end; that because they are what they are they have always won her victories, and always allowed the fruits of victory to be taken away from them; and that *they* have learned, too, so rapidly that this time, by God's grace, they will fight to keep their victory as they fought to win it. In which battle after the battle I shall take my full part.

Yes, I have changed. His experience and mine, and the contact of his with mine, have brought us both to the same gate. Nothing can turn me back now. Nothing can close the eyes which have once been opened to the world's shortcomings. Not that the main objective has changed. Why should it? The path has never turned aside by a hair's breadth from its headlong advance upon the fort of Nazism and Fascism; the only change is that I see beyond now, and the path doesn't end there. When we have taken that strong point there will still be more to do, and it will be useless the old men shouting to us then that we've done our part, that we can throw away our guns and rest, that the war is over. The war will not be over.

What am I going to do? I am going on with my job, of course, with all my mind and strength, while this phase of the battle lasts. And afterwards, when the first victory is won, I am going to write for Strang again, if he will have the sort of column I mean mine to be, as I think he will. Yes, and for other papers, too, wherever and whenever I can. I am going to record the progress of the war.

No, it will not be over when we march through Berlin. It ends only when we have cut away from our own national body all the inequalities and exploitations and snobberies and simonies and treacheries and embezzlements that enfeeble it now, and opened our frontiers to all progressive minds of whatever country and race without distinction; when we have assured not only for ourselves but for the whole world of men of goodwill the right to live in peace, dignity and happiness, as the brothers they should be. Never, you may say. Very well, we will remain armed until we die, and teach the next generation to fight better after us.

I have it in my mind, Nick, that this is going to be a lonely journey for me. One of very many, I said, and so I am; but obviously none of my own people will know what ails me, and I doubt if even you can bring yourself to go where I am going. And he is dead, who should have been my companion. There will not be wanting well-meaning people who will cry me down for a fifth-columnist, a destroyer, a complicator of clear issues, a traitor – as they cry down 'Cassandra' now, and any others of my profession who have the courage and indignation to damn folly and graft and injustice wherever they find it. Let them try to stop my mouth. I want more of my country, yes, and more for her, than they are capable of conceiving. I am ambitious for her as they have no notion how to be. If they realise that they'll curse me all the more. Those who have anything left to lose may well think twice before venturing such a storm. But I have nothing. I shall never be silent, and I shall never turn back. They called me to war. Well, let them be satisfied. I am at war.

I don't ask you to approve of me, Nick. Even that has stopped being of any importance now. I only ask you to go on being my friend. And if you can find it in you to be my companion on the road as well, you know how glad I shall be; and if not – well, I'll render a better account of myself some day, somewhere, when the war is over.

Catherine Saxon.

Headline books are available at your bookshop or newsagent, or can be ordered from the following address:

Headline Book Publishing PLC
Cash Sales Department
PO Box 11
Falmouth
Cornwall
TR10 9EN
England

UK customers please send cheque or postal order (no currency), allowing 60p for postage and packing for the first book, plus 25p for the second book and 15p for each additional book ordered up to a maximum charge of £1.90 in UK.

BFPO customers please allow 60p for postage and packing for the first book, plus 25p for the second book and 15p per copy for the next seven books, thereafter 9p per book.

Overseas and Eire customers please allow £1.25 for postage and packing for the first book, plus 75p for the second book and 28p for each subsequent book.